2020 Vision

The Plot to Change the Catholic Church

A Suspense Novel

Robert J. Betterton

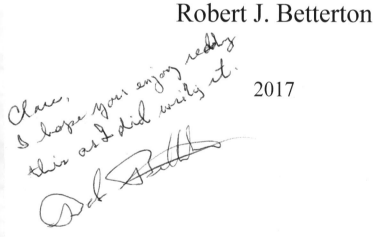

2017

The cover picture is the front entrance to the

Pontifical Apostolic Nunciature (Vatican Embassy)

3339 Massachusetts Avenue NW Washington DC

2020 Vision

The Plot to Change the Catholic Church

A Suspense Novel

Robert J. Betterton

2017

Also by Robert J. Betterton:

The Compliant, Curious and Critical Catholic (2005)

The Familiar Stranger Who Lives in Our Home (2008)

Saving the Catholic Church While Sitting in a Pew (2011)

Dedicated To

The Fabulous Fourteen:

My Great-Grandchildren,

Adrian Lindsay, Jackson Keating, Connor Lindsay,

Ryan Olivia Keating, Greyson Keating, Xander Lindsay,

Caitlin Carson, Duncan Lindsay, Rocco Betterton, Aislinn Carson,

David Carson, Ciará Carson, Noah Betterton, Rome Betterton

And all their future siblings and cousins.

May you learn to love a Church that is truly worth saving.

2020 Vision

Table of Contents

BREAKING NEWS!!

Washington, D.C.—At 6:55 a.m. on Wednesday, July 19, Pope Francis II and Cardinal Parolin, the Vatican Secretary of State, were getting ready for their morning walk. Two Swiss Guards, Franz Buchs and Roland Pfyffer von Altishofen, were waiting for them in the car.

After a couple of right turns, and no traffic in sight, the pope, the cardinal and one of the Guards got out of the car and began walking. The other Guard then drove to the pick-up destination to wait for them.

A Ford with no license plate passed the embassy car and parked a quarter of a mile down the road. When the pope and the cardinal came into view, the Ford's driver left the car and headed toward the walkers. Strangely, he raised both arms and, extending his fingers, turned his open palms toward the walkers, shaking his hands, seemingly to indicate that he was unarmed. Suddenly, continuing to shake his left hand, he dropped his left arm, and his right hand went to his waist.

"GUN!"

Parolin tripped as he moved to grab the pope and take him to the ground.

"Pietro!!"

The silence was broken only by wailing sirens.

"The cardinal was hit. Pope in ambulance headed for Georgetown Hospital for examination. I am with him," Guard Buchs said.

"Cardinal in second ambulance. Seriously wounded. I am with him," said Guard Pfyffer von Altishofen.

The third ambulance took the shooter to the morgue.

Chapter One

Decision

Pope Francis died on February 6, 2019.

The reaction to the news was unprecedented. This very special man had resonated with billions of people—not just Catholics but others as well.

The conclave to select the new pope began two weeks later. Everyone agreed that it would be very difficult to elect a Benedict-like authoritarian traditionalist as successor to Pope Francis.

No one knew that better than The Brethren, a small but powerful group of cardinals, some retired, who were pledged to Benedict XVI's ultra-conservative theology and philosophy. They were not about to change. Instead, their strategy was to search for another man with a Francis-like personality but far less energy and conviction. They wanted someone like John Paul II, someone who could be manipulated as effectively as Cardinal Ratzinger had manipulated his predecessor, someone who old enough for his reign to be short. Then they could return someone to the throne of Peter a man even more traditional than Benedict. It could be the end of the Catholic church, but they didn't believe that. Nor did they care.

Their final choice was John Atcherley Dew, Archbishop of Wellington, and Metropolitan of New Zealand, who was elected pope by a narrow margin on the second ballot and chose the name Francis II. He had been elevated to cardinal by Pope Francis in February 2015. The Brethren were satisfied with their choice.

In his own words, Cardinal Dew was "a fairly ordinary Kiwi kind of a bloke," and many hoped he would remain that as Pope Francis

II. He was plainspoken and gave the impression that he had no personal agendas on anything.

All his priestly life, when his workday was over and he was back at home, he'd make a quick change to faded jeans, a rugby jersey and a pair of well-worn loafers. Where he was not well known, he might venture out by himself to a nearby restaurant. If he were recognized, he'd say lightly, "It's okay ... I'm off the clock."

Dew, now Francis II, was a young-looking 70-year-old with a Facebook page and a rigorous exercise program. He was clearly a pastoral bishop, untainted by the Curia. His election as pope was seen by some as an affirmation of the papacy of Francis. He liked that.

Ironically, after his election, a minority of the Pope Francis appointees, joined by a minority of the so-called Traditionalist Catholics and a minority of John Paul II/Benedict XVI appointees, all seeking to solidify their established but diverse positions, pressed him to take the archaic Papal Oath, which every pope since Paul VI had refused to do.

The oath swore:

> I vow to change nothing of the received Tradition, and nothing thereof I have found before me guarded by my God-pleasing predecessors, to encroach upon, to alter, or to permit any innovation therein;
>
> To the contrary: with glowing affection as her truly faithful student and successor, to safeguard reverently the passed-on good, with my whole strength and utmost effort;
>
> To cleanse all that is in contradiction to the canonical order that may surface;
>
> To guard the Holy Canons and Decrees of our Popes as if they were the Divine ordinances of Heaven, because I am conscious of Thee, whose place I take through the grace of God, whose Vicarship I possess with Thy support, being

subject to the severest accounting before Thy Divine Tribunal over all that I shall confess;

I swear to God Almighty and the Saviour Jesus Christ that I will keep whatever has been revealed through Christ and His Successors and whatever the first councils and my predecessors have defined and declared.

I will keep without sacrifice to itself the discipline and the rite of the Church. I will put outside the Church whoever dares to go against this oath, may it be somebody else or I.

If I should undertake to act in anything of contrary sense, or should permit that it will be executed, thou willst not be merciful to me on the dreadful Day of Divine Justice.

Accordingly, without exclusion, we subject to severest excommunication anyone – be it ourselves or be it another – who would dare to undertake anything new in contradiction to this constituted evangelic Tradition and the purity of the Orthodox Faith and the Christian Religion, or would seek to change anything by his opposing efforts, or would agree with those who undertake such a blasphemous venture.

Pope Francis II refused the oath, choosing to keep his options open. Many on all sides sighed in relief. He was inaugurated on Saturday, February 23, 2019.

Among the first actions taken by the new pope were the reappointment of Cardinal Pietro Parolin as Secretary of State and the reconstitution of his predecessor's advisory council of cardinals with the same nine members.

Francis II also decided to follow the lead of the first Francis, living and doing routine work in a small apartment at Domus Sanctae Marthae and using the papal offices in the Vatican only for formal events and meetings.

He found the weekend between his inauguration and his first day in his new office uncomfortable at first. He tried out each chair in his new apartment and couldn't decide which he liked best. He looked out the window, hoping that no one would notice him. He looked at himself in the full-length mirror in his white cassock, white mozzetta and white skullcap and did not recognize himself.

Suddenly he smiled, and in the back of his closet he found his faded jeans, rugby jersey and worn loafers. He had a momentary urge to slip out into Vatican City and head for a favorite pizzeria, but thought better of it. He just went to bed, sleeping more soundly than he had in weeks.

* * * * *

Cardinal Pietro Parolin, the Vatican Secretary of State, had requested a private meeting with Francis II at his earliest convenience. It was scheduled for eight a.m. on the new pope's first day of work, February 25. The cardinal was a few minutes early and was shown in immediately.

"Good morning, Your Holiness."

"Good morning, Pietro. Sit down."

"Did you have a pleasant, or at least somewhat restful, weekend?"

"Well, I've had better ... this pope business is a bit daunting."

"I would imagine it is, but you will adjust, I am sure."

Parolin took a thick notebook from his briefcase and placed it on the table between them. "Pope Francis instructed me to pass this plan on to you, with his sincere request that you consider implementing it as soon as possible. But first I would like to tell you about its development.

"Almost a year ago, Pope Francis invited Cardinal Ouellet, Cardinal Stella and me to a private and highly confidential meeting in the palace. We were pledged to secrecy.

"He talked about his work on Curia reform, which he said would be in vain if the role and culture of the diocesan bishops were not completely changed to the way it once was and should be. He said

14

that the bishops must become *representatives* of the Vatican and at the same time *advocates* for the baptized. He said they also must become an efficient channel of communications between the persons in the pews and the man on the papal throne and not self-appointed barons.

"He charged us with bringing that culture change about in the more than 3,000 dioceses in the shortest period. In the Foreword to the plan, I have described the process we went through; the research we did; the alternatives we considered; and the conclusions to which we came.

"He was ready to implement the plan, which is described in detail in this notebook, when he learned of his illness. Only we three cardinals—and now you—even know of the plan's existence.

"The plan is dramatic, and for some it will also be highly traumatic, but we believe that it is the best alternative. I suggest that you read it and then we discuss it at your earliest convenience."

The pope stood, picking up the notebook. "Thank you, Pietro. I will read it carefully, thoroughly, and with great interest. As you know, since everyone is here in Rome, I have invited you and all of members of the council of cardinals to a private dinner tomorrow evening in the palace. There is no planned agenda, but after dinner I would like you to make a brief presentation of the proposed plan. It should be no longer than twenty minutes or so, and then I would like you to give each of them a copy."

"I can do that."

"I will then ask them all to meet there again on Wednesday to discuss it thoroughly. Then, after I have prayed for a while, I will decide."

Parolin bowed. "I understand and agree completely."

* * * * *

As soon as he got back to his office, Parolin made a conference call to Cardinals Ouellet and Stella, telling them about the meeting and the plan to consult with the council of cardinals.

"It looks like as much as another week for a decision. Keep next Monday and Tuesday open, please."

* * * * *

Dinner with the pope's council was held in the formal dining room of the papal apartment in the Vatican palace. The atmosphere was light and optimistic about the papacy of Francis II. The conversation over dinner followed that mood.

Afterward, when they had moved to more comfortable chairs, and each had been served an after-dinner drink, the new pope said, "When I invited all of you to dinner last week, I had no idea that I would be saying what I am about to tell you.

"My first official meeting yesterday was with Cardinal Parolin. He told me about an assignment my predecessor had given him and Cardinals Ouellet and Stella about a year ago, to develop a plan to change the church for the better and forever. After a struggle of several months they completed the plan and Francis accepted it.

"Sadly, by that time Francis knew that his days were numbered, and he asked that Cardinal Parolin pass the plan on to his successor with a strong recommendation that it be adopted. Pietro did that yesterday morning and I read it last night. I must tell you that it is a remarkable piece of work and my first inclination was to adopt it, but that would be a foolish way for me to begin our new relationship.

"Therefore, I have asked Pietro to give us an overview of the plan, which he assures me will take no more than half an hour. He will also give you a copy of the plan to read." He said gravely, "You are not to share anything you read in it with others outside this room or to make a copy.

"We will convene here tomorrow morning at nine for a discussion that will last as long as it takes. Then you will return all the copies to Cardinal Parolin, who will destroy them. Any leaks of the contents of this plan will be treated both quickly and harshly.

"Following tomorrow's discussion I will spend some time in prayer and consideration before making a final decision.

"I have one more thing before Pietro begins. Several of you will find that the plan will seem to personally affect you significantly. Be assured that we have given that considerable thought and you will see how that will be handled later in the plan you will be reading. Cardinal Parolin, please take the floor."

Parolin spoke to a transfixed audience for twenty-seven minutes before distributing the plan books. Then, strangely, the council members spontaneously applauded, and left with a quick "Good night." Neither the pope nor the cardinal could say what that meant.

* * * * *

During the next day's intense discussion, it was difficult to determine approval or disapproval. Except for the usual bathroom breaks, which were always followed by quick updates for the absentee, the men never left the room. Boxed meals appeared for lunch, then for dinner.

The new pope stayed all day, saying very little and listening intently. When asked a question, he usually deferred politely to Parolin.

There was occasional humor and some repartee among the participants, but they fully understood the magnitude of the issues being discussed and displayed a genuine desire to reach the right decisions and interpretations rather than those they might personally prefer. They all deferred the details of how some things would be handled to the Secretary of State.

They finished just short of ten p.m. The discussion could have run longer, but they felt that the Holy Father had all the information that he needed to make his decision.

When Council had all left, Francis offered Parolin a nightcap and asked, "If I had asked for a vote of favorable or unfavorable, what would the result have been?"

"I have absolutely no idea."

"Nor do I ... and I think that is how it should be."

The Secretary of State heard nothing for the rest of the week. That pleased him to some extent because he felt the pontiff was probably giving full attention to it. However, The Brethren would be meeting on Sunday evening, and he knew they would ask him about the secret meeting.

* * * * *

The Brethren were a diverse, complex and, in some ways, incongruous group. Some had serious, contentious relations with one another in the past. Their fierce belief that the church should be highly conservative in everything it does held them together. They hated the memory of Vatican II and worshiped the papacies of John Paul II and Benedict XVI. Almost all of them despised Pope Francis.

Pope Emeritus Benedict XVI had passed away in the spring of 2018, but his death had energized their desire to return to the conservative path he had laid out for the Catholic church. In truth, they were determined to "out-Benedict Benedict," if possible, ensuring that Pope Francis II would accomplish as little as possible during his papacy, which would lead to the election of a more

Benedict-like pope next time around. They had vowed to be extremely wary of anything that would make the church even more liberal than the first Francis had left it.

Their core members were four Rome-based American cardinals: Bernard Law, James Stafford, Raymond Burke and William Levada. The leader was Cardinal Law, 87 who had fled his Archdiocese of Boston in the dead of night to avoid arrest as the "worst of the worst" protector of priests who raped children. Given a posh job of little practical significance before his retirement, he had cultivated the myth that he was a sort of brilliant elder statesman.

Cardinal James Stafford was also 87. Although years before he had been Bishop of Memphis and Archbishop of Denver, he has been a career Roman Curia member since 1996, most recently as Major Penitentiary Emeritus of the Apostolic Penitentiary, from which he retired in 2009.

Next in age at 84, Cardinal Tarcisio Bertone was formerly Secretary of State and one of three Brethren who previously had problems with one another.

Cardinal William Levada, 83, had been Archbishop Emeritus of San Francisco and Cardinal Prefect of the Congregation for the Doctrine of the Faith. MSNBC once reported that Cardinal Law was "the person in Rome most forcefully supporting" the investigation of the Leadership Conference of Women Religious, a large group of American nuns. Cardinal James Stafford strongly supported Law in this, and the investigation had been handled by Cardinal Levada. Now retired and no longer eligible to vote to select any future pope, all four men were still strong believers in Benedict XVI's authoritarianism.

Archbishop Carlo Maria Viganò, 78, was currently the only non-cardinal in The Brethren's leadership and certain to remain so. He had previously had trouble with both Cardinals Bertone and

Parolin. Viganò was assigned by Benedict XVI to investigate corruption in the Vatican Bank, where he was doing too good a job. To prevent him from exposing any more incriminating information, Bertone sent him to the United States as apostolic nuncio. During Pope Francis I's first trip to the U.S., Viganò arranged for an anti-gay activist to be present at a meeting with the new pope. The press was all over it. Since he was just a few months from retirement, Bertone's successor Cardinal Parolin had allowed Viganò to retire, but it was clear that he would have preferred to fire him.

Bertone and Viganò had put all of that behind them in their zeal for the work of The Brethren. At that point, they still thought Parolin shared their enthusiasm.

Cardinal Pietro Parolin at 64 was the youngest member of The Brethren. A rising star in the Curia, he had replaced Cardinal Bertone as Secretary of State. He and Gerhard Müller were among the first to be elevated to cardinal by Pope Francis, although Müller was considered more of a Benedict leftover. Cardinal Law watched Parolin very closely.

Cardinal George Pell, 78 had been both a supporter and a critic of Benedict XVI and represented a challenge to Cardinal Law regarding leadership of The Brethren.

On the surface, Cardinal Marc Ouellet, 75, appeared to be a prototypical Benedict XVI partisan and therefore a strong member of The Brethren—or at least Law thought so.

Cardinals Gerhard Müller and Raymond Burke, both 71, were protégés of Benedict XVI and rabid Brethren.

Cardinal Law lived in a large, luxurious apartment in the Palazzo Della Cancelleria, a palace built in the fifteenth century that became the home of the first Medici pope, Leo X. The Palazzo, in Rome just outside Vatican City, was owned by the Holy See, so those who lived there were beyond the reach of U.S. legal authorities.

The Brethren met for dinner and conversation at Law's opulent residence at least once a month and whenever events of interest occur. This particular evening, they were tired of rumors about the new pope and hungry for facts when Cardinal Parolin arrived.

When the greetings were over and each was relaxed in his favorite chair with a drink in hand, Cardinal Law looked at the Secretary of State and said, "Well, Cardinal Secretary, I understand that you were the first to meet officially with His Holiness."

"Since I don't know anyone else who has the extensive access to the Pontiff's appointment book that you seem to have, Your Eminence, I will accept that as true."

"And what did you boys talk about?"

"I am sure you know precisely how long I was there. It was strictly routine business."

"When are you going back?"

"When I am called."

Both men were chuckling throughout this fencing match.

Burke jumped in saying, "Come now, Pietro. There are no secrets among the Brethren," but was ignored.

The meeting went on, but Parolin made an excuse that he hoped they accepted and left shortly after dessert. When he arrived home, a message from the pope's secretary asked him to meet on Monday for breakfast after Mass.

* * * * *

Breakfast on Monday, March 4, was in the pope's office.

"I must compliment you and the others on the plan. Its detail seems flawless and very complete. Doing it quickly will assure that no one can develop a counterplan in time. We must do it now."

"Thank you, Your Holiness. I will have the nuncio, Archbishop Pierre, make the arrangements with the university. And for my part, I will start immediately on the final details of our portion of the plan since it must be in place first."

Francis nodded. Parolin continued, "It is still risky, Your Holiness, and it demands much sacrifice from you. You will become a hated man among many of your friends and colleagues. We need to talk more about that as we go forward. You may be in physical, even fatal, danger. You must keep me advised of anything that seems out of the ordinary, no matter how trivial it may seem.

"I don't know if you are aware of this, but there is a dinner group of ten or so that meets frequently on Sunday evenings at Cardinal Law's residence. It began rather innocently during the papacy of Pope Benedict as a sort of support group for some of his policies. To the outside world, they are known as The Brethren, but when they are together they call themselves Benedict's Brethren. This group worked quietly behind the scenes for your election as pope—not because you were their choice, but because they were sure that they could not elect a conservative. They look at the long term, these men.

"Cardinals Ouellet, Pell and I are members. We have considered resigning from The Brethren, but decided that remaining on the inside might be beneficial. I believe that to be the case. I am not suggesting that anyone among The Brethren would physically harm you, but they are powerful and well-connected enough to make that happen without anything being traceable back to them. You must also tell me when someone seems to know something that they shouldn't."

"I understand," said Francis.

"I will have a highly secure phone connection between us installed to reduce the need for too many private meetings."

"Whatever we need to do for the plan to succeed, we will do," the pope replied.

"There is one more thing. We must be prepared for everything. I think that you should plan on staying in the United States at least until November, and you should ask the American President for temporary political asylum while you are there."

"Are you sure that is necessary?" Francis asked softly.

"Yes, I do."

"All right—if you say so."

Parolin added, "Archbishop Pierre is still in town visiting friends. In fact, he is coming to my office this afternoon. I will go over the things we need him to arrange and at least part of his role in it."

* * * * *

When Parolin left, the pope called his secretary, Monsignor Carlos Menendez Serra, into the office. "Msgr. Menendez, I'd like you to find out if Cardinal Mamberti could stop by to see me today for a half hour or so."

A few minutes later Menendez returned. "Cardinal Mamberti will be here at two today."

"Thank you, Carlos."

Cardinal Dominique Mamberti was from France and had spent a good part of his career as a nuncio. Pope Francis I appointed him as Prefect of the Apostolic Signatura in the Roman Curia to replace the embarrassing Cardinal Burke. In 2015, Francis I made him a cardinal in the same group as John Atcherley Dew. They were the first who were purely Francis's picks for cardinal. When they learned about the Benedict Brethren, they labeled themselves the

Francis Fellows. Unlike the Brethren, hardly any were based in Rome, so they rarely met in person; however, they did conduct an active e-mail network and have an occasional videoconference session. Their group was much larger than the Brethren, though heavily outnumbered by Brethren supporters. The Francis Fellows had reached out to all the Francis I cardinals, even to some known as the "Benedict Leftovers." Francis II enjoyed their support, but today he worried a bit that he might be letting at least some of them down.

Cardinal Mamberti and Dew had become close friends in recent years, often confiding in one another. When Dew became pope, they agreed this would not change. Francis II was about to test that.

Martini bowed, "Good afternoon, Your Holiness. What can I do for you today?"

Francis replied, "Good afternoon Dominique. I would like to ask a favor from you."

"Popes don't ask favors, they express wishes. What do you wish?"

The pope laughed and replied, "I suppose that is correct, but not between friends."

"You must always be sure that you know who your friends are and who only appear to be, Santità."

"I will heed that advice, my friend." The pope explained to his friend about the plan prepared for Francis I. "Here is my copy of the plan. I would like you to read it and get back to me as soon as possible"

"I will do that and may be back to you tomorrow."

"Thank you, Dominique. I appreciate that."

* * * * *

Cardinal Parolin went directly to his office from the meeting with Francis. He took a card from the desk drawer and calculated the time in Washington, D.C. Then he pulled out his cell phone and called the number on the card.

"Hello, this is Cardinal Parolin calling."

"Good morning, Cardinal ... I just walked in."

"I'm calling about our real estate project. You may begin now, and your deadline is April 12."

"That will be no problem. Thank you."

"The apostolic nuncio, Archbishop Pierre, will be in touch soon. Goodbye."

"Goodbye, Cardinal."

Another step taken.

* * * * *

When Archbishop Christophe Pierre, apostolic nuncio to the United States, arrived a few minutes after eleven in the office of the Secretary of State, Parolin greeted him. "Christophe, thanks for stopping by. What time is your plane home?"

"Not until five."

"Good. I have some important things to talk with you about. As you perhaps know, the Holy Father has been considering an early trip to the United States and just this morning he decided to do that in May. We talked about several things he might do and decided that he would be willing to make the commencement address at a major Catholic college. We talked about Notre Dame, St. Louis and Boston College, but we decided on Catholic University. We would like you to make arrangements for that."

"That is exciting news. I am sure they will be very pleased."

Parolin continued, "The pontiff would also like to have private and confidential dinner with the president of the United States on an evening during the week before commencement. Do you think that would be possible?"

"I will certainly try," replied Pierre, "I know the vice president and will ask him to help. He is a Catholic and a great fan of Pope Francis I. I am sure he will try."

Parolin said, "Finally, regarding the trip, it has been decided that the spring meeting of the Pope's council of cardinals will be meeting in the nunciature in Washington during the week of May 20."

"I am glad you said 'finally.' It will be a busy time."

"Christophe, let me relieve your mind a little by telling you what has already been done and what has been started. I think you probably will be able to take some things off your list."

"That will be very helpful."

"First, I am not at liberty now to tell you any details about the speech until we arrive, but there is an obvious assumption in it that all of us who came from Rome may be there for an extended period."

The nuncio's head shot up. "All of you?"

"Yes," replied Parolin. "Cardinals Ouellet, Stella and I developed a much larger plan for Francis I, and the talk at Catholic University is only the beginning. We will be part of the implementation team and will be staying there along with a fairly large number of additional people.

"It has become obvious that there is not enough space in the nunciature building for us all to operate there. However, the building and grounds are sovereign parts of the Vatican City State, which could be very important. Therefore, the nunciature must operate—temporarily we hope— somewhere else.

Parolin continued, "Several months ago, you requested that we do some minor refurbishing of the embassy, which I suspect you thought I had forgotten. I did not. As soon as Papa Francesco approved the plan, through a third party, I confidentially contracted with a developer to take care of the overcrowding situation and the refurbishing. A building less than a mile from the embassy was leased and the space was designed last year. When Francis II gave us the go-ahead for the plan, I immediately authorized the build-out.

"Although it will be two floors instead of four, every room in this building is being replicated in a building less than a mile from there. It will be completed by the April 12 deadline, when your staff will move there.

"Every room is furnished almost exactly like its counterpart. Prior to our arrival, a team will move all files and personal effects to the new location and your people will move to the new location as unobtrusively as possible. They are to be told that they are moving for us to do the refurbishing and to accommodate the pope, his council of cardinals and others.

Pierre said slowly, "I won't ask how you were able to do all of this without me knowing about it."

"Good. You personally should continue to live at the embassy, for reasons that we will go over when I arrive in early May. I think you should announce this move to your staff when you have made all the arrangements for the commencement address."

"Thank you for sharing this with me and making all the arrangements." The nuncio bowed.

Parolin handed him the builder's card. "This is the fellow with whom I have been working. I have called and told him that you will be in touch. Feel free to make any changes you like as long as you don't delay completion."

"Thank you, Pietro for the information and your confidence."

"Thank you, Christophe, and have a safe trip. I will see you in May."

Parolin asked his secretary to tell Cardinals Ouellet and Stella that the plan had been accepted, and Archbishop Pierre was on board.

* * * * *

Cardinals Ouellet and Stella arrived about nine Tuesday morning. The three gathered in Cardinal Parolin's small conference room.

After they settled in Ouellet asked, "Did he approve of every aspect? I mean specifically the new organizational elements, manpower and budgets?"

"Everything," said Parolin. "Now, I am sure that when we give him the details he may have some questions, and reducing the number of potential questions is a major part of what I want to address in the next four or five weeks."

"All right. What do we do first?" asked Stella.

"I have been trying to decide on that and I don't feel comfortable with anything yet. The danger is that overlooking some less obvious significant element of the plan will complicate what we are trying to accomplish. Let's not rush our thinking."

"Didn't you say that there would be a press conference after the Holy Father's address?" asked Ouellet.

"Well, not immediately after. It will probably be the next day."

"How about using that sort of thing to create a framework for thinking about this?" Ouellet suggested.

"How do you mean?"

"It would be a bit like role playing."

Stella rolled his eyes.

"I still don't understand what you mean," said Parolin.

"Let's go back to our offices and each of us picture ourselves as reporters at the press conference and list the questions we we'd ask in the first round, based on what we have just heard. Then we will make a list of those questions, deleting the duplicates and grouping by topic. We go back to our offices and list the follow-up questions we'd have. We repeat that process until we can't think of any more questions and then we answer them all."

"Now that is a great idea!" said Stella.

Parolin said, "I agree, with a couple of additions. In the second round and later, we should also include all new questions as they occur to us. We also should establish a schedule for our follow-up meetings, remembering that we really want to concentrate on the answering on all questions."

"I say we meet every morning, with a one-hour limit," offered Stella.

"I agree—first thing in the morning. I will have my secretary set up a mutually agreeable schedule."

Cardinal Ouellet's plan worked very well, and by the end of the second week they were running out of questions. They grouped the questions by topic and then into three sets of related topics, each taken by one of them based on their individual expertise. They set a deadline of March 29 to answer all the questions in a coherent way and to prepare addenda to the plan in the form of policy statements, procedures and courses of action.

In the process, the three men bonded in a way uncommon for clerics in Rome, with a level of mutual trust rarely found in the Vatican. They began a habit of meeting casually for lunch occasionally to discuss things other than the plan or other Vatican matters. More importantly, although they did not talk much about it, they concluded that their task was not only the right thing to do, but the only thing to do if the church was to be saved.

One day toward the end of a meeting, Cardinal Stella said, "Before we leave, I'd like to talk about something we have never really discussed. I understand why it makes sense for the pope to stay in Washington until things settle down. And Pietro, I understand why it makes sense for you to remain with him. I can understand why Marc and I should be there for a while just for backup. But we both have important jobs and they are here in Rome. Why can't we return as soon as things begin to settle down?"

"What makes you sure that things will settle down?" said Parolin with a smile.

"Well, I suppose you could be right, but I am worried about how things are going back at the office."

"I have some of the same concerns, but of course my day job is working with the people most affected by the actions to be taken," said Cardinal Ouellet.

"And the priests won't be affected?" asked Parolin, "You have both made the case very well for staying in Washington as planned. But allow me to set your minds at ease. I had one of the best IT specialists clone all the Vatican computers onto a server we will bring with us; he will continually update the software with e-mails, documents, everything. You will be able to access it from your office in the embassy just as you would from your office in Rome.

"Another benefit of this system is that you will be able to monitor the 'unofficial' e-mails between any people on the Vatican system that you want. I will encourage you to do that, so we can have a better idea of what is happening in the Vatican on a day-to-day basis than we would if we were there. This is very important."

Ouellet nodded. "I guess I will withdraw my objection, Pietro. You seem to be able to think of everything."

The trio finished hashing out the details of the implementation plan a day or two before their self-imposed deadline of March 29. On Friday, April 9, they would reconvene for one last review.

* * * * *

True to his word, Cardinal Mamberti returned to meet with the Holy Father on Tuesday. They sat down to talk.

"What did you think of the plan?"

"It is very complete and detailed. It is probably safe from any immediate interference from canon law because no one ever thought about doing this before. With all due respect, someone might take the position that you are not mentally competent and should be removed as pope, but that won't work. Your objectives are to involve the laity in governing, changing the culture of the bishops and improving the time for problems raised in the pews to get to the Vatican."

Francis said, "I think I hear a 'But' coming."

"You are correct. It is: 'But then what?'"

"What do you mean?"

Mamberti said, "The plan addresses the procedure for dealing with the bishops very well. Then what? What are the tools you are going to use to change policies that need to be changed?"

"I don't like to answer a question with a question, but what kind of tools?"

"Ironically, since I have been prefect, I have given a great deal of thought to how to resolve the basic issues of how the church has reached the condition it is now in. The world is very different than it was during Vatican II. People are smarter and more sophisticated than they were and many of our brightest people from that time are now on the other side. Science has changed thinking, often in opposition to things we accepted as faith. It was thought that the sun revolved around the earth, and rejected Galileo's discoveries. Scientific advances, ironically in Galileo's own astronomy, have made that belief archaic, limited to traditionalists who cannot explain what they believe."

"So it would appear," said Francis, "and there are many other examples that science should be accepted as modern revelation. How can we bring that about?"

Mamberti explained, "Unlike almost every other organization, the church has no viable constitution delineating the rights and responsibilities of the people, the hierarchy and its various agencies. Yet we have hundreds of canon laws, at least partially because we don't have a specific process for creating or evaluating them.

"If we did have had a constitution, how many canon laws would pass the test of constitutionality? Yet I must apply all canon laws justly. And how many canon laws have demonstrable conflicts between them, which we ignore because we judge each case individually?

"Now let's consider history and tradition. How much tradition would be considered valid if all were subjected to the scrutiny of true church history? Do we not have the obligation for a verifiable and supportable history of the past 2,000 years in one place, written by recognized historians? Shouldn't that history be part of the magisterium, rather than Genesis?

"Finally," said Mamberti, "what about issues that we know are alienating large segments of the faithful—issues like mandatory celibacy, contraception, equality for women, women in clergy, divorce and re-marriage. Shouldn't we hear all sides of each argument and then decide fairly in the judgment of all, and let the chips fall where they may. That is 'then what' as I see it."

There was silence between the two friends.

Francis spoke first. "Thank you, Dominique, my friend. You have done exactly what I wanted you to do. I will take this as a challenge to define all aspects of 'then what' and I will seek your counsel often in the process."

"You will have it whenever you ask, but seek out others as well, even if they don't agree."

"I will, and now I need to get to work."

"I do, too. You are going to need the support of the Francis Fellows and, given the plan you are about to initiate, they will need some assurance of their futures. I would like your permission to make that happen."

"You have it," said Francis, "and thank you."

* * * * *

That evening in his Rome apartment, Cardinal Mamberti began his program to formalize the Francis Fellows, mostly by e-mail and videoconferencing on his personal computer outside of the Vatican network. He had decided to use an "inside out" process to avoid selection of men not committed to the church envisioned by Francis I.

Pope Francis' first group of nineteen cardinals in 2014 had been comprised mostly of candidates left over from Benedict XVI; with Benedict looking over his shoulder, it would have been awkward to pass them over. Ironically, that included Cardinals Parolin and Stella, as well as the ultra-authoritarian Gerhard Müller.

That was partially the case in 2015, the last chance for the John Paul II/Benedict XVI papacy to "pack the court" so that their successor continued their path backward. But although that class of just fifteen were mostly men from underrepresented countries rather than potential popes, it also included Cardinal Mamberti and Cardinal Dew, now Pope Francis II.

Cardinal Mamberti decided to begin his organization efforts with people he knew: those who had been selected as cardinals in 2016 and later, perhaps a total of eighty, with few, if any, career connections to Pope Benedict XVI, and who seemed more pastoral than authoritarian. His plan was to have this first group lead him to others, especially their friends who were currently archbishops. He also had to be careful to not compromise the pope's plan.

* * * * *

At the same, Francis II was organizing the points made in Mamberti's "then what" assessment into an outline for his strategy for survival of the church.

He began by listing of problems facing the church, organizing them by whether they might have a common solution; he researched earlier efforts to make changes and why they had failed. He found the exercise both interesting and challenging, but gradually a broad strategy emerged. When he finished that, he would meet again with Cardinal Mamberti.

* * * * *

Also on Friday, the apostolic nuncio to the United States, Archbishop Pierre, called Cardinal Donald Wuerl to notify him that Pope Francis II would be willing to give the main address at the Catholic University commencement in May. The pope's offer was immediately accepted.

Wuerl, in addition to being Archbishop of Washington, D.C., is chancellor of Catholic University of America, which had been founded in 1887 by the American bishops. It was governed by a board of trustees whose bylaws state: "The Board's membership is limited to fifty elected persons of whom twenty-four must be clerics of the Roman Catholic Church. The Chancellor, who is the Archbishop of Washington, is an *ex officio* member."

That was half, plus the chairman, who is appointed by the board. The current chairman, Michael P. Warsaw, was also CEO of Eternal Word Television Network (EWTN). The remaining trustees— often major donors, named as a reward—were essentially irrelevant. Every American diocesan cardinal and all other archbishops were among the "twenty-four clerics."

The university had an impressive list of successful alumni well known in many categories, including one that was probably unique: "Alumni on the Road to Sainthood," with no fewer than three members modestly listed.

The university was also a bastion of conservative Catholicism, and probably not pleased with either Pope Francis I or II. However, to be its 2019 commencement speaker was a perfect place for Pope Francis II to make his debut and launch his plan. The response to the suggestion that the pope would consider an invitation was greeted with great enthusiasm, but some concern about the venue.

The traditional place for commencement had been on the plaza of the Basilica of the National Shrine of the Immaculate Conception on the university campus, but that would never be big enough for a papal address.

By the grace of God—and the baseball commissioner's office having scheduled the Washington Nationals to be on the road that weekend—the university could move commencement to the Nationals' Park Stadium in Southeast Washington. Chairman Warsaw quickly negotiated with the Nationals to use their permanently-installed TV production equipment and offer free live coverage of the commencement to anyone who wanted it, domestically and overseas.

*　*　*　*　*

The nuncio also reached out to the vice president of the United States. A practicing Catholic, he was pleased to help. Ironically, the nunciature was just across Massachusetts Avenue from the Vice-Presidential residence on the grounds of the former National Observatory.

The President made some changes in the schedule and extended an invitation to Pope Francis II for a private dinner at the White House on May 14, the Tuesday evening of the week before commencement, at the White House. The Vice President and his wife would also attend.

Since that date was earlier than anticipated, Parolin decided to bring the pope into Washington on Saturday, May 11, three days earlier than previously planned, and decided to keep this confidential. At the same time, he changed the council of cardinals to May 15 to May 17.

The plan was falling into place.

Chapter Two

Final Touches

When Cardinal Parolin returned to his office on Thursday March 7, he settled into the only remaining task in the first phase of the process, one that essential to one of the two main objectives of the plan, and Parolin was best equipped to address it.

The objective was to develop a structure that would facilitate rather than impede a dialogue between the pope and the people in the pews. As the institutional church had evolved into an imperial church, bishops had staked out minor domains and, to maintain their minor sovereignty, they had censored and sidetracked issues that should have been handled at the pope's level. An excellent example of this was the clerical sexual abuse calamity.

Early in the conversations with Pope Francis, he and the cardinals thought it wise to use the existing structure of apostolic nuncios to establish a reliable communications network. However, while this was a logical decision, its implementation would place a burden on the nuncios that far exceeded their resources.

As Vatican Secretary of State, Cardinal Parolin oversaw the worldwide activities of the church. He had two major portfolios: The first was the operation of the Vatican's bureaucracy; to do what Benito Mussolini referred to as "making sure that the trains run on time" was the job called the Substitute for General Affairs, whose incumbent was Archbishop Giovanni Angelo Becciu.

The second was overseeing the Vatican State's relations with other states, under the charge of the Substitute for Relations with States, Archbishop Paul Richard Gallagher. The Vatican had ninety-nine ambassadors, called apostolic nuncios, each with responsibility for relations with the governments of one or more of the countries that recognized the Vatican City State.

In today's complex geopolitical world, this was a major challenge for the largest nations, much less a tiny City State of 110 acres and a population of 842, especially when because of its nature it often was an "honest broker" in disputes between nations far exceeding its size.

Most major countries have diplomatic relations with the Vatican City State, but some of those nuncios covered more than one country. However, the Vatican had no official representation in several nations, the largest of which were the People's Republic of China and the People's Republic of North Korea.

In other words, Archbishop Gallagher handled the apostolic nuncios, otherwise known as ambassadors, to the nations with which the Vatican has diplomatic relations. Up to this point, this had been a reasonable distribution of responsibilities.

In addition to diplomatic relations, the nuncios generally oversaw the bishops of the country in which they served, principally to make recommendations on new bishops and the movement of current bishops' careers. However, this was not a chain of command situation in which the bishops reported to the nuncios—and that contributed to the problem.

Each of the 2,851 archdioceses and dioceses in the world was headed by a bishop or archbishop, (some of them cardinals), and all 2,851 of them reported directly to the pope. The pope scheduled meetings with each of them, usually at the time of their mandatory *ad limina* visits every five years. (If a bishop were in his seventies when a new pope was elected, it was possible that they would never meet.)

One of the most important objectives of the Parolin task force was to dramatically improve the communications between the laity in the pews and the Vatican. To do that through the nuncio structure would require a total reorganization and redirection. The plan suggested that would only be practical with a new and parallel structure.

Now Cardinal Parolin had to define this new system for maximum effectiveness.

The pope had authorized a substantial budget for this structure, led by a new Substitute Secretary of State, an archbishop who would report to Parolin. Parolin nominated the current apostolic nuncio to the United States, Archbishop Christophe Pierre, to become the new Substitute for Communications, and the pope had approved. Parolin planned to inform Pierre when he arrived in Washington in May.

* * * * *

By mid-March Francis II had become comfortable enough with his broad strategy for reforming the church, e-mailed it to Mamberti and scheduled a meeting for Friday, March 22 to discuss it.

* * * * *

Many suspected that Cardinal Law had a way of tracking the activities of people in whom he was interested, but no one knew for sure. Years before, the meticulous, cautious, and often paranoid Benedict XVI had a computer database developed that held the appointment schedules of all members of the Curia and certain other people he either liked or feared. It allowed his secretary to schedule meetings more easily, but he could also track who was meeting with whom and how often.

Cardinal Law became aware of this system soon after it was introduced. Very few people had access the system for obvious reason, but one was his former secretary. Since he shared his benefactor's paranoia, he maintained a connection with the secretary and, for a minor monthly stipend, used his services often. Of course, all the Brethren were tracked to determine their loyalty and to see who was talking to whom.

Because Parolin and Pell also had close relations with Pope Francis through their membership on the cardinals council, they were given a little more attention than Burke and Müller, for example.

Irregularities—such as multiple meetings of the same persons—could make a difference.

There would be a meeting of The Brethren on Sunday, so on Friday afternoon the cardinal called his source.

"Good afternoon. Is there anything going on that you think I might find interesting?"

"Yes. I was going to call you. Cardinals Parolin and Ouellet met for an hour every day this week."

"Just the two of them?"

"No, Cardinal Stella was also at every one."

"Have those three people shown a similar pattern before?" Law inquired.

"Just a minute."

"Take your time."

"Yes, there were four such clusters of them meeting in 2018. At that time, each cluster was followed by a meeting between them and the Holy Father."

"Thank you," said Law. "Thank you very much."

* * * * *

Cardinal Mamberti arrived as scheduled at nine a.m. on March 22 at the Pope's office to discuss the "Then What" strategy. The Holy Father greeted him warmly.

"Dominique! Come in, my friend! I can't wait to learn the mark for my essay. Would you like a cup of coffee?"

"Good morning, Santità. I would like a cup of black coffee and your mark was a strong A-minus."

The two men laughed and sat down.

Mamberti continued, "I like your approach and found it quite complete, although we must be constantly aware of other problems and different aspects of those you have identified. As I am sure you understand, it is clear that everything cannot be done at once to remedy centuries-old problems. That said, there is probably an ideal order in which we should proceed. The task is to find the thread which will neatly unravel the hem."

Francis suggested, "I believe that is to change the culture of the Curia. Great progress was made by my predecessor, but we must build on that—and quickly. I will schedule a meeting of the Curia a couple of weeks after the commencement address."

"Where?"

"In the United States. Will you be able to make it?"

"I wouldn't miss it."

The two men talked for several hours and, over lunch, agreed to meet again on April 19.

* * * * *

When The Brethren met on Sunday evening, March 31, it was a full house. After all were settled in with cocktails, Cardinal Law turned to Cardinal Ouellet.

"Well, Marc, you and Pietro have been having several 'play dates' recently."

Ouellet responded, "Yes, you know how it goes. The need for several meetings in a row and then you don't see one another for months except for special events, like a conclave or something."

Law asked sarcastically, "Anything important involved?"

41

"Why, Cardinal, don't you know? Everything in the Vatican is extremely important!" said Parolin.

Everyone laughed and the conversation moved on to other things.

"Well, I have some news," said Cardinal Pell. "Francis II is meeting with our council in the United States during May." Parolin was looking at Law and could tell that Law already knew.

"When did you learn that?" Law asked.

"Friday. It will be in Washington, D.C.," said Pell.

"Why in the United States?"

"The Holy Father will be there to deliver the commencement address at the Catholic University of America."

Trying to recover, he said looking at Parolin "Didn't you know that?"

"Yes, I just didn't think it had been announced yet," Parolin responded, with a bit of an edge.

* * * * *

Shortly after Parolin left, Cardinals Pell and Ouellet followed. After a few minutes, Cardinal Law asked the others, "What did you fellows make of that exchange between Pietro and George about the day when they learned when their next council meeting would be?"

"A difference of opinion on whether council meetings should be discussed here," said Bertone.

"But we talk about when they are scheduled all the time," offered Müller.

"When do you suppose that the date and location of the next meeting was decided upon?" Law asked.

"Probably at the pope's private council dinner on Tuesday of last week," answered Burke.

"But Parolin asked George when he heard it and he said Friday. Almost as if he were offering Pell a chance to cover a mistake he had made." Law was forcing them to think.

"They were both at the council dinner on Tuesday of last week," said Burke, his voice raised nearly an octave. "And if there is a plot, it certainly was discussed at dinner."

"Not necessarily at dinner, Ray. But I have learned that they also met on Wednesday for thirteen hours," Law revealed.

"There *must* be *something* we don't know about going on!" protested Burke.

Law answered, "Whatever there is, both Pietro and George know about it!"

Things appeared quiet and normal throughout April, although Cardinal Law continued to track the activities of Parolin, Ouellet, Stella and, as well as he could, Pope Francis II.

The first three were completely immersed in the detailed, day-to-day scheduling for the implementation and management of the plan. They met for a full day every Friday to assure that they were fully coordinating the process. The process was routine until the address at the Catholic University commencement, but they were dealing with the unknown following that.

During this process, they calculated how many people from Rome, including a small contingent of Pontifical Swiss Guards would be required to go to Washington. They asked the nuncio to arrange for thirty-six guards to be housed nearby. Since it was summer break, he could get eighteen dorm rooms at Georgetown University.

They also asked him to rent enough automobiles to assure they were covered.

Francis II was also working hard dealing with Cardinal Mamberti's "Then What" challenge." The two men talked often on the phone and occasionally over dinner in the pope's apartment. There were priorities to be set; policy to be framed; and the sequence of introduction to be planned.

It was a crucial and significant month in the history of the church, but only a handful of people knew that. At one meeting Cardinal Stella asked, "Does anyone else have the feeling that we are doing something weird?" They all laughed, but no one answered.

* * * * *

When he met with the Pope on the 19th, Cardinal Mamberti was amazed at the depth of thinking and progress that Francis II had made. He made some suggestions but the strategy was complete and ready to go by the end of the following week.

* * * * *

There was a dinner meeting of The Brethren on Sunday evening, May 5, and everyone attended. Cardinal Parolin was amused that, as far as he knew, no one except Cardinal Ouellet was aware of what the next few weeks would bring, though not for lack of trying. Tonight, would be their last evening of fishing for a while.

Cardinal Law was being the charming affable host, greeting all as they arrived and assuring that each had the cocktail of his choice.

"Pietro, glad you could make it, since you are going to be travelling soon. When are you flying out to Washington?"

"I'm leaving on Tuesday. The pilot is doing the flying." Both chuckled at the lame joke.

"Cardinal Müller, I heard you were not feeling well. I am happy that you are able to join us."

"I'm fine and I wouldn't miss it," said Müller.

"And here is the *retired* Secretary of State. Don't you miss all that world travel stuff?"

"Not for a moment," said Cardinal Bertone.

"Cardinal Pell! Are you flying out with Pietro for the Council meeting?"

"No, not unless he wants to cover the cost of a room for a week or so."

When all were seated and relaxed, Law as usual stood to say the blessing. He reminded the group that this was Pope Francis II's seventy-first birthday and that he probably should have invited him to join them. There was restrained chuckling.

Then he turned to Parolin and said, "Pietro, I was just thinking about what George said. The Council meeting is the week of the nineteenth, so why are you going so early? Did you write the commencement address and have to rehearse him?"

Everyone laughed at the several possible meanings in the question. Parolin chose not to correct the dates of the council meeting and glared quickly at Ouellet and Pell to assure they wouldn't. "No, I wouldn't presume to write for the pontiff as you did for John Paul II until Benedict took over that task. I have several things to go over with the nuncio."

"Ah, yes, Archbishop Christophe Pierre. Give him my best," said Cardinal Bertone.

The group laughed.

"And mine," added Archbishop Viganò.

They laughed harder.

"Do you know what the speech is about, Pietro?"

"I suspect it will be pretty basic. He said he was going to deal with leadership, a pretty standard theme for commencements."

45

"Is anyone else travelling with you, Pietro?"

"Oh, I expect it will be a full flight. They all seem to be like that, lately, but no one I know about."

"I heard that some renovations are being made at the embassy," said Cardinal Burke.

Damn! Has Christophe been talking to someone, Parolin wondered.

"I would describe them more as 'sprucing up' rather than 'renovations.' He asked for them months ago."

"Are any others of you going over to hear the commencement address?"

"I didn't even go to my own," said Burke drily.

The interrogation was apparently over.

* * * * *

Cardinal Parolin's May 7 flight to Washington was long and uneventful. Since it was not a charter but a long commercial flight, he tried to do something productive, but thinking about the coming week and beyond made that impossible. He decided that his substantive discussion with Archbishop Pierre should wait until tomorrow; tonight he just wanted to have a good dinner and to go to bed.

The nuncio met the plane and Parolin suggested that they stop for dinner at some nice place to relax before going to the embassy. Pierre chose a quiet and excellent place in Georgetown. The two men had known each other since Pierre had first been a nuncio. Pierre had considerable respect for his boss, and Parolin felt the same for him, especially Pierre's excellent performance as the American nuncio. Their conversation was friendly and general.

When they arrived at the embassy, it was nearly nine and the cardinal was fading fast.

"Do I have my usual rooms?"

"Of course. Remember we are the only ones here."

"I am really tired," said Parolin. "We have a great deal to talk about, but let's start in the morning with breakfast, about 8:30."

"That sounds fine with me."

"Here is a copy of the Holy Father's address next Sunday. Please read it tonight. It will help in our discussion tomorrow. However, it is not to be discussed with *anyone* other those directly involved."

Pierre said, "I had a call last night from Archbishop Viganò, and another just before I left for the airport. May I return them?"

"You may not."

He handed Pierre the manuscript and headed for his room.

* * * * *

Wednesday morning, the nuncio was sitting at a table in the dining room with his second cup of coffee when the cardinal arrived at 8:25. As he sat down, the nun on duty served their breakfasts.

"Did you sleep well, Cardinal?"

"Christophe, I hope that all the beds here are as good as that in my room. Yes, I slept deeply and well. Did you?"

"I did not," answered Pierre. I read the speech four times. My head is spinning. I don't think I slept a full hour all night long. I don't know where to begin with my question! About one this morning I started making a list of things I could think of that need to be done. There seems to be so little time. It is already Wednesday! I am overwhelmed, and full of questions."

Parolin said calmly, "I understand, but my purpose today is to tell you some things that have already begun, so you don't have to think about them, and to lay out some tasks for which you and I will be responsible."

* * * * *

The same day, back in Rome, Cardinals Law, Müller, Burke, Stafford and Archbishop Viganò were finishing a long lunch at Roberto's. Law had told them about his discovery of the daily meetings between Parolin, Ouellet and Stella, as well as their meetings with Francis II. He also described the similar pattern under Francis I.

Law turned to Müller and said, "So, Gerhard, what do you think is going on here? Parolin went out early. Is there a plot of some kind in the making?"

Müller replied judiciously, "Well, there is certainly some kind project underway. Whether it is a plot, I don't really know."

"I think it is definitely a plot," said Burke. "I have never trusted that New Zealander. That is why I voted against him."

"OK, what kind of plot?" asked Law.

"Something we won't like, I am sure," answered Stafford. "I don't trust Parolin either. Isn't it strange that he had to go to the U.S. a week early, not on the charter next Tuesday. You know they are both staying at the nunciature."

"I called Pierre last night, but he didn't call me back," said Viganò.

"Do you think Parolin is a true Brethren, Ray?"

"I don't think he is a true anything. He is an opportunist."

"What about Pell?"

"I don't trust any of those guys on the pope's council, especially since Francis II has kept all of them. Remember, it was the first Francis who gave Francis II his red hat."

Müller commented, "Maybe it is time for a Brethren head count, Bernie."

"I think you are right, Gerhard. In fact, I think it is time we had more younger men, not those retired and who are more into the 'insider' network. I'm thinking of Dominique Mamberti specifically. Any other thoughts?"

"Great choice."

"I'll call him for today and invite him to dinner. When we meet, I'll invite him to become a member of The Brethren."

Later, Law had two phone calls. The first was from Cardinal Burke who said, "Bernard, I think we need to actively pursue the possibility that there is a plot. I have some connections who might be able to find out what is going on and what we might do to stop it, but it will be expensive and you are not going to like knowing about how it is done."

"How expensive, if I may ask?"

"Probably a million euros or so."

Law said, "We could handle that. What would we get?"

"For a million? Information. Anything else would be more."

Law said suavely, "I would not be interested in anything more, nor should you be."

"I will keep you informed."

"You'd better keep me *fully* informed or you are on your own."

The second call was from Cardinal Müller, who said, "Bernard, I think that we should be careful about Burke. He can get crazy ideas and knows some crazy people. He must be kept on a short leash."

Law smiled at Müller's assessment. "Maybe be so, but perhaps that is what we are going to need," he said aloud.

* * * * *

Cardinal Law met for dinner with Cardinal Mamberti on Thursday evening. Mamberti was already at a table when Law arrived at the restaurant.

"Good evening Cardinal."

"Sorry I am late. I had a phone call just as I was leaving."

"That is fine. I just arrived myself."

They ordered and then made small talk, since they did not know one another well. Finally, as they were waiting for dessert, Law began to get down to business.

"Dominique, have you heard about a group in Rome called The Brethren? It is composed mostly of older guys like me to support the Holy Father and to preserve the traditions of the papacy and the Curia. I helped form it many years ago to help Cardinal Ratzinger make the transition to becoming Pope Benedict."

"Yes, I have heard about it. With all due respect, it is rather conservative, is it not?"

"Well, I would say it is somewhat traditional, but we enjoy dialogue of all kinds and respect the positions of everyone."

"How many Brethren are there?"

Law mused, "Well, membership varies from time to time. We are mostly retired and because of the age, illness and deaths the numbers occasionally drop. That is the case currently and that is why I wanted to talk with you. Although we all were in favor of our new pope and most of those eligible voted for him, we don't know him well. I have heard that you are a friend of his."

"I suppose you could say I am. We were in the same class of cardinals and have kept in touch."

"The Brethren meet at 6:30 for drinks and dinner at my place about once a month on Sunday evening. We'd like to have you join us."

"I'd like that."

"Our next meeting will be on the nineteenth. My secretary will call to remind you."

"Thank you," said Mamberti. "I am delighted."

"The pleasure is mine."

Law and Mamberti parted, each liking the way things had gone.

* * * * *

After breakfast on Thursday, May 9, Parolin and Pierre drove over to the temporary nunciature. Parolin was very pleased with the place and Pierre said the move had gone very smoothly. The embassy also looked to be in good shape. When they returned to the conference room, the nuncio was eager to learn more details of the plan.

"I guess I am relieved, at least so far, but I still have many questions," he said, adjusting his rimless glasses.

"That is all right. Let me now tell you some things, about which I suspect you won't have any questions. First, there has been a schedule change. From the beginning with the first announcement of the Catholic University commencement address, we have given the impression that the pope's visit would be an in-and-out event, with no other stops or appearances planned.

"The impression given has been that the Holy Father probably would be back at the Vatican on the Monday following commencement. It has not even been announced that he would be staying at the nunciature, although there were assumptions about that. And obviously, there was also no mention of the size of his entourage.

"It had been originally announced that the papal party would be leaving for the United States on May 16. However, since the Holy Father will be dining with the president on Tuesday, May 14, we decided to change his arrival date to the eleventh, the Saturday before the commencement address. For obvious reasons, this change has not been announced. In addition, since the group coming will be larger than previously anticipated, there will be two planes.

"Now let's talk about what we expect to be accomplished in the long term with this plan. There are three major objectives. The first is to give the laity a legitimate sense of more participation in the decisions of our church. The second is to better facilitate important information between the pope and the laity on many matters. The third, very frankly is to deal with many of those people who have developed fiefdoms for their own aggrandizement."

"That makes sense and is long overdue," the nuncio observed.

Parolin continued, "There is no question that with some of the technology available today, a new structure is necessary—one that supports that technology and is supported by it. About the Holy Father, we decided that a basic structure within the nunciature framework might work—and frankly, we didn't have any other ideas.

"That doesn't mean adding another layer of management between the pope and the bishops, with the bishops and archbishops reporting to the nuncios. In fact, at this point, that probably would just make things worse. The existing system must be made to work infinitely better; however, the nunciature structure cannot take on that responsibility.

"Therefore, we recommended, and the pope accepted, that the Secretariat of State should add an organization parallel to the nuncio system to facilitate the improved communication that is essential. To do that, the pope has authorized a third Substitute with responsibility for Lay Communications. I nominated you for the job and he approved. It will mean returning to Rome to assist me in making all this work."

Archbishop Pierre bowed his head, grasping it with both hands, visibly moved.

"I assume that means you accept, Christophe. Congratulations!" said the cardinal, extending his hand.

"Thank you from the bottom of my heart for your confidence in me, cardinal. I do accept."

"I also assume that you won't mind moving back to Rome in this way."

"I can't wait. Let's get to work."

"The model we suggest is a communications coordinator in each nunciature. They will be of equal rank to the nuncio, but then nuncio will manage the building. Initially, each coordinator will have one layman as staff. Unlike the nuncio, his first language *must* be the language of the country in which he serves, and he should have at least five years of parish experience.

"In addition, you will initially have a staff of about thirty in Rome."

Pierre asked, "Where will all these people come from?"

"We are working on that, as you will soon see," said Parolin. "There are several aspects of this. We are going to reduce the number of things that currently must be decided in Rome by giving local bishops more authority, particularly regarding things such as annulments and laicization. However, that means we must have a high level of consistency among the bishops, and *that* is a challenge.

"Another aspect is the need to identify commonality on issues, and why it may vary from diocese to diocese. There are many moving parts in this project, but I'm sure you understand what I am talking about."

"I do," said Pierre.

"All right, why don't I start by telling you what we think has led us to this point. For at least a hundred years, popes and their close advisors—the members of the Curia—have believed that the strongest and most rigorous magisterium possible is the answer to all potential problems: Tell them what they must believe; punish them if they don't obey; and ignore them when they object.

"However, they failed to realize that in that same hundred years the world, especially the Catholic world, had changed: the people in the pews were often better educated now than those giving the orders; they no longer lived in local or national economies, but in the world economy; science had provided proof that things were not always as they had thought; they are forced to communicate their religious beliefs beyond borders; and they have the right to be heard.

"St. John XXIII recognized this trend sixty years ago, but his successors, mostly for their own self-interests, held the line and then pushed that line backwards to where we are now. Perhaps because of his Jesuit training or perhaps through the Holy Spirit, Pope Francis understood this phenomenon and was determined to make a change. He recognized that he had to transform the magisterium into a dialogue; and to do that he had to first address the source of the magisterium, the Curia. The Curia was a more challenging task than he anticipated. It was based on personal relationships, which, as you and my predecessor know better than anyone, often involved corruption. That is why his council of cardinals includes only one person from the Curia and that person is in a job that Francis created.

"About a year ago, the Pope Francis asked Cardinals Ouellet, Stella and me to develop a plan to change the culture of the hierarchy, especially the bishops. You read about the first step last night. Dramatic as it is, there is much more to be done. The pope has limited contact with the bishops, but virtually none with the faithful, except in huge, impersonal crowds often hand-picked by the bishops. This situation is made worse by the bishops' efforts, consciously or by habit, to impede upward communications by the faithful. Our job is to fix that system. We have about six months to do that.

The cardinal and the nuncio talked the rest of the day and into the evening. Cardinal Parolin was pleased with the way Pierre responded to his new assignment. They spent the next couple of days going over the details of the pope's agenda through the speech at the Catholic University commencement.

* * * * *

While the pope was getting ready to leave for the airport Saturday morning, a private e-mail on his smartphone said: "Have a great trip and impress the Americans. I have been invited to join that elite group." It was from Cardinal Mamberti.

The Italian charter plane arrived at Washington's Dulles International Airport at around 4:00 p.m. on Saturday, May 11, 2019. On board were Pope Francis II; his secretary, Msgr. Menendez; a large group of international journalists; and two Swiss Guards in plain clothes.

Archbishop Christophe Pierre and Cardinal Parolin were there early to meet them. When the plane arrived, a black papal limousine with tinted windows was already on the tarmac, having been flown in along with its backup a week earlier. The limousine that had brought Parolin and Pierre to the airport was also nearby. The popemobile and its backup remained at the nunciature.

The pope, Cardinal Parolin and two Swiss Guards—Franz Buchs and Roland Pfyffer von Altishofen, the pope's personal bodyguards—boarded the papal limousine to take them to the nunciature. Archbishop Pierre and Msgr. Menendez rode in the other limousine, which followed with the luggage.

The pope had been friendly and reasonably candid with the press during the ten-hour trip, but had not made any news. Most of the reporters checked into a hotel near the airport, fully expecting they might get some real news on the return trip May 20. They would be disappointed.

There were no crowds in front of the nunciature when the limos pulled in and the passengers disembarked. After the appropriate greetings and a simple dinner, the travelers went to bed, to deal with the time differential from Rome. The results were varied.

The four-story embassy was at 3339 Massachusetts Avenue NW, directly across the avenue from the old Naval Observatory, now the vice president's residence, and next door to the Finnish embassy. Its 9,787 square feet included the residence of the apostolic delegation on the top floor; chancery offices carrying on business on the next; public rooms for receptions, a chapel, and quarters for visiting prelates on the main floor; and below, living quarters for the service staff.

Later that night, a second chartered plane with a very large amount of luggage and a heavy, covered package in its cargo bay arrived with Cardinals Ouellet and Cardinal Stella, a Vatican IT specialist and a sizable number of Swiss Guards in plainclothes. The guards were dropped off at a dormitory on the Georgetown University campus, where they would be staying. The cardinals and the rest arrived at the embassy while the earlier group was sleeping.

After Mass and breakfast on Sunday, the Holy Father asked the three cardinals, Archbishop Pierre and the commander of the Swiss Guards, Colonel Christoph Graf, to join him in the small conference room near his suite on the top floor. He began the conversation saying, "We are but six men about to make one of the most dramatic changes in the history of our church. I am convinced that this is not only the right thing to do, but the only way to save it. Many others will disagree with us and try to delay or stop our efforts, but we must persist and prevail.

"I think you know that when I have dinner with the president on Tuesday evening I will ask for political asylum for us all. We are likely to be living here together for an extended period. Cardinal Parolin has assured me that we will all be able to conduct our usual duties almost as if we were in the Vatican and that is, of course, essential. However, it is also essential that we share information we learn in that process. To facilitate that, I would like us to meet in this room for up to an hour after dinner each evening."

The men agreed unanimously and left after chatting a few minutes. The pope and the Secretary of State remained briefly.

"Excellent suggestion, your Holiness," said Parolin.

"These are critical times, Pietro, and we must proceed both thoughtfully and boldly."

* * * * *

While the pope, the cardinals, the archbishop and Col. Graf had been talking, the Swiss Guards who were not yet billeted at Georgetown came downstairs; they and the others on the second plane were just finishing breakfast. Captain Hans Fasel, the commander's assistant, was mustering the four sergeants and the thirty-two guards staying at Georgetown to go to their new quarters. They left in four vans.

Parolin asked the rest to join him in the large conference room. When they arrived, he introduced himself and the nuncio.

"First, who is the chef?"

"I am, Your Eminence. My name is Nick Bourg."

"I thought you looked familiar. You have been the pope's personal chef since the first Pope Francis was elected."

"Yes, Your Eminence."

"All right, we are all going to be living fairly close together, under sometimes trying times, and we don't need to be that formal— 'Cardinal P' will be fine. As you may already know, the permanent embassy housekeeping and kitchen staff will be going back to the temporary nunciature shortly. Probably the best use of your time and that of your team would be to become familiar with the kitchen and the things expected of you, so please take your team and go find the nuncio's chef."

Bourg replied, "Thank you, Your ... Cardinal P ... come on, men."

Parolin addressed Col. Graf. "I'd like to start by telling you and the captain about the details and duration of your assignment."

"That would be very helpful, Cardinal."

"It is likely that the Holy Father, Cardinals Ouellet and Stella, and Msgr. Menendez and I will be staying here until November at least. We believe that for at least that long, the pope may be in some, perhaps serious, danger. You and your men must prevent anything bad from happening.

"Thirty-four men, plus the two personal bodyguards, you and the captain was a guess on my part. That gives you four eight-man squads, on a three-day-on-and-a-third-day-off rotation. Your first job is to make a full assessment of the building and grounds and report to me what you need in manpower and equipment. You will get whatever you need."

"How many people will be living here?" Graf asked.

"Those I have mentioned, plus Archbishop Pierre, his secretary, you, Captain Fasel and the pope's two personal bodyguards. The nine members of the pope's council of cardinals will be here for a few days starting on Wednesday evening. There will be a meeting of the prefects of the Curia in the next few weeks. They will probably have to stay and hold their meeting elsewhere. After that, I don't know.

"Your squads and their sergeants will be billeted at Georgetown University, which is not very far away. You will have access to four vans; if more vehicles are needed, they will be provided.

"You should also know Pope Francis is having dinner with the President of the United States on Tuesday evening and will be requesting temporary political asylum for himself, all the rest of us and the embassy itself. We expect it will be granted, but we don't have any idea how that will affect your role."

Graf said, "That is a start. We need to get to work on the security needs within the embassy and its grounds. May we be excused?"

"Certainly."

The men left without a word. Parolin sat for a minute, thinking. "I don't think I need to do anything more about that. It is in good hands."

* * * * *

Unaware of all this, on Monday, May 13, Cardinal Bertone met Law for lunch. Law told him of his concern over the several meetings between Parolin, Ouellet and Stella; their meetings with the pope; and the fact that the same pattern had also occurred during the last months of Francis I.

"What do you make of this, Tarcisio?"

59

"I'd say that the three cardinals were working on a project requested by Francis I but never implemented, and that Francis II either has asked for changes to be made or is in the process of starting its implementation."

Law asked, "What could that project be?"

"With Ouellet and Stella involved, I'd think perhaps something to do with identifying pastors who have the potential of becoming 'Francis-style' bishops."

"What does that mean?"

"I have no idea," said Bertone, flatly.

"Could this be related to the pope giving the commencement address at Catholic University?"

"That would be a good place to announce something new, but probably only if it applied to Americans. Of course, if it were really controversial, it might be announced somewhere other than Rome.

"We need to find out about this. I think it is important, and I don't think I'm going to like it."

* * * * *

Pope Francis II's dinner with the president, the vice president and their spouses on Tuesday, May 14, did not appear on anyone's announced schedule anywhere. At 5:30 p.m., a limousine with tinted windows pulled up at the Vatican embassy and the pope quickly entered, joining the vice president and his wife in the spacious back seat.

The trip to the White House took little time and they were soon ushered inside where the president greeted them. Dinner was delightful and the conversation light.

As the five were relaxing with after dinner drinks, the pope turned to the president and said, "I have a favor to ask."

"It will be my pleasure. What can I do for you?"

"Well, as you know, I am delivering the commencement address at Catholic University on Sunday. During that address I will make an announcement that will dramatically change our church for many years. Many will welcome it enthusiastically. A few, both here and back in Rome, will respond bitterly and perhaps aggressively. Sadly, there have been some instances of violence in our long history and to be frank, some suspicions of such behavior fairly recently.

"My close advisors are fearful that the announcement will place me in serious personal risk of violence, perhaps even assassination. I request political asylum and protection for myself, my four associates and the rest of the party in the Vatican embassy for six months and perhaps longer."

The vice president said, "Of course, this is not a typical case of asylum since the embassy is actually part of the Vatican City State. So, it would involve protection of an embassy, which might be much easier all the way around."

The president replied, "Let's simplify this. Your Holiness, you personally and your people will be protected wherever you go in the United States for as long as you want. I'm not sure whether it will be by USCIS agents, federal marshals, the Secret Service, or some other agency, but it will be done. In addition, the physical integrity of the Vatican embassy will be protected."

"Thank you," said the pope. "I appreciate your kindness,"

"I am dying to know what the announcement is," the vice president's wife said, with a smile.

"You must watch TV on Sunday. Tonight, I can only offer my
    blessings to you all."

"I personally will settle for that," the vice president said.

Francis II was back at the embassy a little after nine. Parolin met
him at the door and they talked very briefly. "Dinner went very
well and the president granted us immunity. Arrangements will
begin in the morning."

"Excellent. I will alert Pierre and tell the cardinals."

"As you see fit. Here is a list of four sets of two all-day meetings
that I have scheduled over the next several days," said the pope,
handing him a list. "I will want to meet here in my conference
room, with lunch served there. The topics are confidential as is the
fact of the meetings themselves."

Parolin asked, "May I share this with Archbishop Pierre and
Cardinals Ouellet and Stella?"

"I will leave that to your discretion."

Parolin took the list, folded it and put it into his pocket, not yet
sure what he was supposed to do with it.

"Good night, Your Holiness."

"Good night, Pietro." The pope headed upstairs to bed. He slept
well.

* * * * *

In Rome, earlier on Tuesday, Cardinal Law learned that the pope's
commencement address at Catholic University of America was
going to be streamed live internationally by EWTN starting at 5:00
p.m. on Sunday, Rome time. Since that evening was the regular
meeting for The Brethren he asked Maria to call everyone to invite
the members to come around 4:30 on Sunday to watch the show—
everyone except Cardinal Parolin, who was already in Washington,

and Cardinal Pell, who was leaving on Sunday for the pope's council meeting starting May 20.

About half an hour later she returned and said, "They all said yes, except Cardinal Ouellet. He won't be here because he is travelling."

"Travelling where?"

"His secretary didn't say."

Cardinal Law never liked being out of the loop. Never. He called his contact. "Hello. This is Cardinal Law. Can you tell me who was on the pope's plane to Washington today?"

"Cardinal, that flight was rescheduled for last Saturday, May 11.

"When was that change made?"

"About a week and a half before, I think. I can look it up.

"No, don't bother. Who made the change?"

"I took the call, Cardinal. It was Cardinal Parolin's secretary."

Law was furious. He paused before speaking. "Tell me who was on that plane."

"Just a minute, Cardinal."

"Take your time."

"Cardinal, the manifest says the pope, Msgr. Menendez and two Swiss Guards."

"That's all?"

"Well, there were a lot of press people. They filled the plane. Do you want their names?"

"No, I don't need them. Are you sure Cardinal Ouellet was not on board? I heard he was going home to Canada this week and I thought he might have hitched a ride as far as Washington."

"No, he was on the second plane."

"*What* second plane?"

"The one that left a couple of hours later."

"Going to Washington?"

"Yes, there wasn't enough room on the first, with all the press."

"So Ouellet flew all alone?"

"No sir. There was also Cardinal Stella, a guy from the Vatican IT department, Colonel Graf, Captain Fasel and about forty more Swiss Guards."

"OK. Thanks," said Law, slamming down the phone. The irritated cardinal poured himself a drink, muttering, "Ouellet, Stella and a small army of Swiss Guards, but not Pell ... *what the hell is going on?*"

Chapter Three
Getting Down to Business

Parolin asked Ouellet and Stella to join him and the nuncio for breakfast early Wednesday. On his way, he knocked on the door of the pope's apartment.

"Come in."

As Parolin stepped inside, he said, "Good morning, Your Holiness. I have some helpful news, a direct result of your meeting with the president. The White House press secretary, Sean Spicer, called this morning to offer the services of one of his assistants to help set up the Monday press conference. He will be here around ten."

"That is very generous. Please express my thanks to the president."

* * * * *

Over breakfast Parolin brought the others up to date with what had happened and would be happening over the next two days. As they were finishing, the Swiss Guard who was manning the front door entered.

"Cardinal P, there is a U.S. Navy lieutenant here to see you; she says the president sent her to talk with you about security."

"Wonderful. Get in touch with Col. Graf and ask him to join us." Turning to his breakfast mates, he said, "Why don't you fellows stay for this. We can't afford to have me the only one who knows everything that is going on."

Graf was in a meeting with the kitchen staff but he joined the cardinals as Lt. Kate Keenan arrived. The athletic-looking lieutenant was in her mid-to-late twenties, tall and very attractive. Exuding confidence, she took charge of the conversation. "Gentlemen, my commanding officer assigned me to plan and oversee the installation of a security fence around the property as soon as possible and to make recommendations about manning the area for its protection. He also told me that I cannot begin until Sunday morning. I have studied the maps and have a sense of what I think should be done. I brought a few men with me to take some measurements and do a layout."

"That is good news and I appreciate it," said Parolin. "Col. Graf here is the head of the pope's Swiss Guards. He has a detachment of forty men here with him, and we can increase that number easily. He is already familiar with the property and may have some ideas for you."

"That's fine, Cardinal. I'm sure that will be helpful."

"I have a question, Lieutenant," said Pierre. "What kind of fence are we talking about here?"

"It will be very much like the one around the White House—black wrought iron, ten feet high. The top two-and-a-half feet will have an electrical charge strong enough to stun and knock down an intruder. In addition, a state-of-the-art surveillance system will cover every square foot of the grounds and the building exterior."

"How long will *that* take?" asked Pierre.

"Sir, the construction crew is a fairly large detachment of Navy Seabees. They will begin early Sunday morning and not leave until it is finished, which is currently estimated at some time before midnight Sunday evening. However, to assure that, I'd like to deliver all the equipment and materials needed on Saturday. We can stage those things out of sight from the street down at the east end of the property."

Col. Graf said, "My assistant, Capt. Hans Fasel, the sergeants of each of the four watch sections and I have made a complete tour of the grounds, especially way back in the rear. It would take many more men than I have here to police it. I'd like your input on that."

"I assume that there will be some sort of gatehouse in the front and perhaps another at the driveway entrance, and I would like to have some input on the design," added Pierre.

Lt. Keenan replied, "Gentlemen, we will address all those questions and more after we make our survey. Col. Graf, I suggest that your captain and I take a tour while my men make some measurements."

"Excellent idea."

"Have him meet me at the front door. We will begin there. Now, if you will excuse me?"

"You are excused," said Cardinal Parolin.

When the lieutenant closed the door, Parolin turned to Col. Graf and smiling said, "I hope your captain is prepared for her."

Col. Graf laughed and responded, "I wish that Hans would leave his cell phone open, but that is not protocol."

* * * * *

Construction was already underway at the commencement site.

In the stadium, the stage and its backdrop were set up on the grass in centerfield with the front about seventy feet behind second base. Seating for the graduates was in three sections running from foul line to foul line and from an imaginary line from first and third bases, so they wouldn't have to deal with the pitcher's mound. Spectators would occupy the main grandstand, with the outfield stands used for overflow.

About six a.m. Sunday, an armored limousine with blacked-out windows would be driven in through the maintenance gate in the left field corner and parked behind the stage.

* * * * *

The three cardinals and Pierre were about to go their separate ways when the guard at the front door came to the door and said, "Two people from the White House are here to see you, Cardinal Parolin."

The cardinal looked at his watch and said, "They are a little early, but send them in." Then looking at the other three he added, "You fellows should stay for this as well."

Parolin was standing when the two entered.

"Good afternoon. I am Cardinal Parolin."

"Good morning, Cardinal. I am David Andreatta, assistant White House press secretary and this is DeeDee Myers. DeeDee was press secretary for President Bill Clinton and now is executive vice president of Warner Communications in Los Angeles. She was in Washington on business and press secretary Spicer asked her to come along. She is Jesuit-educated, so that may help us. We understand that you are going to have a press conference."

"It is a pleasure to meet you both," said Parolin warmly. "Please sit down. These are my colleagues, Cardinal Ouellet, Cardinal Stella, and the apostolic nuncio, Archbishop Pierre."

"I guess my first question, Cardinal Parolin, is whether you have ever organized a press conference before?" asked Andreatta.

"No."

"O ... K. Do you know the purpose of a press conference?"

"I imagine it is to give the press the opportunity to ask about exactly what we are doing."

"No, it definitely is not that. The purpose of a press conference is to tell them *generally* what you are doing, why that is a great idea and, specifically, what you want them to report about without their realizing it. Then you answer their questions the way you want them to understand. The burden is on them. What are you announcing?"

"The Holy Father is giving the commencement address at Catholic University on Sunday and will make a very important announcement. The press conference on Monday will be a follow-up to clarify that announcement and how it will be implemented."

"OK, what is the pope's announcement?"

"Here are copies of the announcement part of the address."

The two newcomers began to read.

"Holy shit!" Andreatta exclaimed, without looking up. "Holy shit! I'm not even a practicing Catholic anymore and I know this is huge! Oh, God, please excuse my language."

The cardinals were chuckling and so was DeeDee.

Recovering slightly, Andreatta continued, "What kind of planning and preparation have you done for this press conference so far?"

"None," said Cardinal Ouellet.

"Holy shit! This is going to be one of the top ten news stories of this century and nothing has been done?"

"We have been very busy," explained Cardinal Stella.

"What should we do first?" asked Ouellet.

Andreatta gained some control, slowly saying, "What should you do first ..." Then sternly, "I'll tell you what you should do first. You should hire someone like DeeDee for the rest of the year. No question about that and don't even *think* of asking her how much that will cost. Tell her to send you a bill when she is finished. That is the first thing you should do. When you do that, she will tell you what to do next."

There was an awkward silence before Parolin said, "Is that agreeable with you, Ms. Myers?"

"Well, it is certainly flattering, and wasn't what I expected when I came here. But David is right. You need good, experienced help, and you need it now. However, I have a great job, and a husband and children in Los Angeles. I can make some phone calls and arrange to stay another week or so to help get you set up and through the press conferences. By the way, I think there should be two: one by you on Wednesday, and the other a set of interviews by the Holy Father next Sunday."

She continued, "I think I know someone who can take over quickly and get you through this. She is a former colleague and good friend named Jackie Ring, who is a specialist in public relations. We're going to need some experienced help, and I was thinking about asking her to do that. She has handled the political campaigns of several congressmen and at least one governor. I believe she is available and I think she will jump at an offer. I will try to have her here tomorrow or at the latest Friday so that you can meet her."

"Holy shit!" said Cardinal Stella, and everyone nearly collapsed in laughter.

Parolin looked at Myers and said, "This is a great relief for me—I had begun to realize that we really didn't know what we are doing. What do you need to get started?"

"I know it is going to be difficult, but I really need a bank of four or five telephone extensions off the main embassy number with an automatic re-direct, and I need them to be operational before the pope begins to talk on Sunday. The phones will start ringing before he finishes."

"I can get that done," said David.

"I need four to six people to answer those phones starting at noon on Sunday, after I have trained them. I will need them until I can hire some people who have done that before."

"We have some Swiss Guards here who could probably do that," said Ouellet.

"Do they speak English?" she asked.

"I'm sure some do."

"Six who speak excellent English will do. Also, I need to look at the area where you were planning to do the conference and I need an office near that. It seems pretty crowded here. Is it all part of the pope's entourage?"

"No, they are the pope's nine-member council of cardinals, and each has a couple of staff members."

"Are they here permanently?"

"No. They are here for a three-day meeting to be briefed on the plans for the things that are going to happen after Sunday's announcement. The meeting ends Friday and they will move out to hotels Saturday morning. They will leave after the commencement."

"That will not work. It is an unnecessary distraction and we are going to need all the space we can find. Postpone that meeting", said DeeDee.

"I will go and suggest that to the Holy Father."

"That's good. It will be a zoo in this building for at least a week."

Parolin left for the pope's office.

"OK. Let's assume that's the plan and go on" said DeeDee. "I think it will be much better for Cardinal Parolin to do the Wednesday press conference and then make better use of the pope on Sunday. Do you know what I'm thinking, David?"

"A full Ginsburg?"

"What in the world is a full Ginsburg?" asked Cardinal Stella, bewildered.

Myers explained, "There are five hour-long Sunday morning news programs in the United States: one on each major network and CNN. Appearing on every one with this is very important. On February 1, 1998, William H. Ginsburg, the attorney for Monica Lewinsky, who had charged then-President Clinton of inappropriate sexual behavior, was the first person to appear on all five shows on the same day. It has been done several times since, but that's what I meant. I am going to get on the phone with the five Sunday talk show hosts immediately after the address and offer them fifteen-minute interviews with the pope for next Sunday morning. They will shoot them here on Thursday and Friday."

"Do you see why I said you needed to hire someone like DeeDee?" asked Andreatta.

Parolin walked back in. "The Holy Father says fine."

"Great news, Pietro," said Cardinal Ouellet, "We are going to do a full Goldberg!"

* * * * *

Capt. Hans Fasel was thirty, tall, very athletic with boyish good looks. He was at the front door in about five minutes.

"Sorry if I kept you waiting, Lieutenant. I was just finishing my notes from yesterday. I would suggest that we take the same route as the Colonel and I did, and let the notes guide us. We began at the side entrance by the driveway."

"Fine—lead the way."

As they began to walk, Lt. Keenan said, "So, Hans, I am not familiar with the Swiss Guards. Tell me about them."

"Well, we have existed for over 500 years," began Hans. "The basic requirements to join are: you must be a Swiss citizen; a Roman Catholic; have a good moral and ethical background; be between 19 and 30 years old, at least 1.74 meters tall and single;

must have either a high school degree or professional diploma and have completed service with the Swiss army; and have attended the military school in Switzerland. Then to get into the Pontifical Swiss Guard Regiment, you must apply and be accepted. In early May of every year we swear an oath to protect the life of the pope. We all did that last week."

"Wait a minute. Are you the guys who wear the funny outfits and carry swords?"

"When we stand guard at the Vatican Palace or participate in official church ceremonies. we do wear the traditional uniform of the Swiss Guard. However, since the attempted assassination of Pope John Paul II in 1981, some of us have served more often in a bodyguard role for the pope, and we have had special training in unarmed combat and small arms.

"We wear regular clothes for that, or fatigues as I do now. Franz Buchs and Roland Pfyffer von Altishofen, who will accompany the pope to the commencement on Sunday, have that training. And by the way, those two men are sons of two former commandants who were close friends, Franz Pfyffer von Altishofen and Roland Buchs. They named their sons for each other."

"I guess we don't have to worry about commitment there, do we?"

"The rest of us are highly trained in military automatic and semi-automatic weapons, such as the SIG P220 and Glock 19 pistols, the Steyr TMP machine pistol and submachine and machine guns like the Heckler & Koch MP5A3. This is why we are here. Now may I ask a question, ma'am?"

"Sure—and it's Kate."

"How did you get into the construction business?"

Lt. Keenan laughed.

"I'm not in the construction business. I'm in the security business like you are, except of course on a much more sophisticated scale. The SeaBees were assigned to me to define and physically secure the area; they'll be gone Sunday night. I'm with Navy Seal Team Four and my unit is assigned for your security."

"How do you see the security assignments being split up between your people and mine?"

"At this point I don't. This is not a ceremonial situation. Until I see that some of your people can shoot, you will handle the gatehouse processing and whatever else you want to set up inside the embassy. My people will handle external security, including during all outside travel."

Hans raised an eyebrow. "And how are you going to determine whether my people can shoot?"

"After a couple of weeks if you have someone you think can handle it, I'll take him down to the range and we'll see. It will be a one-at-a-time qualification procedure."

"That is unacceptable. We have the sworn responsibility of protecting the pope. We didn't come all this distance to answer phones."

"What are you suggesting?"

"Test them now."

"There isn't enough time."

"Can you get range time late Saturday afternoon?"

"Late Saturday afternoon? Sure."

"OK, here is the proposition," said Hans. "Four of your guys against four of mine. Four head-to-head matches using every kind of weapon you are planning to use."

"So are you telling me you have four guys who can shoot?"

"All my men can shoot, and I can give you as many as you want. I'll have all of them standing in front of the embassy when we get back there. You pick the four you want to see work."

"What if the matches end up two and two?"

"One more match. You and me, head to head. Loser buys dinner."

"For ten people?"

"No the other eight men are on their own."

Kate thought briefly before saying, "Deal," and laughed. "We'll bring the weapons we will both use."

"I'll need directions to the range and we will see you at five Saturday afternoon."

"No, you'll see me Saturday morning when we deliver your damned fence."

* * * * *

DeeDee was on a roll. "I'll send a press release to my A-list by e-mail today, simply telling them I have temporarily joined the embassy staff as communications director. Then on Sunday, I'll send one announcing the press conference immediately after the address. I understand that a group of international journalists were on the plane with the pope and they will be included. Do you have a list of Catholic press, domestic and foreign, that you want me to include?"

"Yes, we do. I'll get it," said the nuncio.

"Is Bill Donohue on it?" asked Cardinal Ouellet, to laughter.

"This may for once render him speechless," answered Pierre.

The session finally ended about five, to resume Saturday morning. The Secretary of State was finishing some notes as the others left, and a few minutes later the IT person who had arrived on the second plane appeared in the doorway.

"Cardinal Parolin, I am Luigi Picardi from Vatican City information technology. I'd like to give you a progress report."

"Come in, come it. I didn't expect much progress yet and certainly no report."

"Well I am not quite finished," said Picardi, "but I have a couple of ideas for which I need your approval."

"I would like the nuncio to hear this. Instead of briefing me now, please join Archbishop Pierre and me for breakfast tomorrow morning at 7:30. I will have an additional assignment for you."

"Good. I will be there."

* * * * *

Picardi was already seated when Cardinal Parolin and Archbishop Pierre arrived for breakfast the next morning.

"Archbishop, I'd like you to meet the IT specialist we brought over from Rome, Luigi Picardi. You two are going to be seeing a great deal of one another in the next several months. Luigi, this is our host, Archbishop Christophe Pierre, apostolic nuncio to the United States."

When the three had finished breakfast, Parolin spoke to the matters at hand. "Yesterday afternoon, Mr. Picardi told me he had a report to make on his activities since he arrived late Wednesday night. I asked him to hold off until this morning until you could hear it firsthand, Christophe. Go ahead, Luigi."

"Thank you, Cardinal. As you know, I brought along the pope's personal server with everything on it. It is up and running in his office here right now, exactly as it was in the Vatican. I have made some changes in the firewall so that no one—and I mean no one other than the Holy Father— can get into it. I have also set it up so that all e-mail traffic in the curial offices is gathered and stored here without anyone knowing that has happened."

"Luigi, I'm sure that you know that Cardinal Law has access to a system that Pope Benedict had designed; it tracks the meetings, their attendees and the travel of virtually everyone in a curial office."

"Yes, sir," said Picardi. "I designed and built it. It is already on the server, although no one outside this building has access to what happens here."

"Excellent!"

"I really think that we should back up this server to another one in a remote location, just in case something happens here. I don't have any ideas about where, but we can think about that."

"Go ahead and order it," said Pierre. "I think we should put it as close as possible to what you think is optimum. When we are finished here, show me the options and we will decide."

"Excellent" said Parolin. "Now, Christophe, I'm going to tell you more about Mr. Picardi and what I would like to make his next assignment. He is not just any person from the Vatican's outstanding IT department—he has college and advanced degrees in communications technology and organizational theory; he also is a topnotch systems designer, program developer and systems management specialist. I suspect the archbishop here has already decided what your new assignment must be, Luigi, but I'd like to tell you what the nuncio's is.

"Tomorrow afternoon, in his commencement address at the Catholic University of America, the Holy Father will make an announcement which will shock everyone and greatly change the institutional Catholic church as we know it. Two of the three major objectives are to give the laity a legitimate sense of more participation in the decisions of our church and to better facilitate communication between the pope and the laity on many matters.

"Not including the Curia, there are 2,851 diocesan bishops, archbishops and cardinals who report directly to the pope. No other person in the world has a management span of control that comes anywhere close to that. There is no question that with some of the technology available today, perhaps that can work; but a structure that supports that technology, and is supported by it, is necessary. In connection with the Holy Father, we decided that a basic structure within the nunciature framework might work—and frankly, we didn't have any other ideas."

The cardinal noted with pleasure that Luigi was nodding his head at the mention of using "the technology available today" to solve the problem. He continued, "The model is to have a communications coordinator in each nunciature, all around the world. At that level there is a need to identify commonality on issues, and whether they may vary from diocese to diocese. There are several moving parts in this project, but I'm sure you understand what I am talking about."

"Letters from the people, especially if they are critical of something, are often, if not usually, ignored by the bishops and almost uniformly by the nuncios, if they get that far. Petitions rarely see the light of day. If anyone were to be questioned as to why this is the case, they would probably reply, "The system is slow." Our job is to fix that system. We have about six months to do that. Now let me tell you about a related but separate task with an even shorter timeline."

Parolin described the work that would start immediately after the pope's address at Catholic University and continue until November. The other two listened carefully. When he finished, they seemed stunned, but he pre-empted a response.

"Now I am expecting the arrival of our press conference experts and I suspect that you are going to be discussing things I don't even understand, so I will leave you now with one more request for the archbishop. I have scheduled a videoconference with all ninety-eight of the nuncios of the world at 11:00 a.m. on Sunday, and Luigi, I would like you to be at my side. This may be the largest and most significant task any of us have ever faced."

* * * * *

True to their word, David Andreatta and DeeDee Myers arrived at nine to continue discussions with the three cardinals. Jackie Ring was with them.

"Gentlemen, I'd like you to meet my friend and former colleague Jackie Ring. I was able to reach her last evening on the phone and explain our project. She has decided to come aboard instead of taking another opportunity she was considering. I have the utmost confidence in her, and she is here this morning to start immediately. Fortunately, I only have to teach her about yesterday."

Parolin said, "Welcome Jackie. Unfortunately, we have a great deal more to learn about this than you do. We are sure that you will quickly become part of the team."

"Thank you, Cardinal. I am happy to be here."

"Ms. Ring, it is a pleasure. I have heard good things about you."

"Jackie, please, Your Eminence."

"Then I am Cardinal P."

"Jackie has agreed to the plan we discussed and she is ready to get started," DeeDee said.

"Wonderful. Welcome to the Vatican in exile. I'm sure we are in good hands."

After the additional greetings, they all sat down to business.

Cardinal Parolin began, "DeeDee, I have been thinking about your idea of the Full Goldberg ..."

"No, that was Cardinal Ouellet's idea of humor. It's called a Full Ginsburg, and I too have been thinking more about that. This whole event is so big that, especially for the average person, it is difficult to properly absorb it all. We need to slow things down. The bishops will have been given two weeks to respond to the demand of the pope. Your press conference is Wednesday and we will not have definitive results by then, but you will have them by the second press conference the following Wednesday."

Parolin raised his eyebrows. "*Second* press conference?"

"Cardinal, you certainly didn't think this was a one-and-done process! We need to have weekly conferences until this whole thing has unfolded. Because of that, I think we should do the Full Ginsburg the following Sunday. You set the stage and then the pope follows up."

"That makes sense, unless they lose interest."

Myers continued, "Believe me, Cardinal, they will not lose interest. I think you should plan to do a press conference every Wednesday for the foreseeable future, and we may use the pope occasionally on Sundays."

"Well, then," replied Parolin, "let's talk about your idea of the Full Ginsburg. Could we concentrate on the rationale for different elements of the plan in each of the five interviews?"

"Fair question, but first let me tell you about the five interviewers. Strangely enough, none of the five is Roman Catholic. The closest is ABC's George Stephanopoulos, who is Greek Orthodox. I believe John Dickerson at CBS is a Protestant of some kind, and Chris Wallace at FOX, Chuck Todd at NBC and Jake Tapper at CNN are all Jewish.

"My suggestion to all of them will be that they do a one-on-one interview with the pope lasting up to fifteen minutes, which they can record here in the embassy and then edit as they like, to fit their Sunday schedule. They can then follow that with a live discussion with a couple of their colleagues who are Catholic, such as Donna Brazile and Cokie Roberts at ABC; Norah O'Donnell and Charles Osgood at CBS; Bill O'Reilly and Sean Hannity at FOX; Chris Matthews and Luke Russert at NBC; and Chris Cuomo and Erin Burnett at CNN. This is a common pattern in the broadcasts, so I think it will be easy for me to get them to follow it."

"That sounds very good to me," said Cardinal Stella. "Although the names don't mean much to me, the concept does."

"Good. Now let's discuss the suggestion that each will discuss different aspects of the pope's reasoning for this monumental shakeup of the way the institutional Catholic church operates. I need your help here. Cardinal Parolin?"

"You know, sometimes people of faith dismiss, as if it were simple, the connection between two things that seem to have a cause-and-effect relationship, as 'the Holy Spirit at work again.'

"While I was operating under the assumption of a Monday press conference, I made a list of some possible topics of interest. They were behind the thinking that went into the plan we presented to Pope Francis I. The Holy Spirit has obliged by providing five of them."

"Great," replied Myers, "but we don't want you to steal the pope's thunder in the Ginsburg at your conference. We can talk about the details after later. We need to start concentrating on what you are going to talk about first thing tomorrow morning."

* * * * *

The first two trucks filled with fencing and construction equipment pulled into the embassy driveway at ten o'clock Saturday morning, and Capt. Hans Fasel was there to meet it. His counterpart, Lt.

Kate Keenan, was on the passenger side of the cab of the first truck.

Hans walked over to the truck, and the driver ran the window down.

"Good morning. Good morning, Lt. Keenan. You are right on time. I'll ride down in the second truck."

Getting out of the trucks, Hans and Kate moved out of the staging area, where they could watch safely.

"How many truckloads will this take?" Fasel asked.

"They said six, so I ordered four trucks," said Kate. "Two more are leaving for here right now. If they don't have everything, these two will finish the job. I have to be finished in time to whip you guys at the range."

"Good planning. Would you like to increase the stakes?"

"Umm ... not yet."

"What did you decide on the layout for the fencing?"

"We will be ten feet in from the tree line all the way around so that we can easily see anyone approaching the fence. We will officially request permission to place our people in the wooded areas from the Finnish Embassy and the property owners on 34th and Fulton Streets. That should be easy to get because it makes them safer, too. We could have a remotely operated gate for that rear driveway."

"How about personnel?"

"Boots on the ground in the wooded area, with advanced night vision capability, because an attack during business hours probably isn't realistic."

"How many will you need from me?" asked Hans.

Kate said slyly, "That will largely depend on how many emerge without being wounded at the range."

"You have to raise the stakes after that one."

"No I don't," she grinned.

* * * * *

DeeDee was working her way down the checklist.

"Are the phones all operational yet, Jackie?"

"Yes."

"Operators assigned?"

"Subject to your approval."

"Good answer. Sufficient capacity for the press conference?"

"Yes, but it probably would be a good idea for them to go to the restroom before taking their seats."

"Post-conference reception?"

"Just about set."

"We need it by Tuesday. Credential list?"

"Tentative list by Monday noon. Firm by Tuesday."

"Credentials?"

"Designed. At vendor. Here Tuesday."

The exercise went on for an hour or so. Then Jackie and DeeDee retreated to her office to write press releases.

* * * * *

Except for Hans and the four Swiss Guards at the range, everyone living at the embassy—the pope, David Andreatta, Jackie Ring, DeeDee Myers and anyone else directly involved—had dinner together on Saturday evening. After dessert Cardinal Parolin stood to say a few words.

"Tomorrow will be a day which marks a major event in the history of the Catholic church. The pope's party will leave here at 8:15 a.m. for the stadium, returning immediately after his commencement address. There will be a videoconference with all ninety-eight of the other nuncios in the rest of the world at eleven. The press room will be open and staffed at noon. I now ask Pope Francis II to give us his blessing for this momentous day."

The pope rose, as did everyone else, including the kitchen staff.

"Heavenly Father, we ask your guidance as we begin this noble endeavor to save your church. Please give us the strength to match our ardor; the resolve to resist our attackers; and the charity to treat our adversaries with love to maintain their faith. We ask your blessing of our plan. Amen."

All responded fervently, "Amen!"

* * * * *

The casually dressed Swiss Guards selected by Lt. Keenan, and Capt. Fasel arrived at the range about ten minutes early. Five minutes later, the Seals arrived. Lt. Keenan came in her own car.

After introductions, the enlisted personnel paired up for the match and the guards were given their weapons. They had a few minutes to try out each of the unfamiliar guns. Then the competition began.

Each match was very close; when they were finished, they were indeed tied two and two. It was time for the shoot-off between Keenan and Fasel. The lead changed several times but in the end, Fasel won.

He said, "I noticed that you arrived in your own car. Should I ride with you to the restaurant or do you want my team to drop me off?"

Kate said, "You can ride with me. I don't live on the base, and these guys have to get there for dinner."

In Kate's car, the two bantered back and forth, until she turned down a quiet street in a residential neighborhood and stopped at a small, attractive house.

"Is this the restaurant?"

"No," she said with a smile. "This is my home—and I am the chef."

"I hope you can cook better than you shoot."

"I guess I asked for that, but actually, I can."

When they walked into the house they were greeted with a mixture of delightful odors.

"What are we having?"

"I don't know about you, but I am having a little Jack Daniel's on the rocks."

"That sounds good to me," said Hans, not sure what Jack Daniel's was.

Dinner was spectacular and the conversation delightful. At the end, Hans raised his glass of Grand Marnier in tribute. "I have a question. Where would we have gone if you had won, and what would have happened to all of this?"

"I would not have won," Kate said with that same smile. "And now, I need to take you back to the embassy. We have a big day tomorrow."

When they drove into the embassy parking lot and stopped by the front door, Kate reached into her pocket. "If you need to reach me during business hours, here is my card," she said. "My home number is on the back."

"Thanks. I will give you mine tomorrow. Shall we do this again?"

"If you are prepared to lose," she said softly, reaching over and kissing his cheek lightly.

"I will win, I think. No matter how it turns out. See you tomorrow."

She pulled out of the driveway as he walked to the embassy door, looking at his watch. It was 9:30.

Chapter Four

Commencement

Sunday began with clear skies. Pope Francis, his secretary, and Swiss Guards Franz and Roland rode in the popemobile with a Seal Team escort to the stadium, to the delight of many pedestrians who did not expect to see him that morning.

There was a breakfast at nine in one of the large hospitality suites at the stadium for all those who would be on the stage for commencement. Each of the twenty-five cardinals and archbishops who were university trustees were there. Most of the archbishops had not seen the former Cardinal Dew since he had become Francis II, and an informal receiving line formed to greet and congratulate him.

After some welcoming words from the president of the trustees, they had eaten, then moved to the visiting team locker room nearby to don their academic robes, hoods and caps. Then they lined up in proper order at the door to the dugout, from which they would emerge in procession. The graduates did the same through the home team locker room.

* * * * *

At 11:00 a.m., the Vatican Secretary of State, Cardinal Pietro Parolin, with Archbishop Christophe Pierre at his side, convened an international videoconference with the ninety-eight apostolic nuncios outside the United States. In it he informed the nuncios of the contents of the papal address at Catholic University; the new and increased short- and long-term responsibilities they would have; and the procedures they were to follow.

He also shared with them the changes taking place within the Secretariat of State, the new role of Archbishop Pierre, and the personnel additions planned for all the nunciatures. He urged everyone who could possibly watch the pope's address to do so.

* * * * *

The Brethren not in Washington were assembled before the large TV in Cardinal Law's residence when the commencement procession began to emerge from the dugout.

"Where are they staying?" Cardinal Müller asked.

"At the nunciature," replied Viganò. "I called Pierre again last night, but he still hasn't returned my calls."

"Did you know that Ouellet and Stella are both there, Ray?" Law asked.

"I didn't know anything about Ouellet and Stella," answered Burke, scowling.

"Now, why the hell *are* they there?" Bertone grumbled.

"I haven't any idea." said Law "but I don't think I like it."

* * * * *

There was a huge explosion of cheering when the pope entered. Then it settled down, as most commencements do.

Commencement went smoothly. There were a few short speeches and then it was time for Francis. Properly hooded to mark his honorary degree, he was introduced by Michael P. Warsaw, chief executive officer of the Eternal Word Television Network and chairman of the board of trustees.

Pope Francis II moved to the podium to a standing ovation. He waved in return and then motioned to the exuberant crowd to sit down. When they did, he began to speak.

"Thank you, Mr. Warsaw.

88

"Graduates of the Catholic University of America Class of 2019, congratulations on that accomplishment at this outstanding institution. I welcome you as potential leaders of the Catholic church in America or wherever your futures take you. We need all the leaders we can find.

"I want to speak to you today about the leadership we need in order to bring those who have left our church back to communion with us both literally and figuratively, and to help lead all of us in a church that finds solutions instead of alienating people. That is the way it was in the beginning – pastoral and loving toward all of us.

"But for reasons we felt were beneficial to us—and for a time they were—we cast our lot with those who wielded physical power, military power and oppression. We emulated those people in dress, in ceremony and in philosophy. That worked for a while in a world much simpler than the one we live in today.

"Then the world discovered democracy which predates our church but not our theology. Our protectors lost their power and their ability to oppress, but we continued to use that tool to save our people from themselves instead of giving them the latitude and guidance to do that with us.

"This *modus operandi* worked for a while, often only because our leaders were better educated than the people they led; they were able to defeat our arguments in that far simpler world. We accepted oppression as the cost of salvation.

"But the world became more complex and among our Christians, people were able to find ways to holiness in the absence of oppression."

* * * * *

"Where the hell is he going with this drivel?" asked Cardinal Müller.

"I don't know, but I don't think we are going to like it," replied Viganò.

"It sounds like that John XXIII crap about opening the windows," said Law.

Burke said snidely, "Well, I guess you and Bertone would know more about that than I do. I was just starting high school then."

They all laughed, and Law motioned to Maria to bring another round.

* * * * *

"But we persisted in our ways, declaring science and progress to be symptoms of Modernism, which was to be resisted at all costs.

"Our hierarchy became authoritative. We decided our pope was infallible. If there is one thing I don't believe, it is that I am infallible. Neither were my predecessors."

There was a ripple of cautious laughter among the graduates.

"Since then, by extension, everyone in Rome except the weatherman has become infallible."

A little less cautious laughter.

"And that is a serious part of the problems facing the church today.

"As you all know well, because I am sure you heard on this campus, the first Pope Francis spent the last six years reforming the Roman Curia, a task *his* predecessor, Benedict XVI, said couldn't be done. It had become corrupt in some areas, generally archaic and nearly dysfunctional.

"It took him much longer than he thought it would, and it kept him from addressing what he considered to be not only a larger problem and certainly one more challenging: the operational hierarchy itself.

"Many of our bishops, who in the early years of the church were its leaders, have become its oppressive enforcers. Their primary task became to resist change in any form. The Curia took what they believed a pope wanted—even when his health didn't allow him to know what he wanted—and turned it into doctrine to be handed down to the people by the bishops.

"The faithful lost their voice, concerning their very lives— issues like basic equality, especially for women who felt the call to serve in ordained roles; people of different sexual orientation, who wanted to be recognized as equals; hardworking good parents who could not afford to raise and educate more children so they used any means to prevent pregnancy; priests who were not allowed to be married and ordained, even though that restriction was not observed in some parts of the church; and those who had troubled marriages and divorced, were denied annulment and told that, if they remarried, they could not receive the sacraments.

"There is no 'no' in Catholic and, in fact, the very definition of the word "catholic" makes that clear. Yet few if any bishops deliver that message up the chain of command to the only person who could currently change this. Instead they are very cautious about discussing these things with other bishops."

* * * * *

"Now I know I am not going to like this," said Law.

"We have to stop him, whatever it is that he is suggesting," offered Burke.

"I agree," added Archbishop Viganò.

* * * * *

"If the church is to survive in this changing world, we must change that culture. By that, I mean that our upward communication and support of the feelings of the laity. Our bishops must once again become advocates for their people. If they don't, eventually all those people will leave. That exodus has already begun.

"There are currently 2,851 dioceses and archdioceses in the world. With coadjutor and auxiliary bishops, that means we must change the culture of over 3,000 bishops and archbishops. However, to attempt such a task one bishop at a time, or even in groups of fifty or more, would take years to complete and even then would have to be repeated from time to time—and closely monitored. That is impractical.

"A detailed, more efficient plan must be followed, and in the last months of his life, Pope Francis commissioned such a plan, which he asked to be delivered to his successor for implementation.

"Today I am announcing it."

There was cautious applause from the graduates and the audience. In Law's living room, there was stony silence.

"As I began to speak, envelopes with a letter and a form to be completed are being delivered to the homes of all of those more than 3,000 bishops, auxiliary bishops and archbishops in those 2,851 dioceses and archdioceses. I expect that all those letters will all have been delivered by the time I finish today.

"The letters request that all those bishops and archbishops complete the enclosed form requesting early retirement with full benefits, plus a retirement bonus effective on November

15, 2019. They are to return the signed retirement request in the addressed envelope provided to the apostolic nuncio in their respective countries by the end of the workday on Friday, May 31, 2019. If there is no nuncio in their country, the forms will be sent directly to the Vatican Substitute Secretary of State.

"If his completed form is not returned by that time, the bishop or archbishop will be in contempt of a lawful order of the pope and will be dismissed immediately with loss of all non-mandatory benefits and, of course, the retirement bonus."

There was not a sound in the stadium.

* * * * *

In Cardinal Law's residence, Cardinal Müller was on his feet, knocking over his glass and shouting, "That ungrateful, goddamned son of a bitch! Can he do that?"

Cardinal Bertone said quietly, "I think he can, but the timetable is a nightmare and there will be chaos. He won't be able to pull it off and will look incompetent."

"He must be stopped, no matter what it takes!" shouted Viganò.

* * * * *

The pope continued.

"Similarly and at the same time, letters of instruction will be delivered to the chancellor of each diocese and archdiocese. These letters will tell them about the request to the bishops and archbishops.

"It will also instruct them to form nominating teams of nine people—four lay women, three lay men and two priests—to select two pastors of their diocese or archdiocese who will compete in an election to determine their new bishop or archbishop. All baptized and confirmed members of each diocese or archdiocese will be eligible to vote.

"Details of this process and the qualifications for candidates will be announced in a press conference on Wednesday at the Vatican embassy.

"Beginning immediately bishops will serve six-year terms, with one re-election allowed. All bishops and archbishops will be subject to recall for cause if 75 percent of the baptized and confirmed members of a diocese or archdiocese sign an official petition on a form issued by the chancellor.

"The election of bishops and auxiliary bishops in every diocese and archdiocese will be held every day during the last full week before November 15. Details of this will also be available on Wednesday."

* * * * *

"He's done his homework," said Cardinal Law, grudgingly.

"He must be stopped!!" Cardinal Burke responded.

"That may not be easy," said Bertone. "There are millions of people on his side of this argument."

"He *will* be stopped!! I guarantee it," bellowed the grim-faced Burke, "if I have to do it myself!"

* * * * *

The pope continued.

"These changes are essential. For far too long, many of the baptized have suffered from inequality, especially women; people with different sexual orientations; innocent partners in marriages who have been divorced and remarried and are denied the Eucharist; those abused by their own priests; and even the poor, while church funds are used for less important, often frivolous things. The voices of the baptized have been ignored by the system and the people who run it. Although these changes are fundamentally necessary, I hope that they will bring back many of those who have given up on us.

"I know these changes will be disliked by many, especially by the affected bishops and archbishops; by ardent Catholic conservatives who think that nothing should ever change; and by the large financial contributors whose real interest is to buy our support on political issues.

"I have been warned by friends that this anger constitutes a threat to me and the people who are helping. We cannot allow our fear to weaken our resolve.

"If it does, or those threats turn into action, we will have lost, and our church is doomed.

"Last Tuesday I had dinner with the President of the United States. Because of the concerns I have just mentioned, I have asked for and been given temporary political asylum in the United States for myself and for those who have travelled here with me, until the elections have been completed and the new bishops can be consecrated in time to enter the 2020 church year in office.

"May God bless our church!"

It was silent for a couple of seconds, before thunderous applause broke out. The graduates were on their feet, throwing caps in air. The people on the stage sat motionless. Twenty-five of them had just been publicly fired.

The pope left the podium, and Swiss Guards Franz and Roland each took one of his arms and rushed him to the back of the stage, down the stairs and into the armored limousine, which immediately headed for the gate from which it had entered. Once through the gate, a police escort accompanied it to the embassy.

When they arrived, the fence around the property was nearly half finished. It was a reminder that things were suddenly and dramatically different.

* * * * *

At the White House, the first couple had been watching intently. Suddenly the president blurted, "I'll be goddamned! That pious jerk just stole my trademark!"

"What do you mean?" she asked.

"He just told all the bishops in the world, 'You're fired!' I wonder if I can sue."

* * * * *

As the Catholic University trustees stood to join the recessional, chairman Warsaw asked a couple of them to pass the word that there would be an emergency meeting of the trustees as soon as they could get back to the room where they had eaten breakfast.

The president of the United States Conference of Catholic Bishops, Cardinal Daniel N. DiNardo, Archbishop of Galveston, stopped just outside the meeting room and used his cell phone to call his secretary, who answered quickly. "What just happened?"

"The end of the Catholic church, perhaps. I want you to schedule an emergency meeting of the entire USCCB for Wednesday. In St. Louis if you can, to reduce the travel problems. Set up a meeting of the executive committee for Tuesday evening. Then meet me wherever you can arrange for things tomorrow afternoon. I will go directly from here."

"Done."

"See you tomorrow."

* * * * *

96

When the board of trustees assembled, chairman Warsaw called for attention. "I asked you to come in here for three reasons: I wanted to get you away from all those people who don't know what to say to you ...."

"It sucks!" from the back of the room.

"Yes, it sucks, and I also wanted to ask you what you think this does to Catholic University, and what we have to do about it."

Archbishop Wilton Gregory raised his hand and asked, "Have we also been fired from this board of trustees?"

Warsaw said, "No, I don't think so. At least not until the diocesan successors take office. The by-laws say that except for Cardinal Wuerl, whose appointment is ex officio, half the board must be clerics, but they don't say what your jobs have to be or that you cannot be emeritus."

Gregory said, "Then I move that we say unanimously that we will remain on the board and set a time and place for a meeting to answer your questions. All in favor?"

"Aye!"

* * * * *

DeeDee Myers was correct. All the phones were ringing when the pope's party walked in to strongly felt applause.

Chef Bourg and the housekeeping staff had quickly put together a celebratory reception. The pope raised his hand for quiet and said, "Let us pray that we have done the right thing."

"Amen," was the loud response.

The pope turned to Parolin and said, "After dinner this evening, I'd like to get together with you, Cardinals Ouellet and Stella, and Col. Graf for a private meeting, perhaps in one of the small reception rooms. Could you arrange that?"

"Certainly."

White House assistant press secretary David Andreatta was beaming as he greeted Parolin and said, "I was right! It is a Top Ten story of *several* decades."

* * * * *

Later, Col. Graf of the Swiss Guard was out on the grounds of the embassy watching the construction of the security fence and saw his assistant, Capt. Fasel, and Lt. Keenan, the security director assigned by the president for the protection of the pope, talking with the head of the SeaBee detachment doing the installation. As the SeaBee left the conversation, he walked over to join them. "This is very impressive progress, I must say."

"Thank you Col. Graf. 'Many hands make light work,' as they say," answered the lieutenant.

"I would hardly call this 'light work,' but I understand the principle. Have you and Capt. Fasel come to agreement regarding the allocation of responsibilities for the manpower to provide the proper level of protection?" His smile betrayed knowledge of least some of the unofficial parts of the conversations between the captain and Lieutenant.

"We have, sir, and I will have a plan for your approval in your hands tomorrow morning. I will admit that I had some questions, but Hans—I mean Capt. Fasel—has satisfied my concerns."

Fasel smiled slightly at her choice of words.

The lieutenant continued. "Because we have the state-of-art night vision capabilities, the outside perimeter in the wooded areas and the parking areas will be handled by the Navy Seals. Surveillance within the fencing, including the roof of the embassy and potential drone activity will be handled by the guards. The command post with its closed-circuit displays will be manned jointly, as will the gates and the visitors' entry post. This will demonstrate the presence of the Seals without being overpowering."

"That sounds like a good plan, and I look forward to seeing the final version. Are you satisfied, Capt. Fasel?"

"Yes, sir."

"I have one more thing for you to think about. The Holy Father is accustomed to daily early- morning outside walks of about two miles. Since he has been here, Cardinal Parolin has been accompanying him. They find it an opportunity to keep each other informed of developments, while providing more beneficial exercise than sitting in an office, and they would like to continue that practice. I would like you to come up with a way for them to do that."

"We will try to do that, sir." the captain and lieutenant replied, almost in unison.

"Carry on, then," said Graf, returning to the building.

* * * * *

The Brethren sat stunned and silent for several minutes.

"What are we going to do?" asked Burke.

"First we are going to get rid of those damned traitors Parolin, Ouellet and Pell," answered Müller.

"I will take care of that tonight," said Law, "But we need to replace them quickly with strong people with particular expertise and influence."

"Who do you have in mind?" Bertone asked.

"I welcome your suggestions and will invite them as soon as we all agree. I look at it this way. The resignations don't take effect until November 15. We have six months to change the pope's mind, or make it impossible for his plan to work, or find a way to remove him from office."

"Remember that some candidates are likely to be 'Francis cardinals' and in the same class as the new pope. They might be friends. Those might be positive attributes and provide us a mole in the Francis II camp."

Burke asked, "What could we offer them for that kind of help?"

"Perhaps a chance to be Benedict XVII. Everyone has a price. I will begin tomorrow. Let's call it a night."

* * * * *

Parolin's phone rang and, seeing who it was from, he answered. A voice said, "You are no longer welcome in my home," and the caller hung up. Minutes later, Ouellet received the same call, and somewhere en route, so did Pell.

* * * * *

When Burke arrived at this apartment, his landline phone was ringing. That was unusual enough that he picked it up rather than waiting for it to go into voice mail.

"Cardinal Burke."

"Raymond, this is Salvatore Mastrangelo. What should I do?"

Burke and Mastrangelo had been seminary classmates and had always kept in touch. The little bishop owed his entire career to the cardinal, so it was always important for him to please his mentor. And the cardinal knew it.

Burke said to the worried Mastrangelo, "Salvatore, we are all concerned with this situation. I just came from a meeting of The Brethren. We feel we have six months to turn this thing around and we are dedicated to doing that."

"How could it be turned around?"

"Well, we may be able to convince him that it is a terrible idea and he will stop. Or we may be able to make the case that somehow he has suffered mental breakdown and he can be removed from office, as the liberals tried with John Paul II." He paused. "Or he might die."

There was a moment of silence at both ends of the call before Salvatore spoke. "I would be willing to do anything to make one of those possibilities happen."

"Anything?"

"Absolutely anything," said Mastrangelo. "But what should I do right now?"

"Sign the request for early retirement immediately. Then, without disclosing your destination or return date, come to Rome as soon as possible and plan to stay for a while. You can stay here with me. I will tell you what you can do to help."

"I will be there Tuesday morning."

"I will look forward to seeing you, Salvatore. Goodnight."

"Goodnight, Raymond, my friend, and thank you."

Burke then called Archbishop Viganò and said, "Carlo, we need to talk. I have an idea."

"Breakfast tomorrow morning at the usual place?"

"I'll be there at eight."

* * * * *

"Cardinal Parolin, could I have a few minutes of your time?"

"Certainly, DeeDee. In your office?"

"That would be great. Jackie is already here." She closed the door behind them, not in the interest of privacy, but noise. "I'd like to get some idea about what you will be covering in the Wednesday press conference."

"Good!" said Parolin. "There are several items we should talk about."

"That was what I was afraid you'd say," replied DeeDee. "We need to concentrate on what they don't know, what we want them to cover on the evening news, and that is all. Let's look at your list."

"Okay. First, we need to explain why we are doing what we are doing."

"They already know that. The pope told them very eloquently this afternoon. Cross it off your list. Next?"

"We need to tell them that in the future, popes will be elected only by cardinals serving active dioceses."

"Wait a minute," said DeeDee. "That is a big change and affects many people. Doesn't that require an official proclamation of some kind? And unless the pope is planning on dying in a few weeks it may be news, but it isn't big news."

Parolin said, "Of course. The pope will release that proclamation in a couple of weeks."

"Then it isn't news yet and it is important that the pope announce it. Cross it off. Next?"

"The next couple are similar changes over the next few months."

"Important, but not news yet. Cross them off. Next?"

"I don't have any more," said Parolin.

"Good. How much is the retirement bonus the bishops will get?"

"One hundred thousand euros."

"Why don't you let the bishops just run for election instead of throwing them out?"

"Well, they can, but only in the diocese in which they entered the priesthood, and they would have to be nominated by the nominating committee."

DeeDee said, "Both of those items are news. Write them down. What if the bishop is a cardinal archbishop, and his home diocese doesn't rate a cardinal, and he gets elected?"

"He'd still be a cardinal."

"That's really news," she said. "Write it down."

"What about a bishop who is not the ordinary of a modern diocese, like those in the Curia, who might like that early retirement idea?"

"They will be offered the same kind of deal, but the bonus will be less. The pope will be announcing that during the Full Ginsburg next Sunday."

"No, no, no," exclaimed DeeDee, "That should be announced by you on Wednesday. We don't want anything to detract from the five different and important plans and programs he will be announcing on Sunday. What, if anything, are you going to do with the bishops who would like to stay even if they don't have a diocese?"

"That is part of offering early retirement to the bishops not in modern dioceses. We will try to place those who want to stay and do not have other issues."

"What other issues?"

Parolin said, "Well, we won't be placing people like Archbishops Nienstedt, Myers or Finn."

"I get it. I think we have enough for your press conference. Let's work on those things tomorrow."

"Great! Thank you."

Jackie, who had been silent during this exchange, observed, "Well, the cardinal is very, very impressive. I like this job already."

"But he is a cardinal, Jackie. Keep that in mind and don't get yourself, or me, in trouble."

"But he sure is good-looking. I wish I had worn something different."

"Stop it."

* * * * *

After dinner, the Holy Father, the three cardinals and Col. Graf met in a small parlor off one of the reception rooms. Always on the alert, Chef Bourg provided a simple coffee service for them. When they were comfortably seated, the pope spoke.

"Today, the five of us have begun the implementation of a process which, for good or bad, will change our church forever. In the next several weeks, nothing that happens will be trivial, and we cannot run the risk of being uniformed about anything. Pietro, Marc and Beniamino, you have magnificently executed a plan that provides the church with the opportunity to rebuild a new ecclesial hierarchy with a new way of doing its pastoral work. For the next several months I have the responsibility for influencing its culture.

"One day Pietro made the comment that this project has many moving parts. I didn't understand the reality of that description at the time, but I am beginning to and it is impressive. In addition, we each have a day job six time zones away, in Rome.

"We will not succeed unless everyone is aware of everything, because everything affects everything else. Tonight, I would like to begin a daily practice. I would like us to gather here after dinner each night and for each one of us to tell the group at least three things that they don't know—not problem-solving, just information sharing, and we will not exceed one hour."

"Great idea," said Stella, "But we need to include the gossip we hear from Rome regarding reactions."

"And pertinent ideas we have about everything, especially about what others are doing," added Parolin.

"I agree with both points, but I think we should include impertinent ideas as well," said the pope. "Gentlemen, we have torn down the temple, and we must rebuild it quickly into a much more modern and functional edifice. My predecessor realized that for the church to survive, the culture of its hierarchy must change in many ways. Pietro, Marc and Beniamino devised and implemented a plan to begin that transition and it is now half-completed. Your primary goal for the next several months is to complete the renovation by installing more pastoral replacements. I am confident that task will be completed on time.

"On the day that we decided to follow this path, I began thinking about the work of this new hierarchy and the non-personnel changes we must make to meet our objective of a dynamic adult church reflecting both historical and modern values. I have been praying over this task and have developed a framework, which I am ready to implement. For example, I am concerned that though we have a very large Code of Canon Law, we have no list of the rights and privileges of either the church or its members against which to test the laws. The Church needs a constitution. I will be appointing a commission to work on that within the next couple of weeks.

"It is also true that there is not an up-to-date, church-approved, authoritative, independently written history of the church available to the faithful—or to the clergy. I am working on a proposal to offer a highly qualified, internationally recognized historian complete access to anything and everything, including the complete Vatican archives, in return for preparing a comprehensive and extensively history of the church. They would have the rights to revenue from its sale, but we will own the book."

The banter went on until the hour was up. The pattern had been established.

* * * * *

Lt. Keenan and Capt. Fasel were still out at the construction site.

"Do you have any thoughts about Col. Graf's challenge with the walkers?"

Kate said, "I thought you might want to handle that one, since he is your boss, not mine."

"OK. How about this: They walk at seven a.m. They wear casual clothes. At 6:45 a car, driven by one of the personal bodyguards, takes them and the other bodyguard out the driveway, right on 34th Street, right on Fulton Street heading south into Normanstone Park, directly behind the embassy. The pope and Cardinal Parolin get out with the guard who's not driving. They begin to walk south on the left side of Fulton, the guard five paces behind and on the right, out of conversational earshot from them. The driver continues two miles down Fulton, makes a U-turn and parks. He stays there until they reach him. They get in the car and come home."

"I think I'd like them more disguised than just in casual clothes, but that would work. I love it when you are creative," said Kate.

"Should we go someplace and toast my creativity?"

"Not I. I have to set the watch at midnight and then be back here early in the morning to review the night logs."

"Well, *that* isn't very creative."

"Hey, what you see is what you get," said Kate.

"That's good. I like that," said Hans, smiling.

The fence was completed, the system operational and the first watch set at 11:53 p.m.

Chapter Five

Rush to Judgment

A little before eight on Monday, May 20, Monsignor Carlos Menendez Serra, the pope's secretary, came down for breakfast where he was surprised to see Carl A. Anderson, Supreme Knight of the Knights of Columbus and a trustee of Catholic University, standing in the lobby tapping his foot impatiently.

"Good morning, Mr. Anderson. What brings you here this morning?"

"Good morning, Msgr. Menendez. I am here to see His Holiness."

"With all the confusion of yesterday, Papa Francesco must have forgotten to tell me you were coming. I'm sorry, but you don't have an appointment, and His Holiness is booked solid all day."

"I am here to see the pope and I don't need an appointment!" said Anderson, steaming.

"You seem angry, Mr. Anderson, and there is no need for that. The Holy Father's first appointment is at 8:30. I will ask if he can see you for a few minutes before that."

"You are damned right that I am angry, and you had better call whoever he is meeting with and tell them their meeting will not begin until *I* decide to leave!"

Msgr. Menendez turned and headed back upstairs. Anderson followed.

The secretary said, "Please wait in the lobby. I will call you."

Anderson bellowed, "Like hell I will!"

The two men continued up to the pope's office. When they arrived, Anderson barged right in. Francis looked up and said, "Carl, what are you doing here?" Standing, he extended his hand, which Anderson ignored.

"I'm sure you know why I am here. You have lost your mind!"

Turning to Msgr. Menendez, the pope said, "Leave us for a few minutes please, Carlos. We won't be long."

Menendez went to his office and called the duty sergeant of the Swiss Guard. Within three minutes, two guards were there.

* * * * *

"Now Carl, what can I do for you?"

"I demand that you immediately revoke your edict of yesterday."

"The answer is no. And I have an appointment, so you may leave now."

"Do you have any idea what I can and will do if you refuse? The 1.9 million people I represent will cut off all contributions and we are your largest single source of money."

"I'm certain that you will not take that path, Carl," said Francis. "It would be in neither of our interests."

"Firing of all the bishops is outrageous!"

"You will change your mind as you see the plan unfold."

"Never!"

There was a single knock on the door by Menendez, who opened it. The two Swiss Guards were standing behind him. "Your Holiness, your 8:30 appointment is here, and I have an escort for Mr. Anderson."

"Thank you, Carlos. Nice to see you again, Carl. Keep in touch."

Anderson left, fuming.

The duty sergeant had also arrived. "I apologize, Your Holiness. The guard at the gate recognized Mr. Anderson and since it was before your first appointment, he let him wait inside. He has been reprimanded and the standing orders have been changed."

"Thank you, Sergeant. Dr. Kearns Goodwin, please come in."

* * * * *

The phone calls from the press began again just before eight o'clock. Cardinal Parolin and the nuncio asked DeeDee about that when she walked past them in the dining room.

"The number of requests for credentials is already twice the space available in the largest room in the embassy. We could try a video feed to other rooms and select occasional questions from there, but that can get awkward. Do you have any ideas about that, Cardinal? I have assumed that taking it off-site was a non-starter."

"Yes, it is. We don't want to go off-site."

"Then how about doing it outside in a tent? It looks like a pretty big backyard."

"We could do that," replied Pierre. "We have held large receptions using a tent."

"I am just concerned with the optics," DeeDee said. "A crowded room looks much more impressive to people watching at home than does a half-empty tent."

"Is this response unusual?"

"Yes, but it is not totally unexpected. I started with the list of the White House press corps which is a little over fifty, and then I added my personal list that included several people who used to be at the White House and are now freelance writers with multiple magazine and social media contacts. Then your list of the Catholic press was added. So there are well over a hundred people out there with 'personal invitations,' and who knows how many have heard

111

it on the grapevine and have called, or will do so soon. This is a big deal. There will be some no-shows but I believe we should expect at least a hundred."

"Sounds to me like we need the tent," said the cardinal.

"Just listen to those phones ring. I'm going to order the tent right now!" she said, reaching for her phone. "And while I am thinking about it, Cardinal, we'll be ready in half an hour to talk about your agenda for the press conference."

"Good. I'll see you in the conference room."

Jackie Ring arrived as they were finishing. "Good morning, Cardinal."

"Good morning, Jackie. You look very nice this morning."

"Thank you," Jackie said as the cardinal left. "The cardinal is quite handsome," she said to DeeDee.

"Jackie, you're incorrigible!"

Both women laughed.

* * * * *

A little later in the morning, Lt. Keenan asked directions to Col. Graf's office. She knocked on the door and asked if he had a few minutes for her.

"Come in please, Lieutenant. The fence looks great and the control center is operating like clockwork. What can I do to help you?"

"Thank you, Commander, I will pass your comments on to the SeaBees and my people. I am here to talk about the pope's daily walks with Cardinal Parolin."

"Oh, good. The cardinal asked me about that again this morning. Tell me your current thinking and how we might make that happen."

"I am happy to report that the plan proposed by Capt. Fasel has been approved by my CO, with one condition. In addition to the casual, non-clerical clothing, he would like some facial appearance disguises, specifically a beard for the pope and a wig for the cardinal."

They tried to keep a straight face. They failed.

"And just how do we accomplish that?" asked Graf.

"Well, it probably would not surprise you that we have people who do such things. One of them will be here in about an hour, with different colored samples in several sizes to fit them immediately."

"Lieutenant, would it surprise you if I told you that I would like you to personally handle that process, without me being involved?"

"No sir, it would not. In fact, I anticipated that. Should I contact the cardinal?"

"Yes, and thank you."

With still a slight smile the lieutenant left in search of Parolin. She found him in his office.

"Hi, Cardinal P! I have some good news for you. Everyone has signed off on the plan for your daily walks with the pope, with only two provisions."

"Excellent. What are the provisions?"

"The first is that in addition to the casual clothes, they want you both to wear facial disguises. Simple ones. A beard for the pope and a wig for you."

"A wig? Is that necessary? It's summertime."

"I'll see if I can get you an air-conditioned one. Seriously, with the materials they use these days, heat is not a major problem. I have an expert coming here around noon to fit you both. It won't take long."

"Have me paged," sighed Parolin.

"I will."

"And what is the second provision?"

"It is more of an operational matter, but you should be aware of it. We are locating two very fast motorbikes in the woods behind the embassy, near the road, and clearing a short and hardly visible path for them onto road. On a rotating basis, two of the Seals will be assigned to them from the moment your car leaves the embassy for your walk until you return. If anything, unusual occurs, the Seals will be dispatched to your location as backups for the two guards."

"That sounds like a good idea to me," Parolin said.

The pope had no problem wearing a beard, considering it an extension of his fondness for his rugby jersey and jeans.

One of the Swiss Guards was dispatched to buy running shoes for each of them and "something appropriate" for the cardinal to wear. The pope whispered a suggestion to the guard, who grinned back at the pope.

* * * * *

Parolin, DeeDee and Jackie met to discuss the press conference. DeeDee had four press releases on the desk in front of her.

"Cardinal, I have written a press release for each of the points you are planning to cover in the Wednesday press conference. Our task here is to control what we can control, and plan for what we cannot. I have put parts of each of the releases in quotation marks. You should consider them as announcements you should make; they serve as the *minimum* you can say about that subject. This way, you make them work for more information with their questions. The worst thing to happen in a press conference is for them to not ask any questions.

"However, that doesn't mean you should hide something you want them to know. But remember, people rarely forget the answer to their own questions. In whatever they write, they will always try to get what you say right when you answer them personally.

"Think of the questions I asked you the other day. These are smart people and this is a big story. They will ask all the questions you want them to, and some you'll wish they hadn't. You need to be prepared for both, while still controlling what you tell them."

"Okay. I think I understand that," sighed Parolin. "What do we do now?"

"Why don't you read aloud the four statements in quotation marks one at a time. After each I will ask you a few questions a reporter might ask. You decide how you are going to handle them."

"Fair enough."

After nearly an hour and a half, they all felt quite comfortable.

* * * * *

Cardinal Burke and Archbishop Viganò met Monday for breakfast.

"How do you feel about the pope's speech after thinking about it overnight, Ray?"

"I feel the same way I did last night. Something must be done. That something must be strong enough to stop this nonsense in its tracks, and it must be done quickly."

"Do you think that Law agrees with that?"

"I'm not sure any more what he thinks. I don't know whether it is because of his age or not, but he doesn't have the sense of urgency about things that he once did."

"Should we ask our friends on the island if they might be willing to help with the situation?"

"I already tried that with Law."

"What did he say?"

"He said no violence."

"But that is what they do," said Viganò. "Is it a question of money?"

"I don't think so. He was fairly receptive to having them do some surveillance. He didn't say so, but I think some scare tactics might be also acceptable." Burke added, "By the way, Salvatore Mastrangelo will be in town tomorrow morning."

"Sal Mastrangelo couldn't scare my hypersensitive aunt."

"I was thinking more about us having him travel to Catania as our representative to learn what services are available and at what cost."

"Could he do that without screwing up? That could be a problem."

"It could. I will make a call and get the protocol for Mastrangelo to meet with our friends. If it is not too difficult, we might try it. Let's meet again on tomorrow for lunch and we will decide."

* * * * *

The press tent for 120 people, with a podium, was erected on Tuesday, May 21. DeeDee said the conference, which would be at ten the next morning, would be standing room only by Tuesday afternoon, although she managed to find seats in the first four rows for several big-name latecomers.

DeeDee and the cardinal inspected the setup that afternoon.

* * * * *

Bishop Mastrangelo arrived at Cardinal Burke's apartment early Tuesday morning.

"Salvatore, it is great to see you and I see you brought enough things to stay a while. I hope that second suitcase has plenty of non-clerical clothes. The things I might ask you to do will require that."

"But I don't own any non-clerical clothing—even all my shoes are black."

"Then what is in it?"

"My vestments. It is difficult to find them some places when you are as short as I am."

"Hard to find vestments in the Vatican? Did your crozier fit in there?" Burke asked, trying unsuccessfully to keep a straight face.

"Oh, it would ordinarily fit. I had it specially designed. It's only five feet tall and telescopes down to thirty inches, but it still wouldn't fit. I should have carried it on, but it is hard for me to reach the overhead compartments. The airline sent it on the wrong flight. It will be delivered here tomorrow."

"Fine. We have a great deal to talk about. I know you might be tired, but let's have some breakfast while I tell you what we have in mind."

The two men sat down at the table while Rosa was still preparing their omelets.

"Salvatore, I'm sure you remember the unfortunate confrontation several years ago between the first Pope Francis and some of our loyal and generous benefactors from Sicily."

"I do."

"Well, since my reassignment to Patron of the Knights of Malta, Archbishop Viganò and I have been very diligently trying to heal those relationships—on an unofficial basis of course—and we have been quite successful. We have now returned to very good terms with several of the most powerful families of that community. You may recall in our phone conversation the other night, I mentioned several ways we believe we might be able to turn around the direction in which the Holy Father appears to be taking us; but if that's unsuccessful, we might need to introduce another course of action."

Burke continued, "The task that Carlo and I would like you to undertake is to travel to Sicily as our personal ambassador to find out from them the cost of them conducting the closest possible surveillance on His Holiness and the anticipated cost of a, um, *stronger* alternative, should that become necessary."

Mastrangelo flinched. "If you are suggesting what I think you are suggesting—you are terrifying me."

"Then you really didn't mean it when you told me that you would do 'absolutely anything" to help us do what we must do?" Burke asked silkily.

"I did mean it, Ray, but aren't you are talking about assassination here?"

"I am not suggesting that you or Carlo Viganò or I would do anything of the kind, just that you would find out the cost of having it done. That is an enormous difference! I must leave now and will be gone all day. I want you to consider this assignment carefully and to re-assess your willingness to help."

"I promise that I will do that," bleated Mastrangelo.

"Fine. But don't unpack your things until I return."

* * * * *

When Burke returned home around five, Mastrangelo was seated in the living room with a drink in his hand.

"Ah, Salvatore, I see that Rosa has taken good care of you. Have you made a decision yet?"

"I would like a full explanation of what it is that you want me to do."

118

"Fair enough. Let me get a little more comfortable. Ask Rosa to bring me my usual." Burke returned to the room in a few minutes in his idea of wearing something more comfortable: a pair of worn bedroom slippers adorned with the Vatican seal.

"You wanted to know exactly what you are to do?" Burke continued.

"Yes, every detail."

"These instructions were given to Carlo Viganò by one of our friends. I think you will be relieved to learn that there will be no discussion of arrangements directly by you. Your only role will be that of a courier. You will not know the contents of what you are carrying."

Bishop Mastrangelo looked dramatically relieved. The cardinal continued. "These instructions must be followed to the letter. There will be no improvisation of anything at any time. Any mistake will result in cancellation of your meeting. I suggest that if that happens, you should get out of wherever you are immediately.

"You will take a train from Rome to Catania using a round-trip ticket I will give you. Although the trip to Sicily from Rome takes ten times longer by train than by air, you can travel almost anonymously by train; a plane ticket would have your name on it and require screening before boarding—and you might be remembered. You will carry a large sealed envelope, with a sealed smaller envelope inside. When you are on the train, you will remove the smaller envelope and discard the larger one. The inside envelope contains the specific questions we are asking and you do not need to see them at any time.

"When you arrive in Catania, you will make a call to a phone number written on the inner envelope. The woman answering the call will be expecting it. She will tell you where to meet her. When you meet her, say 'I am the courier from Rome.' She will ask you how long you will be staying in Catania and you will answer 'Five days,' and hand her the envelope. As soon as she leaves, you will take the first train back to Rome, pick up your belongings here, and return directly and immediately back to the States and home."

"That is all there is to it?"

"Yes."

After a long pause, Salvatore said, "OK."

"Buy some casual clothes tomorrow. You will leave early on Thursday morning."

"Then what?"

"You are to forget everything you saw or heard."

* * * * *

Cardinal DiNardo's secretary, Gloria Romeo, had called him on Monday afternoon to report that because of the short notice she was not able to find a place large enough, with enough sleeping rooms, for the emergency meeting of the USCCB in any major city. Then someone mentioned the Franciscan University of Steubenville; because of summer break, they could accommodate the group, although most of the bishops were probably going to be unhappy with the idea of dorm rooms. And though Steubenville was in Ohio, it was located near Pittsburgh so transportation would be reasonably convenient.

The cardinal flew to Pittsburgh late that afternoon and Ms. Romeo picked him up at the airport. She had booked rooms for them at a nearby hotel; over dinner she explained the arrangements and he gave her a thumb drive for her laptop containing his agenda, his remarks to the group and other related materials.

DiNardo spent the next morning on the phone with various members of the archbishops' committee, making sure they were all on the same page on the issues.

Ms. Romeo put into order the mini-chaos of the cardinal's notes and instructions, and used one of the hotel's printers to make them look like they had been finalized several days earlier. After lunch, they drove the thirty-five miles to the Steubenville campus across the river.

The Tuesday night meeting of the archbishops was scheduled as a private dinner at six, then a meeting in an adjoining room. All except Boston's Cardinal Seán O'Malley were present.

"Good evening," began DiNardo "I will spare you the irony of saying that I am pleased to be addressing you this evening, but I *am* pleased that almost all could make it except for Cardinal O'Malley, who has an excuse. He is in Washington for the pope's council meeting."

One archbishop said, "I thought the council meeting had been postponed to next week."

"Well, actually it was, but I decided not to call Seán at the last minute and require him to rush." They all understood and laughed.

DiNardo continued, "The question before us is simply: what the hell are we going to do about the pope's demand that we all resign? I can assure you that at this point I do not know the answer. What am I—what are we going to say tomorrow morning to the full membership?"

"What alternative do we have?" asked Archbishop Cordileone of San Francisco. "I say we take him up on the offer and then sit back and watch how he handles the chaos he has created."

"Is anyone in favor of refusing to sign?" asked New York's Cardinal Dolan.

"And give up the benefits? Hell, no!!!"

They all started chiming in.

"And there is that 'retirement bonus'—does anyone know how much that is?"

"Some are guessing a million each."

"No way. That would be three billion euros!"

"Assuming that all bishops would get the same. Certainly, cardinals should get the most, then the other archbishops, and then the bishops. Aren't we getting the most?"

"I would hope so!"

"Someone said the auxiliaries aren't going to get anything."

"I think we should demand that we get a million, the non-cardinal archbishops should get five hundred thousand, bishops a hundred thousand, and the auxiliaries maybe fifty," said Cordileone.

"We could offer to agree that he definitely wouldn't have to give any more than fifty thousand to the auxiliaries."

"Why should the auxiliaries get anything?"

"You fellows are sounding like you think this is a bargaining situation. What leverage do you think we have?" asked Chaput, Archbishop of Philadelphia.

"What do I recommend to the rest tomorrow morning about whether they should resign or not?" asked DiNardo, trying to get them back on track.

"I'd like to say something before we decide, if you don't mind," said Chaput. "I think we are ignoring something very important. We are forgetting that in signing this request we are essentially giving the pope six months' notice that we are leaving. A great deal can happen in six months. And we lose the advantages of those six months if we refuse to sign.

"We have many strong intellects in the USCCB, and not all are in this room. Many of them, if not most, are very proficient in canon law. I am not convinced that despite his absolute power, the pope's request is consistent with canon law. Some have said that the pope has acted irrationally in this matter. Once again, that may be a consideration to be tested against canon law."

"So what are you saying, Charles?" Cardinal DiNardo asked. "What advantages do we have?"

"I am saying that tomorrow we should strongly suggest to our members that they sign the request for early retirement. I further suggest that we ask them to sign a pledge to join in anything we do in the next six months to derail this plan. What I have said should not go out of this room. I have drafted a plan that I think we can implement; and I'd like Tim Dolan and Jose Gómez and perhaps one or two others to work with me for the rest of the evening and review it tomorrow morning prior to the meeting. Then we ask the entire USCCB to endorse it."

"That sounds good to me," said Dolan, and Gómez nodded in agreement.

"A pretty damned good committee," DiNardo thought. Chaput was thinking the same thing.

"One more thing before we finish," said Chaput. "I want you all to consider this entire discussion to be covered by the seal of confession. Not a word. And I would extend that to our beloved colleague Seán O'Malley. As a member of the pope's council, we must spare him the conflict."

The meeting of the entire USCCB was subdued. There was fear among those of a certain age, who hadn't planned well enough to ride out an early retirement. There was concern over the amount of the retirement bonus. There was anger, especially among some of the younger men who have been trying to do what they were supposed to do. And there was relief among those who had secrets that now might never be disclosed.

In the end, all the USCCB members agreed to resign and to support Chaput's plan.

* * * * *

After the meeting Chaput called Cardinal Law, whom he knew well. He also knew Raymond Burke, but chose Law as a more rational contact. He told Law of the USCCB and their development of a plan to upset and defeat the pope's coup. Law was fascinated.

"In effect, we are all planning to go on vacation until November 15. Out of touch. Whereabouts unknown. We will travel if we feel like it. We are also considering refusing to ordain the newly-elected bishops, because the process of their election by the laity is not prescribed in canon law. And we will close all diocesan schools for the fall semester, and furlough all diocesan employees, including those in social services. An extension of this could be to forbid all baptisms, weddings and funerals until after November 15. Others are under consideration.

"We will grant paid furloughs to all employees of the USCCB, and the chanceries of our dioceses and archdioceses will be closed for the duration. The Catholic church in the United States will be shut down until the new cadre of bishops takes over and, by the way, I don't know how the elections will be held with all the chanceries closed."

"In other words, you are going on strike for the remainder of your episcopates," said Cardinal Law. "Can you e-mail me a copy of the plan? I will review it and get it out to all the bishops worldwide by the weekend."

"You will have it within the hour."

"Fine, I'll get back to you if I have any questions."

"Bernard, before we hang up, I have a favor to ask."

"Certainly. You have earned that. What can I do for you?"

"Well, I'll be out of a job on November 15. Could you find a spot for me in Rome?"

"I'm sure that can be arranged. I will talk to Müller and Mamberti tomorrow."

* * * * *

By 9:30 Wednesday morning, the press tent was almost full. DeeDee walked out onto the platform at 9:59. "Thank you all for coming this morning. We have a lot of ground to cover today, so let's get started."

There was an appreciative burst of applause; talking over it, she continued, introducing Cardinals Parolin, Ouellet and Stella, giving some of the background on their involvement in the plan.

Parolin stepped to the microphone. "Good morning. Before we get to your questions, I'd like to provide you with some further clarifications of the Holy Father's announcement on Sunday. I am prepared to address questions on these issues as well as those you have prepared, perhaps in a somewhat limited way. There will be press releases on each of these issues as you leave."

There was a slight murmur at that, but DeeDee leaned over to White House assistant press secretary Dave Andreatta and said, "So far so good." He nodded, as did Jackie.

"First, about the current bishops and their eligibility to run for election under the new system: They *will* be eligible to run for the office of bishop, but *only* in the diocese from which they entered the seminary, in order to be consistent with the intent of the change, which is to have them serve in their home dioceses.

"Each must signify his willingness to serve to the chancellor of that diocese by July 1 and the nominating committee will consider it, but they are not required to nominate him. However, if he is elected, he *will* be limited to no more than one six-year term.

"While I am at it, regarding the length of the terms, while the standard is six years, we don't want to go through the trauma of elections in every diocese every six years. Therefore, we will do things like the U.S. Senate, electing one-third of them every two years.

"To implement that plan, we listed all the bishops in each country by age. The oldest third will be running for a two-year term with future six-year terms and they will be allowed two possible re-elections. The middle third will run for a four-year term, also with two possible re-elections if they are young enough. The youngest third will run for a six-year term with one possible re-election.

"In the United States, each group will consist of sixty-five dioceses. If you are interested, we will tell you how to find out the plan for each diocese.

"The second topic is related to the first. Cardinals running in dioceses, as opposed to archdioceses, will of course still be cardinals. And just so you won't have to look it up, Cardinal Dolan could lead St. Louis; and either Cardinal DiNardo, Cardinal O'Malley or Cardinal Wuerl could end up in Pittsburgh, *if* they were nominated. And won.

"The third is the question of how we can retain good people who would like to remain active, some of whom are actually better qualified for positions other than diocesan bishop. With the general shortage of clergy, this is of serious concern to us. We are looking for places that are understaffed and, frankly, for positions that will be created by our new way of doing business.

"Finally the question has been raised as to why early retirement has not been offered to bishops and archbishops who are not the ordinaries of active dioceses. While this has always been part of the plan, Pope Francis did not mention it in his commencement address so as not to confuse things. Doing this will help us find places for the people I mentioned in the last question.

"Now we are going to take questions. Let's deal with questions related with topics in order, beginning with bishops running in their home dioceses. And since DeeDee Myers knows your names and affiliations far better than I do, I have asked her to call on those who have questions."

"Okay," DeeDee said. "We have a very large crowd here and in fairness, we need to stay on topic. We will begin with each topic in the order that Cardinal Parolin presented them. When they are all complete, if we have time, we will have a free-for-all round. So, about bishops running in their home dioceses, let's begin."

The hands went up and DeeDee called "Ed Henry from *Fox News*."

"Cardinal, with all due respect I assume that the objective of the pope's announcement was to get rid of all of the current bishops. Why then are they now given the opportunity to come back in through the back door?"

"Part of the answer is that the pope does not consider himself infallible. We know that despite the generosity of the retirement offer, some percentage of the sitting bishops may be willing to stay in active ministry as bishops. The pope wanted to give them the opportunity for them to have his decision reviewed by the people, and so he offered this option. The bishop would be considered for candidacy by the nominating committee of the diocese in which he grew up. He is subject to their scrutiny along with other candidates. He may or may not be chosen as a candidate. I don't think of that as a back door. "

DeeDee called, "Susan Page from *USA Today*."

"Cardinal, you mentioned the generosity of the retirement offer. Just how much is the retirement bonus? And I have a follow-up question."

"The retirement offer is 100,000 euros for each archdiocesan bishop, diocesan bishop, co-adjutor and auxiliary bishop."

"Thank you, and my follow-up question is: who will pay for this bonus?"

"That is an excellent question. In most cases, the bonuses will be paid from diocesan resources. Where that is not possible, the Vatican will provide some assistance."

DeeDee called, "David Corn from *Mother Jones*."

"Cardinal, when these pastors are suddenly elected bishops, will they be sent to some bishops' boot camp to be trained?"

DeeDee and the cardinal joined in the laughter.

"David, I can assure you that is a question that neither DeeDee nor I anticipated. I think the answer is simple. The Holy Father believes that the primary role of a bishop or archbishop is not to be part of a Vatican management training program. The role of the bishop is, by example, to develop and train the shepherds of his diocese. Now, he will have been a pastor in that diocese, and many of the people in that diocese know whether his example is pastoral. He should know how that works because he has been doing it. He needs to be looking down, not up.

"That is what has brought us to this point. A high percentage of the 2,851 bishops in the world are extensively trained—some would say excessively trained—in canon law and theology, but have little or no pastoral experience, and that is their *primary* job.

"A diocesan bishop or archbishop can hire all the canon lawyers and theologians they will ever need. They can hire financial experts and personnel people. None of those jobs require ordination. We want pastoral bishops, not administrative bishops."

That drew spontaneous applause.

DeeDee said, "All right, last question on this topic, Chris Jansing of *NBC News*."

"Cardinal, I would like to explore the 'career path' notion a bit more, and I have two questions. The first is: Since the Archdiocese of New York is significantly larger than, say, the Diocese of Ogdensburg, are you sure that you can find someone for the bigger job by just nominating and electing from who happens to be available? And the second question is: Isn't the potential of a path to becoming a cardinal like yourself, or even a pope, a strong motivator for every bishop to do the best job they can?"

Parolin turned to DeeDee and said into his microphone, "DeeDee, these people are really good. We didn't rehearse any of these questions!"

The laughter was louder. Andreatta whispered to DeeDee, "Now he *really* has them!"

"Chris—if I may call you Chris? I'd like to answer the second question first. For centuries, most of our young men haven't entered the seminary with the idea of becoming pope. We have proved that the potential for making a successful career is an awesome motivator for high-level performance, but that success has often come at the expense of the people in the pews, who already have a pope. They want and need pastoral bishops.

Parolin continued, "Regarding the first question, I think we are going to be the beneficiary of the law of large numbers. Large dioceses are large because they have many Catholics in many parishes, staffed by many pastors. We think we can assume that the percentage of capable people is a constant. In addition, we must recognize that in the current system, talent is not necessarily the criteria for promotion, but who you know often is. The diocesan electorate will make some mistakes, and that is why terms are for six years; only one re-election is allowed; and there is a recall process."

DeeDee stood up and said, "Okay, we are going to change topics now. If we have time at the end, we will have a free-for-all round. So, about cardinals, let's have a show of hands ... Major Garrett of *CBS News*."

"Cardinal, for as long as I can remember, cardinals have headed specific archdioceses and served as metropolitans of provinces. Isn't this automatic?"

"Major, what branch of the military are you in?"

Some laughter.

"None, Cardinal; Major is my real given name."

"Really? I have never met anyone named Major before. But I believe that you had a singer a few years ago called Prince."

More laughter.

"In any case, thank you for your service."

Strong laughter.

"Now, getting back to your question. I would say that it is more traditional than automatic. When a cardinal dies, his successor usually becomes a cardinal, although if a cardinal retires, his successor usually must wait until his predecessor dies, before being given that honor.

"Being made a cardinal is supposed to be an earned honor rather than a job. The diaconate, priesthood and episcopate are Holy Orders. The cardinalate is an individual honor not intended to just go with the job.

"It is not a promotion to a higher order as is promotion from priest to bishop. I am not aware of any canon law that prevents Chris' Bishop of Ogdensburg from being designated as a cardinal if he merits the honor. However, that is not the way it works now. It's that same old career path thing again. That is the mindset that our pope is trying to change."

"Does that mean that ordinary bishops or pastors might become cardinals in the future?" continued Garrett.

"Perhaps, or even priests who are not pastors. Your own Cardinal Avery Dulles was never made a bishop or archbishop because, as a Jesuit theologian, he successfully petitioned the pope for a dispensation from episcopal consecration. For that reason, he was not allowed to participate in the election of Pope Benedict XVI."

"How about women?"

"Canon law does not prevent it, and in fact, Pope John Paul II offered Mother Teresa that honor, but she declined. More recently Cardinal Dolan has suggested it could happen in his lifetime."

"Is that an announcement?" Major pressed.

"No comment."

DeeDee picked up the cue and said, "Jim Acosta of *CNN*."

"Cardinal, I think this is in order in this segment. Do you have any significant returns of the resignations by bishops as requested by the pope?"

"Not really. Remember that it has only been three days since the bishops received his request. Because of the number of things that have happened, it seems that a long time has passed. It hasn't. The resignations are being returned to the nuncios—that is, ambassadors—in each country. We asked them to check them and send them here in large batches. I would guess we should start to receive them early next week and we will announce results as soon as we have them."

"Do you think that many will refuse?"

"No."

"OK," said DeeDee, "let's shift to the third subject: how we plan to retain and place good people who want to stay. Let's have a show of hands ... Joan Walsh from *The Nation*."

"Cardinal, will all the bishops who resign be considered for placement elsewhere? And a second question: would the same true for those who refused to resign?"

"Joan, I'm not sure why I seem to want to answer questions in reverse order, but the answer to the second is No. By refusing a request of the pope they are excluded. As for the first question, the answer is that we hope many of them will be."

"Then, if I may," said Joan, "I have two follow-ups: how will you be able to do that, and will people like Archbishop Nienstedt, Archbishop Myers or Archbishop Finn be considered?"

"Once again, Joan, the last shall be first—and the answer is again No. Regarding the first, it is that we frankly do not know how difficult the placement task will be. If the number is small, meaning a couple of hundred, we can do it in a matter of days. For example, the new system will create an immediate need for people in the Secretariat of State. In addition, many part-time jobs in the Curia are held by diocesan bishops for training purposes in addition to their primary jobs. That is just another example of the 'career path syndrome,' and many can be combined and converted to full-time jobs.

"Our plan is to work from the youngest to the oldest because that seems fairest. However, if they are placed, they will not be retired and will not get the retirement bonus until they retire, which would be easier for the younger men."

Walsh added, "Have you thought of breaking up the archdioceses into two or three 'bishop-sized' dioceses?"

The Cardinal feigned searching for a pen, saying, "No, we haven't, Joan, but that could be a very good idea. Thank you."

Over the laughter, DeeDee said, "Now we will shift to the question of early retirement for bishops not heading a diocese, such as those in the Curia, teaching in universities and seminaries and those serving in other ministries ... John Allen of *Crux*."

"Cardinal, what about what DeeDee just said?"

"Yes, they will, John."

More laughter.

Parolin continued, "With perhaps a few exceptions, we will offer early retirement to such bishops who are sixty-five years of age or older on December 31, 2020. It will carry a retirement bonus of fifty thousand euros. It will not be mandatory that they accept. Those people should be receiving letters to that effect. The offer will be good until July 1, 2019 with their last day being December 31.

No hands were raised, so DeeDee said, "Thank you, Cardinal Parolin, and thank you all for coming. The press releases are on the tables at several locations outside the tent. And for those of you who are not fighting a deadline, we have a lovely buffet set up behind you at the back of the embassy. Because this is an unfolding story, for the next several weeks we will be holding Wednesday press conferences every week at ten a.m. This is a busy place. Next week, from Monday to Thursday, the pope's council of cardinals will be here for a meeting and during the week of June 10, the Roman Curia will be meeting here. Welcome to the Vatican beat!"

Turning away from the microphone, she said to Parolin, "You knocked that out of the park, Cardinal."

"I'm not sure I know what that means, DeeDee, but I really enjoyed it."

"I just hope that the Holy Father does half that well in the Full Ginsburg," Andreatta added.

"Speaking of the Full Ginsburg, said the cardinal, "there are some interesting new developments that the two of you need to know. We should talk this afternoon. I will accommodate your schedule."

DeeDee said, "Dave, Jackie and I need to do some schmoozing with the press for a while. How about two in my office?"

"I'm sorry, what does 'schmoozing' mean?" asked Parolin.

"You'd be great at it," said Andreatta. "Come along. It'll be fun. We'll show you."

* * * * *

The four schmoozers reached DeeDee's office at two.

"You were right, Dave; schmoozing was fun, and very interesting."

"I told you so. Now what are these new developments that we need to know about?"

"Well, last Monday after his dinner with the president, the pope gave me a list of some very important people with whom he had scheduled individual two-day meetings starting the next day. Each of these four meetings has been dealing with a different one of the topics he will be talking about in the Full Ginsburg series.

"Wait a minute. You said four meetings. The Full Ginsburg has five topics," said Andreatta.

"I know, and I have a way to handle that."

DeeDee voiced her concern. "You do know that the five hosts involved are doing their research as we speak. I am meeting them starting early tomorrow on content and timing and we start recording early Friday morning. Timing is important. Postponing for a week would be a disaster."

134

"Hear me out. I think you will be pleased. The first is the need for a Catholic church constitution. There are hundreds of canon laws, but no constitution with which to evaluate them. The church has many documents that are called 'Constitutions,' but what I mean is a document that delineates the rights, privileges and obligations of the faithful in the way that constitutions of countries do; a similar description of the duties and responsibilities of those in authority; and a process for establishing laws and regulations, as well as resolving conflicts between these elements. With these guidelines, an agency of the governing body would be able to determine the legitimacy of any canon law. The Holy Father is willing to discuss and describe the way in which this issue will be addressed.

"As you know, next Monday through Wednesday morning, the pope's council of cardinals will be here for a meeting. Cardinal Seán O'Malley will be here tomorrow. They hope to convene a constitutional commission comprised of cardinals from the four other democracies around the world with the largest Catholic populations, to produce a consensus of what is needed. Since Cardinal O'Malley has already personally presented his request for early retirement, he will have the time to undertake this task.

Parolin continued, "The second is, in a sense, related and the Holy Father will soon be also announcing another new commission to address it. The church does not have, in one place, a complete and verifiable history that acknowledges what we know; what we think we know; and what, legitimately, we cannot know. This leads to the dilemma of the relative importance of tradition and fact in establishing doctrine.

"Examples of the latter are the only two doctrines of the church officially declared to be infallible. One is the Corporal Assumption of the Blessed Virgin into heaven; this developed from the request by a fifth century emperor that some of his soldiers find the remains of the Mother of God who, it was believed, had died somewhere near Jerusalem about 450 years earlier; he wanted her to be buried in a crypt under a great cathedral he was going to build. They searched for a couple of years and found nothing. Terrified to report to the emperor that they had failed, they developed a theory that Jesus had arranged for her body to be assumed into heaven. The emperor bought it.

"Another thirteen hundred or so years passed until the First Vatican Council in the 1860s, when the notion of papal infallibility was introduced. Since then, two doctrines have been proclaimed infallibly since then. One was the Assumption.

"Today, the belief in the corporeal assumption of Mary is universal in the East and in the West; according to Pope Benedict XIV, it is a *'probable opinion, which to deny were impious and blasphemous.'* However, it had only become 'universal' because it had been repeated for thirteen hundred years."

"*That* is impressive—and weird," DeeDee said.

"On Monday and Tuesday of this week, His Holiness met all day with world-renowned historian Doris Kearns Goodwin on the subject of the lack of a definitive history of the Catholic church. He is willing to offer complete and unfettered access to the Vatican archives, including the famous 'secret archives,' as well as other incentives for whoever undertakes the project."

"Will Dr. Kearns Goodwin be that person?"

"That has not been determined yet, but she is interested and will be considered."

"Will she be required to reach out to Old Testament Jewish scholars and historians and Protestants?"

"Yes and to Muslims, as well." Parolin went on, "The third meeting topic is 'Embracing Science as Revelation,' and in this case, a new prefecture in the Curia will be founded to address that issue. On Thursday and Friday of this week, Pope Francis will meet with Jesuit Father George V. Coyne, who is the former director of the Vatican Observatory and head of the observatory's research group based at the University of Arizona in Tucson, Arizona. Father Coyne currently holds the McDevitt Chair of Religious Philosophy at LeMoyne College. He will be here to discuss the role of science in revelation, and how to resolve conflicts such as between evolution and Genesis.

"The fourth meeting topics deals with the concept of the equality of the faithful, and by that, I mean between genders, among sexual preferences, between those who are divorced and those who are not, and myriad other examples. Again, this will be addressed by a new prefecture in the Curia. On Monday and Tuesday of next week, leading theologian Sister Elizabeth Johnson is meeting with the pope to talk about ways to bring more equality in the church regarding women and LGBT issues.

"Finally, there is the question of communications between the pope and those in the pews. At least part of that is organizational, but it is also philosophical."

"So, there would be five different exclusives?" asked Andreatta.

"Why not?" countered DeeDee. "That is quite a lineup, but what about the fifth exclusive?"

"That can be an explanation of the thing that ties this all together, our new way for the faithful to communicate more simply with the pope, which is what this is all about. Now, there is one caveat. The concepts and the fact that there will be meetings about them can be discussed, but not the names of the individuals concerned. It is much too early for that, and none of the people I mentioned have been asked to do anything but discuss the concepts.

"I will be talking to the five anchors this afternoon and I will tell them what we want to do," DeeDee said. "I think they'll like it, especially because there will be five exclusives. We will start recording tomorrow afternoon here and finish up on Friday."

"I can't wait until next Sunday to watch the Full Goldstein," added Cardinal Stella, with a big smile.

"I have to tell you, Cardinal P, this is getting so damned interesting I'm sorry I'm leaving," said DeeDee.

"And I'm excited to be here," added Jackie.

* * * * *

On Thursday morning, May 23, Bishop Salvatore Mastrangelo left for Catania. The trip was pleasant enough, a ride through parts of Italy that the little bishop had not seen before. The entire train was ferried across the Strait of Messina, which took about an hour. He disposed of the large envelope by tearing it up and dropping the pieces into the water. The train arrived in Catania around seven p.m.

He called the phone number on the envelope, and the woman who answered directed him to a small restaurant just two blocks away. She told him that she was already there and was wearing a black dress and a red scarf. He saw her as soon as he entered, went quickly to her table and sat down, saying, "I am the courier from Rome"—suddenly thinking that might have been a line from a movie he saw when he was in high school. She was too young to make the connection, he guessed.

She asked how long he was staying in Catania.

He replied, "Five days."

She held out her hand and he gave her the envelope. She slipped it into her purse and left without saying another word. Salvatore was relieved and he didn't know why. He checked his watch and saw that he had time to have something to eat before the train back to Rome left.

* * * * *

A basic temporary set for the recording of the five Full Ginsburg interviews was erected in a room used for small nunciature receptions. The five networks brought in their own furniture and set items. Three interviews were done on Thursday and the other two on Friday. Both DeeDee and Jackie were very pleased with the results.

* * * * *

Cardinal Mamberti had been recruiting, slowly and deliberately, members of The Francis Fellows. He began with close friends whose stance regarding authoritarianism he knew well. Then he asked them for recommendations regarding others, personally vetting them as he went along. He now had a list of thirty-seven cardinals and archbishops who had been solid supporters of Francis I and were cautiously optimistic about his successor.

He was pleased with that because it was a larger number than the hardcore committed members of The Brethren, and he believed he was ready to give the Francis Fellows some additional information regarding the intentions of Francis II. He had been doing this in a series of teleconferences every week or so, assuring them that the pope's actions to date had not destroyed their careers. It was dicey at first, but he gradually had gained their nearly complete confidence.

Now he was urging them to help extend membership to more and more people, while building a list of those who leaned toward the thinking of The Brethren. He had urged all who had access to American television to watch the pope's Full Ginsburg and found an expert to put together a series of videos that he could send to others for use as a recruitment tool. At this point, he did not think The Brethren were aware of The Fellows or his own involvement.

* * * * *

The train from Catania arrived in Rome before daylight on Friday, May 24. Salvatore took a taxi to Cardinal Burke's apartment and had the driver wait while he picked up his two suitcases. At the front door, he met Burke's housekeeper Rosa coming to work.

"Good morning, Bishop Mastrangelo. Are you leaving?"

A bit flustered, Salvatore answered, "Yes, I visited a friend down south yesterday, and while I was there I learned that a problem back home needs my attention. I returned last evening after you left for the day. Now I am heading for the airport."

With that he got in the car and shut the door.

Rosa shrugged, and went into the cardinal's apartment.

Mastrangelo arrived at the airport in plenty of time to catch his Chicago flight connecting to Rochester, Minnesota, and then a rental car to Winona and home. He went to bed and stayed there for two days.

Chapter Six
The Full Ginsburg

There was an emergency meeting at Cardinal Law's condo the evening of Thursday, May 23 to discuss the Chaput proposal. All remaining members of The Brethren were in attendance, as was Cardinal Mamberti.

Law spoke first. "I don't know about you fellows, but I feel a great deal more comfortable with our new membership than I did with our departed friends. Please welcome again our newest member of The Brethren, Dominique Mamberti."

There was unanimous applause.

"Now, we need to get moving on a plan that will stop Francis II in his tracks and reverse this travesty. I'd like to hear from Cardinal Mamberti regarding any legal action we might take."

"Well, I must say that I anticipated that question and did a little homework. The basic problem is that, as we have all known since we were children, the pope is the supreme authority in the Roman Catholic church, so the chances of overturning his decision in this matter are practically nonexistent."

"Since the decisions of bishops can be overturned, why can't those of the Bishop of Rome?" asked Cardinal Burke.

"Interesting thought, Raymond, but how would you go about proving that he was acting not as pope but as Bishop of Rome, when the premise on which you are basing your argument on that is the Bishop of Rome doesn't have that authority?"

"That might be the reason that Ray doesn't still have your job," suggested Levada to much laughter.

"How about a vote of 'No Confidence' by all the prefects of the Curia?" asked Müller.

"If you could get everyone to sign it, it would probably have some moral authority, but you would get probably get fired for doing it. In any case, as you know, it would not be binding on the pope."

"Is there any possibility that we could make the case that he is not mentally competent to be pope?" asked Cardinal Bertone.

"That would be difficult. In the first place, you must remember that he is merely carrying out a plan that was commissioned by his predecessor, whom it would be difficult to prove insane. Secondly, it is only three months since the conclave elected him. There is no evidence of mental impairment."

"Except on the part of the conclave," said Law, contemptuously. "What does that come down to, then?"

"Why is no one willing to mention the historic means for dealing with a rogue pope?" asked Burke, to a murmur of disapproval.

"Because these are not the Middle Ages and we are not going to do that," said Law decisively. Burke looked annoyed, but he always did.

Law continued, "You have all received copies of a plan written by Archbishop Charles Chaput and adopted by the USCCB. I propose that we distribute it to the heads of all such conferences worldwide, recommending that they adopt and implement it immediately."

What if he becomes angry, immediately fires all 3,000 of them and saves himself thirty million euros?" asked Burke.

"Then he would have total chaos and besides, the bonus is to be mostly funded by the dioceses. I don't think he would risk the chaos," replied Law.

"I think we should do as Bernard suggests," said Levada. There was a loud and enthusiastic response.

Law said, "I think we have unanimity here. It's done."

In their enthusiasm, no one noticed that Cardinal Mamberti had been silent.

After a celebratory toast of Law's best champagne, they all headed home.

* * * * *

Returning to his room, Cardinal Mamberti made a call to Washington.

"Good evening, Dominique ... how are you?"

"Good evening, Your Holiness. I am fine, but I have some news that you are not going to like. I have just e-mailed you a document, written by the American archbishop, Chaput, that was adopted yesterday by the USCCB; and tonight The Brethren, with great enthusiasm, voted to send it to every conference of bishops in the world urging them to immediately adopt it as written."

"Thank you Dominique. I will read it immediately and call you this weekend."

"Good night, John ... I mean Your Holiness."

"You were correct the first time, Dominique ... good night"

* * * * *

Law called Archbishop Chaput to tell him about the result of the meeting. Chaput was delighted to know Law appreciated his efforts. His job prospects were looking good.

* * * * *

On Saturday morning, May 25, Francis II and Cardinal Parolin were ready for their first walk under the new regimen at 6:55 a.m. Swiss Guards Franz Buchs, the driver, and Roland Pfyffer von Altishofen, the bodyguard, were waiting for them in the car.

143

"Good morning, Franz and Roland," said Francis happily.

"Good morning, Your Holiness and Your Eminence," they replied.

"Good morning, gentlemen," said the cardinal, a bit uncomfortable in his wig, running shorts and Washington Redskins sweatshirt.

Franz turned right out of the embassy compound onto 34th street and right again onto Fulton. At the rear of the embassy, he stopped and the pope, the cardinal and Roland got out. The pope and the cardinal began walking along the left side of the road facing traffic. Roland followed on the right side, walking five paces behind, out of conversational earshot. Franz continued two miles down the road, made a U-turn and parked facing the walkers, who obviously were not yet in sight. Finally, the walkers reached the car. As they got in, the pope said "Bravo. That was perfect!"

The cardinal agreed, with less enthusiasm.

Lt. Keenan and Capt. Fasel were waiting for them at the embassy.

"How did it go?" asked Lt. Keenan.

"Very well," answered Parolin.

"I agree. Very efficient," said the pope.

He and Parolin headed inside, and Francis suggested that they have breakfast in his quarters. When they were out of earshot, Lt. Keenan said, "Well, we have some adjustments to make. You were off the grid for about half an hour, and that is not acceptable."

"How is that possible? Wasn't the GPS working?" asked Franz.

"Oh, we knew where you were, but not what was happening. Buchs, were you not briefed by any of my control room people on the voice procedures and protocols of this mission?"

"Just that we were good to go."

"OK, I will deal with that right now." She called the control room and had the crew leader report to the car, where, with some major embarrassment, he properly briefed Franz and Roland regarding vocal verification of every turn, stop and unusual situation.

Although he was enjoying this episode fully, Fasel didn't say a word, but he could hardly wait to speak privately to Lt. Keenan.

* * * * *

When the pope and the cardinal finished their breakfast, Francis II pushed his chair back, a sign that the conversation was going to change a bit.

"Pietro, how are you feeling these days?" he said with a smile.

"I feel fine, Santità. Why do you ask?"

"Because you should be very proud of all the wonderful work you, Beniamino and Marc have done to plan and organize this extraordinary project. And you must all be exhausted."

"Thank you—and thank God you are not aware of some near-disasters."

"Amen to that, but some evening when we are all back in Rome, I want the three of you to tell me about some of the close calls."

"We will, but not all of them."

"All right. I can understand that. But now I have another task for you."

"We are ready," said Parolin. "What is it?"

"I want you to develop a plan and a detailed agenda for a meeting of the Curia in the next few weeks. I am thinking of an arrival during the afternoon of Wednesday, June 12 through the afternoon of Tuesday, June 18, so they can fly back to Rome that evening. We need to bring them up to date regarding how all we have done comes together and why that is a good thing for Holy Mother the Church."

"Are you thinking of trying to do it in this area?"

"Yes, somewhere in the Washington area would be fine. And I think we should provide them beforehand a general idea of what we are going to be discussing."

"With their help," added Parolin.

"Of course, but without it if necessary. I will begin with inviting the people involved to attend. I'd like to have a proposed agenda and schedule in two weeks."

Parolin replied, "That is good timing for us. As you know, DeeDee Myers will be leaving us that second Saturday to return home in California, and I'd like to have her participate in the planning."

"Good idea. She has been a valuable resource for us all. Since she is leaving the next day, perhaps our planning group could have a private farewell dinner for her Friday evening?"

"I will arrange it," said Parolin.

"Thank you, Pietro."

"Thank you, Santità."

"And Pietro, you can remove the wig now."

* * * * *

Parolin knew that even though it was Saturday, DeeDee was going to have a final rehearsal for the Full Ginsburg with the pope during lunch, so he called to ask if she could stop by to discuss a serious matter whenever she was available. Then he alerted Col. Graf, who lives in the building, to stand by for a call. DeeDee arrived a little after one, and Col. Graf joined them a few minutes later.

Parolin began, "I will make this as quick as I can. I had a long discussion this morning with the Holy Father and he wants us to develop a schedule and proposed agenda for the Curia meeting June twelfth through the eighteenth. Since DeeDee will be leaving us in two weeks, I wanted to have us all up to speed on Monday."

DeeDee said, "He mentioned that to me at lunch when we were doing a last-minute tune-up for the Full Ginsburg, but he didn't share what he wants to cover."

"Do you suppose he would give us a few minutes now to get us pointed in the right direction?" asked Graf.

"Good idea. Let me ask him," said Parolin. "I'll be right back." When he returned, he said, "Good news. He will meet with us now in his conference room."

Francis said, "When I asked Cardinal Parolin to put together a plan and agenda for our meeting with the Curia, I didn't expect such a quick response. This is wonderful. How can I help you?"

"What do you want to address?" asked DeeDee.

"Much of what we are going to talk about in what you call the Full Ginsburg tomorrow. For example, I want to carefully and clearly define the role of the laity. And then to define a new role of the Curia: moving from dictating the way the church operates to implementing the informed will of that laity without causing chaos."

"With all due respect, that could be an impossible task," remarked Parolin.

"Unless you consider that our church holds that the pope has ultimate authority."

"Are you sure that you want to do it that way?"

"No. I am not sure that I do," said Francis, "but I know that perhaps I must."

"What if they don't agree?"

"Then they don't agree and they will not matter."

"You are not making this easy," said Parolin.

"I didn't say I would."

"Let's get specific. What do you expect from Cardinal Müller?"

"Strong resistance. Perhaps even his resignation."

"Why don't I just let you describe what you want discussed," said Parolin.

Francis began, "I want to begin by talking about why the Curia must change from being the will of the church to being its conscience and counsel. For centuries, it has concentrated on discerning efforts to change doctrine and countering it with more intransigent doctrine. They have done it sometimes by selective use of scripture to shore up their arguments and ignoring the basic pastoral elements regarding equality, charity and love.

"Our plan is based on the premise of listening and considering the voice of the faithful. That is now impossible due to the culture of the bishops, trained extensively in canon law that opposes any prospect of change. We had to remove the bishops, but allow them to try to return on different terms through election in their home dioceses. The Curia must set aside authoritarianism and become responsive to the needs of the people. It is called being pastoral.

"That does not mean that we do not need the Curia, or that it can be ignored. It plays several roles: counsel to the pope, responsive to the people and keeper of the faith. But it cannot ignore that things change over time, like the emergence of feminism—which can become the savior of the faith—and science, which has become the ultimate modern source of revelation. In fact, although I do not want to announce it at this meeting, I am considering adding two new congregations: equality of the baptized; and science and other forms of revelation. And perhaps a third.

"We also need to stop rejecting concepts simply because 'they are not firmly based in scripture.' We need to explore and assure that the *concept* is correct. The church cannot survive solely on the thinking and understanding of the first century."

"Are you going to give them any specific action items?"

Francis replied, "Oh, yes, and I am completely open to suggestions, even if it were to explore and develop one or more historically and theologically supported pathways to the priesthood for women or for a married clergy. There are other social issues such contraception, in vitro fertilization and stem cell research, including the use of millions of frozen embryos that are still in storage although in some cases their owners are no longer alive. These must be similarly addressed, although not in this meeting. Have I given you enough to get started?"

"This has been extremely helpful, Your Holiness," said DeeDee, "but could we spend a little time on style?"

"If you're asking if I am going to wear my beard, that hadn't occurred to me, but if you think that will help, I will consider it," Francis joked.

"I hadn't thought of that either," said DeeDee. "Obviously, I have never been to one, but I picture Curia meetings as very stuffy, everyone in full clerical regalia, and completely devoid of humor, fellowship and spontaneity."

"Neither have I, and I have the same mental image," said Francis. "I myself have only attended two rather brief and rather informal Curia meetings in my conference room.

DeeDee asked, "Can we do some things to change that perception?"

"We can certainly consider it."

"Thank you, Your Holiness. This has been very helpful," said Cardinal Parolin, signaling the end of the meeting."

As the three made their way back to Parolin's office, Commander Graf, who had been silent during the meeting, spoke up. "There is an issue that we never got to, which could be a showstopper."

"What do you mean?" asked Parolin.

"I made some calls to Rome a couple of weeks ago to determine how many people will be attending the meeting. There is no way the meeting can be held in the nunciature and, of course, no place for them to eat or sleep. We have searched a radius of nearly fifty miles from here for a suitable and *secure* facility to handle the lodging, dining and meeting. Because this is the vacation time of the year and many people want to visit Washington, there is nothing available that meets our standards or those of the Seals, for the pope's security."

"This needs to be the first topic at Monday's meeting," replied Parolin.

* * * * *

That evening, DeeDee thought back to her days at the White House, hoping that she might think of a similar instance when she needed an appropriate place for an important meeting and how she solved it. After an hour of fruitless thinking, she called David Andreatta at home.

"Hi, David, sorry to bother you at home, but I have a question."

"Not a problem, DeeDee. I hope I can help."

"Well, I am completely out of ideas on this one and as you know, I am heading home in a couple of weeks. I hate to leave them with a huge problem."

"I understand."

"Do you remember me telling you about the Curia meeting that is planned for a couple of weeks from now?"

"I do and I remember we had different ideas about how large it might be."

"Well, you were right about its size. It will be fifty people or more. There is not enough room here in the embassy, but it is critical for it to be held. Col. Graf of the Swiss Guards has been considering hotels as far as fifty miles away, but it is short notice and there are major security issues. Lt. Keenan is concerned about even taking the pope off-site and has said that her commanding officer must sign off on any plan."

"Has she made any suggestions?"

"Not yet."

"OK, let me think about it overnight," said Andreatta. "What are the dates again?"

"Arrive on June 12. Planned departure on June 18."

"I'll call you tomorrow afternoon as soon as the Full Ginsburg is over."

"Thanks. Oh, call me on my cell phone or at the office. I'll be watching it at the embassy."

* * * * *

When Archbishop Chaput returned to his quarters from Mass on Sunday, the twenty-sixth, and sat down to breakfast with his secretary, Father Murphy who said that a message arrived from Msgr. Menendez asking him to meet with the pope Monday at the nunciature in Washington. Chaput said out loud, "Bernard Law is a man of his word, and his punctuality is exemplary."

"I don't understand," said Father Murphy.

"I asked Cardinal Law for a favor and it appears that he has come through."

"Something I should know about?"

"Not yet, but you may be very pleased on Monday afternoon."

Chaput called Cardinal Wuerl and asked if he could stay overnight.

* * * * *

A large screen TV was set up in the main reception room in the embassy, and all the staff, including DeeDee Myers, Jackie Ring, Lt. Keenan, Capt. Fasel and off-duty members of the Swiss Guard, gathered to watch the Full Ginsburg. The three cardinals and Col. Graf watched with the pope in his quarters.

The plan was to record the five programs because some were simultaneous and others overlapped. By doing this they could start at ten and finish all five by one p.m.

* * * * *

"Good morning. I am Chuck Todd. It is Sunday and this is *Meet the Press* on NBC. This morning we are going to begin with an exclusive interview with Pope Francis II, which we recorded at the Vatican embassy here in Washington on this past Thursday. The pope will be laying out one of the five elements of efforts to modernize the Roman Catholic church: communications. Following my interview with the pope, I will be joined here by our own Chris Matthews and Luke Russert, both of whom are Catholic, for a discussion of what we have heard.

"Good morning, Your Holiness,"

"Good morning, Chuck."

Todd began, "Now in the interest of full disclosure, I am not a Catholic, so I may ask some questions which betray my ignorance.

"As you in the audience know, Pope Francis II delivered the commencement address at Catholic University last Sunday and announced that he had requested the resignations of approximately 3,000 bishops and archbishops around the world in a move to jump-start major changes in the Catholic church.

"His plan for the church is based on a new way to look at things in five different areas: better communications with the people in the

152

pews; the rights and the responsibilities of the faithful under canon law; the conflicts between science and theology; the conflicts between tradition and history; and the fundamental issue of gender equality for all of the faithful.

"Your Holiness, why was it necessary to remove all the bishops and archbishops—around 3,000 of them—to establish better communications with the people in the pews. Couldn't you just have changed the system?"

Francis answered, "The problem was and is far more complex than that, Chuck, and the decision to do what we have done was not made frivolously. As you may know, my predecessor, Francis I, made significant progress in reforming and modernizing the Roman Curia, a task that many thought impossible. The Curia is charged with maintaining the integrity of the dogma and doctrine of the church, through its various secretariats, congregations, tribunals and councils. It makes and adjudicates canon law. It serves the administrative needs of, and is subject to, the authority of the pope.

"A major part of this reform in the areas of overlapping jurisdictions was completed in the latter part of last year. The next task, in ways more complex, was to change the culture of the diocesan bishops to better involve the laity in the decision-making of the church.

"For most of the first five centuries of the church, the faithful elected their own bishops. Then for several centuries kings and emperors of countries named them, subject to the approval of the pope, who almost always gave it in return for their protection of him.

"In 1917, the Code of Canon Law affirmed that the choice was to be made by the pope on the recommendation of the Curia, working through the papal nuncios. Vatican II tried to insert more collegiality on the part of the clergy and laity in the governance of the church, including the selection of bishops, but that was substantially curtailed by later popes.

"The existing bishops became part of the problem. Promising seminarians are selected for completing their education in Rome and that means heavy emphasis on canon law and theology at the expense of the pastoral training that is critical for ministering to the faithful. When they finish their studies, sometimes, but not always, they are sent home for a year or so of pastoral work and then return for graduate work in canon law or theology before being assigned to jobs within the Curia.

"The apostolic nuncios in each country—who report to the Vatican Secretary of State and therefore are extensions of the Curia—monitor the selection of bishops. Rarely are these men appointed as bishops in their home dioceses, which makes them strangers to their flocks and more importantly, their flocks are strangers to him. And many bishops operate their dioceses like entities separate from the church. They have become administrators rather than shepherds."

"But with all due respect, Your Holiness, you have the power. Wouldn't it be easier to issue a decree ordering them all to change?"

"How could that be monitored? There are 2,851 dioceses spread across the world."

"Aren't they organized into national conferences? Couldn't you work through those?"

"Those conferences are often part of the problem," said the pope. "They are also organized into provinces. In the United States, there are thirty-five, but thirteen—mostly in the northeast but two in California—control the majority vote of the entire United States Conference of Catholic Bishops."

"How will that be eliminated under your new plan?"

"The bishops will be term-limited, and the members of any diocese can hold a recall election."

"Fascinating. Your Holiness! I know you have a busy morning, and thank you for visiting *Meet the Press*."

"Thank you, Chuck. I enjoyed it."

Francis left, and Todd announced to the audience, "Next, after a short break I will be joined by Chris Matthews and Luke Russert for more discussion."

After the commercial Todd sat at a table across from Matthews and Russert. "Well, I've never interviewed a pope before, but I found that to be both interesting and enjoyable. When you think about it, this is man was elected the leader of more than a billion people, in a church that was seriously in trouble in many ways. Instead of settling in and continuing the status quo, in three months he has staged a potential counter-coup and thrown out most of the human infrastructure. I'm glad to have you two insiders to help me sort it out, but this must be an interesting time to be a Catholic."

Chris Matthews responded, "I am fascinated by the political courage and acumen that he has shown. There is no way to change the culture of the bishops, so throw them all out and let the faithful elect their leaders with term limits and right of recall. This is a brand-new kind of Vatican politics!"

"I agree" said Luke Russert, "but I am wondering where the Curia stands in all of this."

"I suspect that there is more change to come," said Chris. "Remember, that Francis I spent a major portion of his reign reforming the Curia, but many have said that the task can't be completed until significant changes are made in the culture of the bishops. I don't believe that the changes in the Curia are yet complete."

"Do you mean the Curia will have a different role, Chris?" asked Todd.

"Probably," was the reply.

"What will it be?"

"I have no idea."

Turning to Luke, Todd asked, "Do you think firing the bishops will be met with any substantive resistance?"

"I doubt it. It has long been understood that the pope is the supreme ruler of the Catholic church. That would be difficult to overcome."

"Maybe not" said Matthews. "Everyone knows that I'm from Philadelphia and some say I never left. But I do know a lot of people there, many of whom are Catholics, and I have talked to some of them. I have not been able to find anyone who will confirm this, but two different people, who are not connected to each other as far as I know, have told me that during a hastily convened meeting of the USCCB early this past week, Archbishop Chaput from Philly offered some kind of resistance proposal to the conference, which was accepted."

"With that bit of news to think about, thank you, Chris and Luke. As I said earlier this must be an interesting time to be a Catholic. We will be back in a few minutes with more of *Meet the Press.*

* * * * *

"Good morning and welcome to CBS and *Face the Nation.* I am John Dickerson. We have the great honor this morning to have as our guest Pope Francis II for an exclusive interview, which we recorded at the Vatican embassy here in Washington on Thursday. The pope will be laying out one of the five elements of efforts to modernize the Roman Catholic church.

"Following my interview with the Pope Francis II, I will be joined here by our own Norah O'Donnell and Charles Osgood, who are both Catholics, for a discussion of what we have heard.

"Good morning, Your Holiness."

"Good morning, John," said the pope.

"Your Holiness, in your recent commencement speech at the Catholic University of America, you said that the historic action of retiring all the diocesan bishops in the world and replacing them with bishops elected by the baptized and confirmed residents of those dioceses was done to 'change the culture' of the bishops. How is that going to work?"

"John, that is just the first step in the planned transition. We determined very early that it was unlikely that trying to teach old dogs new tricks was a viable strategy."

"Then what is the next step in the strategy?" asked Dickerson.

Francis replied, "There are several, and they must be done practically simultaneously because they will take varying lengths of time. I'd like to start with discussing two of the cornerstones of our faith: history and Catholic tradition."

"Aren't they pretty much the same?" Dickerson asked.

"One would hope so, although it is more of a verification relationship, assuring that the tradition is consistent with the history. Tradition, in this case, was established by dedicated early Christians, borrowing heavily from the Jews they once were. Certainly, some of them could be considered historians, or at least they had an awareness of history. However, we have some anomalies that challenge reality.

For example, in scripture many people are described as having lived well over one hundred years, yet we know that there was disease, leprosy for one and virtually no medical care. That is a greater life expectancy than exists now, and it challenges the credibility of what scripture says. Dedicated non-Christian modern historians are likely to be more objective and better able to distinguish between the way things were and the way the Christians thought they were or ought to be. We need to narrow that gap by revisiting tradition."

"We must also remember that, as we know now, there was a great amount, perhaps most of the history of the world occurred before man devised a method to record it in a form that could be read by people who had not witnessed it. It is probable that the Vatican has one of the largest, if not *the* largest, archives of the history of the church, and yes, that includes the famed secret archives. We are going to commission the definitive history of Christianity, to be written by the most credible and honored historians we can obtain; we will give them freedom to hire as many people as they need, give them and unlimited access to everything in every single archive."

"How long will that take?" asked Dickerson.

"That remains to be seen. That is why they will have hiring freedom. The result will certainly be many volumes, and we will make it available online to anyone who wants it, at no cost. The time for mystery is over. History and tradition must become aligned."

"Will the history of Judaism also be researched?"

"Yes, to the extent that it is related to Catholic tradition. The same with Islam and Protestantism."

"Have you selected someone to lead this enormous effort?"

"Not yet," Francis answered, "but we are considering several people."

"What happens if history shows that some element of Catholic tradition is completely wrong?"

"It will no longer be considered as Catholic tradition, but the bar will be high."

"Thank you, Your Holiness, for a very interesting conversation. I said at the outset that this was an honor, and it certainly has been."

"Thank you, John. I enjoyed it very much," said the pope.

Dickerson said to the audience, "Stay tuned until after a short break when Norah O'Donnell and Charles Osgood will join me to discuss this interview."

After the commercial, O'Donnell and Osgood were seated across the table from Dickerson, who asked, "Well, what do you think?"

"That was wonderful," said Norah. "It is clear that this holy man is determined to bring about change."

"Finally," added Osgood. "However, this is going to be a monumental task."

Dickerson asked, "Any idea who will get the job, Norah?"

"Apparently, there was a Doris Kearns Goodwin sighting at the Vatican embassy on Monday, but he was clearly not confirming that today."

"This will be a career-maker for someone and a clear shot at a Nobel Prize," Osgood suggested.

"I think this could be a five-or six-year project, or even longer. He may be looking for someone in their late fifties or early sixties," Dickerson offered.

"Fascinating," said O'Donnell.

* * * * *

"Welcome to *This Week on ABC*. I am George Stephanopoulos. Our special guest today is Pope Francis II, in an interview we recorded on Friday at the Vatican embassy in Washington. As you know, the Holy Father startled the world last Sunday at the Catholic University of America, by asking for the resignation of all 2,851 diocesan bishops around the world. Today we will discuss this initiative to increase the confidence in the Catholic church.

"Following my interview with the Pope Francis II, I will be joined here by two of our Catholic colleagues, Donna Brazile and Cokie Roberts, for a discussion of what we have heard.

"Good morning, Your Holiness."

"Good morning, George," said Pope Francis.

"This morning we are going to discuss some of the anomalies between science and revelation."

"I prefer to think of science *as* revelation," said the pope, "despite the great irony in that reality."

"What is the irony?" asked Stephanopoulos

Francis said carefully, "It goes back to the treatment of Galileo by the church, and our refusal to accept the reality that the earth revolves around the sun. We didn't get around to admitting that until a few years ago.

As recently as 1990, Cardinal Ratzinger claimed that the church was correct in ostracizing Galileo and that to apologize would be just political opportunism. In 1992, before he was under Ratzinger's control, John Paul II expressed sadness of the treatment of Galileo. But the real irony was that Galileo made his discovery with a telescope, and the church has long been involved in astronomy through the Vatican Observatory—which operated a site also in this country in Arizona. We have been a part of the

Hubble Telescope program and are involved with its current offspring. Yet Galileo has not yet been fully accepted."

"Your Holiness, I am a member of the Greek Orthodox Church, which shares much doctrine with Roman Catholics. How do the discoveries of the programs you have mentioned square with the account of creation found in Genesis?" asked Stephanopoulos.

"Obviously, they don't, but they certainly cannot be denied. That is the whole point of our initiative in this area."

"Will Genesis be dropped from the Bible?"

The pope laughed. "Not likely soon, but the emphasis may be changed and some caveats presented.

"How would that be done?"

"The church does not reject evolution, per se. For many years, Catholic scholars, some who are teaching in seminaries have found stories like the Genesis version in folk tales that had been taught in many other civilizations. It is likely that they were originated by leaders to explain something that they had no way to understand."

"Thank you very much, Your Holiness. It has been an honor and a privilege to talk with you."

"Thank you, George. I have enjoyed it as well, especially with your connection to our theological colleagues from the East."

Following the commercial, George was joined at a table by Donna Brazile and Cokie Roberts.

"George, I want to first thank you for inviting me this morning," Cokie said. "This is a very special man. In my life, through my family I have had the opportunity to meet several popes and interview a few. This may be the best of them, and he is certainly relevant."

"I agree completely," said Donna. "He is not afraid to bring up issues and embarrassments, from Galileo to evolution."

George asked, "Is evolution an issue for you?"

"Not for me personally," said Cokie. "And not for most, if not all, of my Catholic friends. It is more the Genesis thing. On the one hand, they believe in evolution, but Catholics are not open to their fellow believers. It is almost like 'don't ask, don't tell.'"

Donna laughed. "I know just what you mean. This past Holy Saturday, I thought I was taking care of my Mass obligation by going to a Saturday evening service. It turned out to be an Easter Vigil service. It took two hours and consisted of a very dramatic reading of Genesis I, accompanied by a spectacular video of each of the six days."

Cokie chuckled and asked, "Did they have light the first day, but no sun, moon and stars until the fourth?"

"Of course," said Donna, also laughing.

"What was the reaction?" George asked. "Did they believe it, Donna?"

"I have been a member of that congregation for about thirty years. It is an educated group of people. I would guess that no more than five percent believed it and they are all over eighty-five, but the rest were all smiling and saying 'Wasn't that wonderful?' I admit that I was one of them. That kind of makes the pope's point, doesn't it?"

"It certainly does. Thank you for joining me this morning, Cokie and Donna."

"Thank you, George," they replied.

* * * * *

"Good morning. I am Chris Wallace. Welcome to *Fox News Sunday*. This morning we are going to begin with an exclusive interview with Pope Francis II, recorded earlier this week at the Vatican embassy here in Washington. The pope will be laying out one of the efforts to modernize the Roman Catholic church, specifically regarding equality for the baptized.

"Following my interview with the pope, I will be joined here by our own Sean Hannity and Bill O'Reilly, both of whom are Catholics, for a discussion of what we have heard.

"Good morning, Your Holiness."

"Good morning, Chris."

"Since you have shaken up the Catholic church with your commencement speech at Catholic University last Sunday in which you literally fired your 3,000 bishops, serving over a billion people, many people are wondering what your ultimate objective is."

The pope smiled and said, "We refer to that as the 'Then What' phase, and it has already begun. We have five immediate objectives, as you know. Let's talk about one of them, equality of the baptized, which is fundamental to our success."

"Okay, what do you mean by equality of the baptized?"

"Since you live in a democracy, I am not surprised at that question. In the United States, you believe that all people are created equal because they were born here or have gone through the naturalization process.

"All Catholics should be considered equal because they were baptized. But they are not, and have not been since the first few centuries of the existence of the church. Even Saints Peter and Paul had to have a summit conference on circumcision to settle part of that. A baby baptized this morning is every bit as much Catholic as

163

I am," said Francis, adding wryly, "except, of course, if it is a baby girl".

He continued, "We have an all-male clergy, an all-male hierarchy and an all-male Curia. But the parish and even some diocesan staffs have majorities of women. We need to change that imbalance quickly."

"Female priests?"

"Why not? It may take time, but why not? In the norm of things, they would become deacons first, which would also open the door for female permanent deacons."

"Female bishops?"

"Once we start, that would be inevitable."

"Then why don't you start?"

"We have started, but we can't do everything at once. That would produce chaos and perhaps even violence. Patience and good judgment are required."

"And good timing?"

"And good timing," agreed Francis II.

"Changing the subject a little, what has been the grassroots reaction to the firing of all of the bishops?"

Francis answered, "From the unscientific and incomplete analysis of the feedback from the diocesan chancellors, we think it has been greeted with guarded optimism. Many people had given up hope that any fundamental changes would occur. We had anticipated that, but it seems stronger than we thought. It may be different after the new bishops have been elected and served a couple of years.

"My opinion is that we must follow through with significant cultural change throughout the hierarchy. Culture has no direct connection to doctrine, canon law or theology. It has everything to do with attitude, charity, understanding—you know what I mean: being pastoral. Once that is set right, the rest is just plain common sense. Just look at the current situation.

"At the top, the culture of the hierarchy has been to stay steadfastly devoted to intransigence and otherwise maintaining the status quo. At national levels, the conferences of Catholic bishops seem dedicated to keeping their jobs, assuring an elegant retirement and not rocking the boat. And at the diocesan level, it is 'my way or the highway and don't bother me with facts.'

"The result is that from the great promise of Vatican II, the church has moved steadily back to the nineteenth century by the action and inaction of Popes John Paul II and Benedict XVI. We have a consistently boring magisterium that provide us weekly, ten-minute rehashes of the readings of the day, with zero relevance to what is going on around us in the world.

"Some wring their hands that so many of the younger people leave the church when they leave for college. I suspect that many leave when, usually as high school freshmen, they take Earth Science and then try to reconcile it with the first chapter of Genesis. The irony here is that in some dioceses, this is at about the same time they are preparing for confirmation.

"In this country, the USCCB has two conferences each year, and all we know about them is a picture of the perfect attendance of all 350 sitting in the auditorium of a posh hotel. There's no agenda, no minutes and no assured record of any decisions. A few years ago, they staged a televised session that was more like a commercial.

"Would it not serve the church better—and the laity, who really *are* the church—if they used those three or four days to develop a Catholic position on gun control within the construct of the Second Amendment, or health care, or immigration, or poverty, or the relationship between the police and those they are sworn to protect? And then publish the agenda, minutes and decisions with a mandate that pastors must address them in two successive weekly sermons, with equal time for men and women homilists?

"Ironically, if you recall the TV series *Rome*, the time of Christ was far more violent than it is now. Does that come across in the readings? We have many idyllic scenes of wells, pleasant roads, vineyards and large dinners, but no street crime or violence or demonstrations until the crucifixion. The reality? Jesus was a rebel, not just the local storyteller.

"Women in the church have been ignored, abused and discriminated against for centuries and still stay. And after more than forty years we still have child rape and cover-ups.

"This is the culture of our church. Fixing one or two of these situations is not going to work, because the system is broken and corrupt. It's not a very promising situation."

"Your Holiness, it has been a pleasure and great honor to have you here this morning. I'm certain that you have given our viewers, Catholic and no-Catholic, a great deal to think and talk about."

"Thank you, Chris. I enjoyed it."

After the commercial, Sean Hannity and Bill O'Reilly joined Wallace to discuss the pope's comments. Hannity was smiling but shaking his head when he sat down, saying "I have never heard a person in the Catholic church hierarchy, much less a pope, talk like that in my entire life. This man is crazy! Something needs to be done about this or the church is doomed."

"Well, it certainly is a different approach, in some ways to some real problems," O'Reilly remarked.

"Problems? He *is* the problem!"

"Don't you agree with much he said about the culture of the church hierarchy?" asked O'Reilly.

Hannity retorted, "I do not, and neither should you. They are doing their jobs."

"Don't you agree that the church has rolled back much of Vatican II?"

166

"Vatican II was another disaster—liberalism redefining the core values of our religion. It drove millions from the church!"

"I didn't agree with everything about Vatican II either, but I think backing away from it, with which I mostly agree, has been responsible for many more of the departures. Just look at who is there at Mass on Sunday—mostly conservative Catholics and a few Vatican II diehards."

"What's wrong with that?" snorted Hannity.

"Sean and Bill, as a disinterested Jew, this exchange has been very entertaining, but I thought the pope made some very good points. What is wrong with making the hierarchy more pastoral?"

"The Catholic church is governed by canon law, the scriptures and tradition, not by liberal pastoral bishops!" said Hannity.

"Well, I am not sure I agree, but thank you, Sean and Bill."

* * * * *

"Good morning, I'm Jake Tapper with CNN's *State of the Union.* This morning we are going to begin with an exclusive interview with Pope Francis II, which we recorded at the Vatican embassy here in Washington on Friday. The pope will be laying out one of the efforts to modernize the Roman Catholic church, specifically regarding the laws of the Catholic church.

"Following my interview with Pope Francis II, I will be joined here by our own Erin Burnett and Chris Cuomo, both of whom are Catholics, for a discussion of what we have heard.

"Good morning, Your Holiness."

"Good morning, Jake."

"Your Holiness, with all the things you have on your plate, why is the subject of canon law one of your priorities?"

167

"Well, actually, while this is an extremely important part of our program, it will not take much of my personal time. In January 1983 Pope John Paul II promulgated the 1,752 canons of the new Code of Canon Law. However, the church does not have an agreed-upon document like your constitution, which defines the duties, responsibilities, rights and privileges of the governed. Each canon law stands on its own.

"Now you might argue that the church is not a democracy, and you would be correct. However, we have nothing we can consult when canon laws conflict with one another, or to decide whether a canon law is consistent with our collective position.

"But what can you do about that at this point?" Tapper asked. "The church has never had a constitution, yet is has survived more than 2,000 years, longer than any other form of government."

"That is true," replied Francis. "However, we have a parish in this country, in Jamesville, New York, that was closed over ten years ago under questionable circumstances. For the past ten years, the members have disputed this and the disposition of the funds they had at the time, and still do not have a decision."

"What do you propose to do about that?"

"Popes don't have to propose things, Jake," Francis said with a smile. "I have appointed a five-member constitutional commission to draft a Roman Catholic church constitution for my approval."

"Can you tell us who they are, and why they were selected?"

"Did you know that there is an official list of the world's democracies in order of excellence?" asked Francis.

"I did not."

"Well, we obviously want the best possible advice on this. However, the top four and the ninth were Scandinavian, if you consider Iceland to be Scandinavian; however, none of them had large Catholic populations. The fifth was New Zealand, my homeland, and I did not want to bias the process, so I skipped them. Number six was Australia, and Cardinal Pell will chair the commission; seventh is Switzerland, and Cardinal Koch will be the sub-chairman. Cardinal LeCroix from the eighth, Canada, will also serve. The ninth, Finland, was Scandinavian and will be not included; but tenth is The Netherlands, and Cardinal Eijk will serve. That makes four members. Although the United States is ranked fifteenth in excellence, it has the largest Catholic population, so Cardinal O'Malley of Boston will complete the team."

"Do they have a deadline?"

"We will set a deadline together, after Cardinal Pell and the others have a chance to define the task. I will be very pleased with June 30, 2020."

"Well, I think we made some news this morning, Your Holiness. Thank you for your time."

"I think that was our objective, Jake. I enjoyed it. Thank you for the opportunity," responded the pope warmly.

When the commercial finished, Erin Burnett and Chris Cuomo were at the table with Jake.

"Well, what do you two Catholics think?"

"I think we got the most interesting topic," said Cuomo.

"I agree. This is a subject I never expected to hear mentioned, much less discussed. You said you made news, Jake, but you made history."

Jake replied, "I really think we did. He was very well informed and very clear. He has an interesting team assembled and made it certain that they are not just going to edit the U.S. constitution."

"Definitely not. I agree with Erin. This is a new direction."

169

"At least they won't have worry about the Second Amendment," Erin said, laughing.

Chapter Seven

Solution to a Dilemma

On Sunday, May 26, shortly after Jake Tapper and *State of the Union* ended, DeeDee had a call from Dave Andreatta.

"Good afternoon, DeeDee. I have a solution for your Curia meeting dilemma."

"Wonderful! What is it?"

"I talked to the chief of staff and he talked to the president. Both agree that because of the president's pledge to safeguard the pope, an off-site meeting could be problematic. The president prefers a venue that is controlled by the government. Their first thought was right across the street from you on the Naval Observatory grounds. However, that does not resolve the logistics problems related to where people might stay. So they checked the schedule and the place they chose is free at that time, even possibly a couple of days longer."

"Sounds great, but you're driving me crazy with the suspense. Where is it?"

"The president is probably on the line with the pope right now, offering him the use of Camp David, but there are a couple of conditions attached."

"Oh my God! I am so familiar with Camp David, and I never thought of it. What are the conditions?" exclaimed DeeDee.

"We'd like you to refer to the location just as 'an off-site location.' If someone figures it out, so be it, but we'd like to make it difficult for them and, if possible, retain deniability. It's a church and state thing.

"Here are some suggestions: The Holy Father, his secretary and body guards and LT. Keenan should arrive in the afternoon of the eleventh; bring the European attendees into BWI; we'll have a fleet of Secret Service vans to take them to Camp David. Cardinals Parolin, Stella and Ouellet, Ms. Ring, Capt. Fasel and you should travel the same way, leaving as soon as the press conference ends, while the press is still distracted and milling around.

"You are my hero. Thank you *so much!*"

"Act surprised," said Dave.

"Oh, I will. Talk with you soon."

* * * * *

About ten minutes later, Parolin called DeeDee, asking her to come to the pope's office to meet with him, Col. Graf, Lt. Keenan and Capt. Fasel.

They all arrived together and were greeted by the smiling pope.

"I have just received a phone call from the president. He has invited us to use the presidential retreat at Camp David for the meeting of the Curia. I don't know anything about it, but it sounds very nice."

There was great excitement from the group, although Graf and Fasel looked a bit bewildered.

The pope continued, "I understand this is a highly secure and very well-equipped facility first used by President Roosevelt during World War II, and the site of many historical events by every president since. Now I can guess how this came about since he said that the assistant press secretary, David Andreatta, mentioned our need to the chief of staff. I appreciate your help, DeeDee."

She replied, "I wish I could say it was my bright idea, Your Holiness, but it never occurred to me. David asked me where the meeting was going to be held and I told him we were having

172

problems finding a place. He called me with a 'heads-up' a few minutes before you asked us to join you. David said that there were some things about the arrangements for the meeting that they'd like us to consider. I made a list.

"Tonight, if you have a chance, everyone should go on the Internet and google Camp David. You will get a pretty good idea of the place and its history; although the security features are not disclosed they are second to none. That will prepare us well for the planning we must do."

"And it's run by the U.S. Navy," added Kate with a smile.

"I will leave the details to Cardinal Parolin," said Francis. "Is that all right with you, Pietro?"

"Excellent. Is everyone free to meet in my conference room nine tomorrow?"

They all agreed and left, except DeeDee, who asked Parolin if she could speak with him for a moment.

"Thank you again, DeeDee. You saved us from a lot of confusion. What can I do for you?"

"Cardinal, as you know, I had planned to return to California on June 8. But with this new development, I just can't do that. Why don't I plan to leave on the Friday after the Curia meeting?"

Parolin replied, "You have just answered the silent prayer I have been saying for the past hour. I know you have other obligations. How can we help with that?"

"Be understanding when I have to take certain calls and have to take an occasional morning off."

* * * * *

173

Archbishop Chaput arrived at the nunciature on Monday, May 27 at 7:45 a.m. He was admitted to the pope's office at eight a.m. He emerged red-faced nine minutes later.

As soon as he was in his cab headed for the train station, he made a phone call to Rome.

"Cardinal Law speaking."

"That goddamned son of a bitch fired me! He *fired* me! I wasn't in his goddamned office ten minutes! And he *laicized* me! He de-freaking-frocked me!"

There was silence.

"Bernard! Are you there? Did you hear what I said? What do you have to say about that, you pompous bastard?"

More silence.

"Bernard ... what do you have to say?"

"I guess I'm glad he wasn't pope in 2002."

Chaput hung up on him.

* * * * *

When the group, plus Cardinals Stella and Ouellet, re-convened on May 27 at nine, they did so with considerable excitement. They all had looked up Camp David on the Internet, and agreed that there was probably no better place for the Curia meeting.

Cardinal Parolin restored order. "Since DeeDee has been to Camp David many times during her days in the White House, and since she has most graciously agreed to stay on with us until the end of the Curia meeting, I think she should chair this entire project. DeeDee?"

The statement was met with enthusiastic applause, and Jackie looked very relieved.

DeeDee said, "I am pleased that you all were able to familiarize yourselves with the features and advantages of Camp David. In my opinion, it is the perfect spot for the Curia to meet. I think the president is happy to be able to help, but for internal political reasons they would like us to refer to the location as 'an off-site location.' If someone figures it out, so be it, but he'd like to make it difficult for them and, if possible, retain deniability.

"The attendees coming from Rome will come into BWI; a fleet of unmarked Secret Service vans will take them to Camp David, about an hour's trip. Capt. Fasel and a small detachment of guards will leave from the quarters at Georgetown after dinner on Tuesday evening to be on site when the Holy Father arrives. The Holy Father, his secretary Msgr. Menendez, Col. Graf and Lt. Keenan will leave by car early in the morning on the twelfth, preferably before dawn.

"Cardinals Stella, Ouellet, Parolin, Jackie and I will leave as soon as the Holy Father's press conference ends, while the press is still milling around. All Washington-based personnel will be at Camp David when the rest of the Curia arrives." DeeDee continued, "Now, I have a couple of suggestions of my own. They may sound strange, but in the past couple of weeks I think I have developed and understanding of what the pope is trying to do and the environment in which he personally operates comfortably. He is trying to break a centuries-old mold to save the church. This meeting with the Curia, the first since most of them were surprised by his speech at Catholic University, is obviously critical to doing that. Now they are all probably rather uncomfortable and as we say, waiting for the other shoe to drop.

"Successful companies and organizations, in such situations, have often found merit in changing the environment and increasing fellowship with conditions and activities they don't usually experience. There is an old and true proverb that 'all work and no play makes Jack a dull boy.' I suggest that you try to avoid that, and here are a couple of things to consider."

The others were quiet but interested in seeing a different side of DeeDee, as she continued, "Last evening I had an outrageous image that I couldn't make go away. It was, with all due respect, many older, proper, boring men in cassocks and beanies wandering around Camp David, which I know so well. They keep their thoughts and feelings to themselves and that does not inspire change.

"Psychologists know well that it is sometimes a good idea to force people out of their comfort zone; they tend to become more alert and creative in their thinking. We all know about Pope Francis' penchant for relaxing in casual clothes—but we usually don't talk about it. He has even made Cardinal Parolin become comfortable in running shorts and a Washington Redskins football jersey."

"*Somewhat* comfortable is more accurate," Parolin remarked.

"Somewhat, but you are not the problem, your Curia colleagues are. You and the pope should make casual dress a requirement throughout the meeting.

"My second recommendation is that the meeting should have a concise and always visible goal statement. My suggestion would be something like, 'Instead of Thou Shalt Not, Together We Will Find a Way.'

"My third suggestion is that the time should be spent on group problem-solving on specific and clearly defined projects. Working together, compromising, finding creative solutions—these all change relationships for the better. As a PR person, I will happily prepare the issues, including a schedule of special events for the week."

"I would be happy to review such a plan, and now we should all get back to work," said the cardinal.

The group broke up, leaving Parolin, DeeDee and Jackie. He spoke first.

"I have a feeling that you have some specifics already prepared."

"I do, but they need some refining with your help. I should warn you, they may be controversial."

"I am sure they will be," said Parolin, "and would have been disappointed if they were not. Let's meet in my office."

"I'd like to suggest instead that the three of us, plus Capt. Fasel and Lt. Keenan, head for Camp David right now. I made a call earlier and only the staff will be there today. We can have lunch and our meeting there, and the captain and the lieutenant can meet with the permanent security people there and start developing their plans.

"It is ten-twenty now. Can we leave at eleven? If so, I'll call and tell them we will be there for lunch."

* * * * *

When they had left the meeting earlier, Col. Graf asked Capt. Fasel and Lt. Keenan to join him in his office.

"This Camp David solution sounds ideal, but it is not something with which we have much familiarity. The material on the Internet was very interesting, but we are going to rely on your experience and insights, Lt Keenan, in developing our security plan."

She replied, "I am pleased to be of service, sir. I have already requested a classified detailed map with all structures specified. It should be in my office now. As soon as you have a complete list of the attendees, we will assign quarters for each person, which is a start. Then we are going to have to determine where to post our security people, which Capt. Fasel and I can do. The next step would be to determine meeting space requirements, followed by any special events and dining facilities."

"That is a good start. We also need to keep up with the plans DeeDee is developing so we can accommodate the logistics."

The phone rang. It was Jackie asking Kate and Hans to join them for the trip to Camp David.

* * * * *

Chaput arrived in Philadelphia around two. He hadn't talked to his secretary, so he took a cab to the residence. He was fumbling for his keys when Father Murphy opened the front door.

"How did it go?"

"Not well."

"Should we talk about it?"

"Yes ... I guess so ... I'll meet you in the living room for a drink and I'll tell you all about it."

When Chaput returned, Murphy asked, "What happened?"

Chaput took a long drink and set his glass on the table. After a pause, he said softly, "The Holy Father removed me as archbishop and laicized me."

"What? *Why?*"

"He found out about the plan to block his removal of all the bishops."

"Who would have told him?"

"I have been thinking about that and I don't think it was anyone from the USCCB. I know them too well. It probably was one of The Brethren. I am going to call Law this afternoon."

"I thought you said you had already told him what happened?"

"Yes, but I have to apologize for what I said."

"What are you going to do?"

"I called Archbishop Myers from the cab. He's going to let me stay in his place until I figure that out. As you know, he has plenty of room. I am driving to Camden early tomorrow morning."

"What can I do to help?"

"Pack up everything I personally own, all my personal files and anything else that someone might like to see, and ship it all to Camden. I want no trace of me in this house after tomorrow."

* * * * *

The Monday afternoon trip to Camp David was mostly spent with DeeDee answering questions about Camp David, although she kept reminding everyone that she hadn't been there for twenty-five years. When they arrived, they had lunch and a guided tour. After that, Lt. Keenan and Capt. Fasel met with the director of security for a briefing.

Cardinal Parolin, Jackie and DeeDee settled into a small conference room to discuss her ideas for the Curia meeting. Parolin smiled, "My curiosity about what I am about to hear is almost unbearable."

"I'm happy to hear that, Cardinal P. I hope you enjoy what I say. It is an extension of what I said this morning, but reflects what I have learned in the two weeks I have been here. As a Catholic, I have opinions and feelings about our church, which are somewhat negative when it comes to relations with the faithful and the lack of recognition of the need for serious change, rather than just tweaking.

"Frankly, that first day I thought that the pope's speech was an interesting concept and certainly newsworthy, but would soon collapse of its own weight. I thought the reaction to it would not only fail to produce real change, but perhaps drive us to an increase in the level of intransigence. However, since then, I have begun to believe that with the combination of Francis I's initial work with the Curia and Francis II's energy and creativity, the grand plan has a good chance of success, at least in the short term. I haven't seen that before and I want to be a part of it."

"DeeDee, we—and by we, I mean the Holy Father, Cardinals Stella, Ouellet and myself, as well as Cardinal Mamberti, whom you have probably have never heard of, much less met—refer to what you are talking about as the 'then what' factor. We know that if we cannot deliver on that, this will have all been for naught," said Parolin.

"Thank you, Cardinal. That makes me much more confident. This morning I gave you some thoughts I had about changing people's ways of approaching problem-solving. The second was to always have a visible goal statement. My suggestion was something like: 'Instead of Thou Shalt Not, Together We Will Find a Way.' After what you just said, I think that statement should be a reflection on 'then what?' Perhaps 'Now what?' would work better. I'll work on that, but all suggestions will be welcomed.

"Now my first suggestion was that we insist on people dressing casually at all functions. There is a priest in our parish whose idea of casual is no coat, a short-sleeved black shirt with one button unbuttoned at the neck, with that white thing that looks like a tongue depressor in his shirt pocket. I can't imagine what a Curial cardinal's idea of casual is."

"You might be surprised," said Cardinal Stella, drawing a large laugh.

"That may be, but I'd guess that at this event what they bring to be casual will be closer to what my parish priest does. I suggest that when they reach their rooms they will find three pairs of jeans and six rugby jerseys in different colors."

"I will suggest it to the Holy Father," chuckled Parolin.

"Would you care to place a wager on it?

"No."

"My third suggestion was to introduce the concept of group problem-solving on specific and clearly defined projects. It is my understanding is that the current practice is essentially to have a problem stated with a little discussion, and then each person develops a position paper, which is discussed until a conglomeration of all is produced, which is voted on paragraph by paragraph. No one is offended and little change results. Is that a fair assessment?"

"Well, perhaps a bit exaggerated, but pretty close," responded Cardinal Ouellet.

"For the past fifty years there has been a great deal of research into group dynamics and problem solving. It is considered by most of the experts that working together, compromising, finding creative solutions— all change relationships and results for the better. I'd like to help the Roman Curia into the twenty-first century, even if it is twenty years late."

"That sounds revolutionary for some of our colleagues, but interesting. Go on."

"Their governing premise is that change is, by definition, wrong," DeeDee said. "You inherently believe that any change will be cataclysmic. The truth is that with many, if not all, it could be beneficial."

"But how do you know that with certainty before you make the decision?" asked Parolin.

"Cardinal P, you are a great straight man. Thank you for asking that question."

"What is a straight man?" the cardinal asked.

"You'll see. Have you ever made a decision and later discovered it was the wrong thing to do?"

"Of course."

"Did you do the same amount of research on what could and would happen if you did it as you did on whether you should do it?"

"But how do you know what will happen in the future?"

"That is what a straight man is," DeeDee cheerfully.

"I think I get it. Please continue."

"The idea is that you pretend that you are committed to doing it, which takes the 'whether I should do it' element out of the process. You then concentrate on the implementation phase, which nearly always reveals both benefits and problems that you hadn't anticipated. In the process, you usually find many more benefits and solve the problems, validating your original decision."

"Interesting. How would we implement this?"

"Let me put together a general schedule for the week-long meeting and then see what is possible. I could have that tomorrow morning. Could we get ten minutes or so with His Holiness to get his approval and then go from there?"

I will try for tomorrow morning at nine," the cardinal answered.

* * * * *

Chaput called Cardinal Law at around ten, Rome time. "This is Charles Chaput calling to apologize for my behavior earlier today."

"Not necessary, Charles. I completely understood your level of shock and frustration. I am so sorry for what has happened. How do you suppose he found out? Do you have any enemies in the conference?"

"I have given that a great deal of thought and I don't think it came from there. If it had, it would have happened quicker, and you never would have even seen the plan. He ordered me to

Washington on Saturday morning and ironically, I thought it might be for a new job through you. I was completely blindsided."

"Whom do you suspect?"

"I hate to say it, but I believe that one of The Brethren may have told him."

"Mamberti!"

* * * * *

When DeeDee arrived at her office at eight, Tuesday, May 28 she found a note that just said "Nine" taped to the door. She smiled.

The door was open when she reached the pope's office at a little before nine; Msgr. Menendez said, "Go right in, Ms. Myers. Everyone is here."

"Good morning, all. I almost feel like I am late."

"Come in and sit down. I understand you have a preliminary plan for us," said the pontiff.

"I do indeed, but I would like to emphasize *preliminary*," she replied, passing out copies to the pope and the three cardinals. "I have made some assumptions, but they can be changed. The first assumption is that we should have some variety, and it should not be all work and no play in the Camp David environment."

"Take us through it, please,"

"Breakfast and lunch each day will be cafeteria-style, with two cook-to-order options each morning. Dinner will be a different style each evening, outside when possible, but not if it is too hot, too cold or raining. First day dinner will be an American-style cookout. We will try to bring in appropriate professional entertainment each evening and I'd like to have some suggestions as to what you would like.

"On Thursday, the group will be randomly divided into two. Cardinal Stella will chair one and Cardinal Ouellet the other. Located in separate rooms, each group will discuss the same issue and develop a plan to address it, which they will not disclose until Friday. On Friday, the two groups will come together under Cardinal Parolin and spend the day working out the differences in the two plans.

"On Saturday, the Stella group will be chaired by Cardinal Ouellet and the Ouellet group by Cardinal Stella. Both groups will discuss new and different issue as before.

"Sunday will be a day off, and I will provide a list of possible activities for the day.

"On Monday, the two groups will come together again under Cardinal Parolin and spend the day as they did before, working out the differences. On Tuesday, the two groups will again come together under Cardinal P to resolve any conflicts between the two basic issues."

"Will I be able to sit in on any of the sessions, DeeDee?" Francis asked.

"Absolutely, Your Holiness and I hope you will as much as you can."

"Will I be allowed to comment?"

"Hey, you're the pope!" Everyone laughed.

"Have you two issues in mind?"

"Yes."

"And they are?"

DeeDee said carefully, "The first is ordination of women, and the second is optional celibacy."

There was silence.

"You don't pull any punches, do you?" the pope said.

"I wasn't aware that I was supposed to, Your Holiness."

"You weren't," he answered. "I like it. Do you have anything else for us?"

"Well, yes. I assume that Cardinal Parolin has mentioned the topic of casual dress."

"He has and I like the idea," said Francis. "However, knowing a little about this group. I'm not sure how they will react. I wonder if we can convince them to do much more than your parish priest example."

"The best way is to make it look like a done deal before they have talked about it and can organize against it. However, I have a couple of ideas about that, like early in the session having activities in which it will be difficult to participate in a dress—I mean a cassock. I will develop a plan which I think will work with about 90 percent of the attendees."

"Do you have a guess as to who might be in the 10 percent?" asked the pope.

"I do not, but I suspect *they* might be the ones who are embarrassed."

"Finally," DeeDee continued, "I'm hoping you can help me with something. I'd like to have a goal statement for the event. Something we could put on small posters all over the place. My first thought was '*Instead of Thou Shalt Not, Together We Will Find a Way,*' but I think that is too preachy even for the Curia. Then one of the cardinals told me about your 'then what' thinking, but I can't quite come up with anything. But I'll keep working on it," she said getting up to leave.

"DeeDee, could we do the press conference meeting in about half an hour?" Cardinal Parolin asked.

"Good idea," she said.

As she was about to go out the door, the Holy Father said, "DeeDee! How about '2020 Vision'?"

Her blonde hair flew out as she spun around and said, "I absolutely love it! I guess that is why they pay you the big bucks!" The men all laughed.

* * * * *

When DeeDee got back to her office, Jackie was there with a list of topics for the next day's press conference. In a few minutes Parolin arrived.

"What are your initial thoughts about what bones you want to toss them?" asked DeeDee.

"Well, I think some announcements are in order, such as: we have responses from a little over 98 percent of the bishops; the pope's council of cardinals is in town for four days of meetings; a fairly large portion of the Roman Curia will be here for a week-long meeting with His Holiness. I suppose there might be some questions about something the pope did yesterday; he has relieved Cardinal Jean-Louis Tauran of his duties as Camerlengo of the Holy Roman Church, and given them to me; and he has sent a follow up letter to all the archbishops and bishops worldwide. Why don't you go ahead with that list, and we'll go over some of your answers now."

"Good idea."

* * * * *

The press conference began Wednesday, May 29 promptly at ten. Some of the attendees were new, but the overall number was slightly higher than the previous week. DeeDee greeted the group, made the general introductions and turned it over to Cardinal Parolin.

"Good morning. Thank you for coming back for some more discussion. I have three announcements to make and for us to discuss. After that, I will be open to clarifying questions regarding the Pope's five TV interviews last Sunday and then we will have a free-for-all round on any subjects.

"First, we have so far received responses from over 98 percent of the world's diocesan bishops regarding the Holy Father's requests for their resignations. Secondly, the Holy Father has transferred the duties of Camerlengo of the Holy Roman Church from Cardinal Tauran to me. And finally, members of the Roman Curia will be arriving on June 12 for meetings with His Holiness and they will return to Rome on the late afternoon of June 18.

"Now, to avoid embarrassing myself I will ask DeeDee to call the names of the questioners."

"Major Garrett of *CBS News*," said DeeDee.

"Thank you, Cardinal Parolin. With your permission, I'd like to start with a question not on the agenda."

"All right, but then you go to the end of the line," the cardinal said with a large smile. There was laughter.

"I'll accept that, Your Eminence. One of our reporters has filed a story this morning reporting that there was a moving van late yesterday afternoon at the residence of the Archbishop of Philadelphia. Has Archbishop Chaput been re-assigned, and if so, where and why?"

"I counted three questions there, Major but I will respond. Mr. Chaput has been removed as Archbishop of Philadelphia for gross disobedience to the pope." There was a gasp.

"*Mister* Chaput?"

Silence.

"Yes, Mr. Chaput. The Holy Father laicized him on Monday morning."

More silence.

"With great respect, may I ask why this was not on the agenda?"

"Fair enough. First, DeeDee heard it just now, as you did. Secondly, we are accustomed to considering such things as private matters, and thirdly, as you said, it just happened yesterday afternoon," Applause.

"Thank you, Cardinal Parolin. I understand," said Garrett. "I will yield the floor."

"No Major, ask your question."

"Cardinal, my colleagues will never let me forget this, but I have no idea what it was."

Laughter and loud applause.

Andreatta leaned over to DeeDee and said, "Pure class on both sides."

She nodded, walked to the microphone and said, "On the topic of the response by bishops to the request for their resignations. Jonathan Karl of *ABC News?*"

"Cardinal, what is the ratio of yes and no to the request?"

"I would have wagered any amount that would be the first question. I am pleased to report that with 98 percent having been received, there were no refusals of the pope's generous offers."

"What will happen to the other nearly 2 percent?" Karl asked.

"They have the rest of today, tomorrow and Friday to respond. We will be in touch by phone on Saturday to all of those not responding, to determine their answers."

"Kristen Welker of NBC News."

"Did anything surprise you about the response?"

"Yes."

Welker asked, "And what was that?"

"Thirty-seven percent included a request for voluntary laicization."

DeeDee leaned over to Dave Andreatta and said, "He didn't tell me that!"

Welker continued, "Do you consider that to be a criticism of the action taken by Pope Francis?"

"No, I consider them to be requests for voluntary laicization, which will be processed with priority."

DeeDee stood and said, "Cardinal, would you explain for the group what laicization is?"

"Surely. Laicization is the process by which an ordained bishop, priest or deacon is returned to being a layperson. He is no longer an ordained person, and is not allowed to preach, say Mass, or administer the sacraments."

"Thank you. Next question, to be fair and balanced, Ed Henry of *Fox News.*"

"Have any of the other 63 percent asked to be considered as a candidate for bishop in his home diocese?"

"I don't know. Such a request is to be submitted to the chancellor of the diocese in question. It's a little early for that."

DeeDee said, "Let's move on to questions about the recent meeting of the pope's council of cardinals. Peter Baker of the *New York Times.*"

"Was the purpose of the meeting for the pope to explain his actions in the commencement address and his plan for the future of the church?"

"The council of cardinals is a group strongly trusted by the Holy Father for their capabilities and support of his actions. They meet often and on a broad range of topics. This meeting was just one in the regular series of such sessions."

"But they obviously have not met since he fired all the bishops."

"The council of cardinals has been fully aware for a long time of the plan to request the resignations and the reasons for that in the framework of the long-range plan."

"Could you be more explicit regarding 'a long time'?"

"Since the evening of the pope's second day in office."

"Did the council sign off on the plan?"

"They were not asked to."

"Why were the council members not made available to the press?"

"Because the council is just that. They are not members because of their office; they are personal advisors to the pope—and remember, he can always invoke the seal of the confessional, which I guarantee is more effective than your Fifth Amendment."

Andreatta whispered to DeeDee, "These guys have done a great deal more of their homework than they did the first time, and the cardinal has handled it with conviction and humor. Good job."

DeeDee stood and said, "Now let's talk about this Camerlengo appointment. Susan Page of *USA Today*."

"What does the Camerlengo of the Holy Roman Church do?"

"It's a very old office with only one real duty. In the early days, when people thought the pope had died, the Camerlengo was called; he lightly tapped the pope on the forehead with a small silver hammer to verify the death. Later, they did away with the hammer and he just called the pope's name three times. Nowadays, we let a doctor tell us."

"Why was this change made now? Is the pope expected to die soon?"

"No, it is just one of those ceremonial things. Cardinal Tauran is in Rome. Usually the task is assigned to the Secretary of State, which I am. The Holy Father is here in the U.S. and so am I. We just wanted to save Cardinal Tauran a trip if something should happen."

DeeDee said, "I think that is all there is to that subject. The next subject is the meeting here of the Curia from June twelfth to the eighteenth. Questions? Chris Jansing of *NBC News.*"

"Cardinal, when did the Curia know about the pope's plan for firing the bishops? And a follow up question, are they fully aware of the entire plan now?"

"Chris, Cardinal Pell, who is a member of both the Council and the Curia, has known since February, as has one other cardinal. Cardinals Stella, Ouellet and I are also members of the Curia; we worked on the plan, so we knew much earlier than that. The rest learned about it when they heard the commencement address. One of the purposes of next month's meeting of the Curia is to bring them all up to date."

Jansing immediately said, "I have another follow-up."

"Go ahead."

"Who was the 'other cardinal'?"

"A personal friend of the pope."

DeeDee cut off the conversation. "Next question, Jim Acosta of *CNN.*"

"How many people are in the Curia? I also may have a follow-up."

"The Curia is like a combination of your executive and judicial branches of government. For meetings, such as this, the heads of

191

the nine congregations—you call them departments—are invited. Cardinals Ouellet, Stella and I are all in that group. The heads of the three tribunals are also invited. In the church, we have a one-man Supreme Court—the pope. Tribunals are somewhat like the federal courts, dealing with different types of issues. They are all invited.

"DeeDee, would it be possible for us to get a press release out concerning the Curia meeting?"

"I'll have one out tomorrow."

"Thank you DeeDee," said Parolin. "I see a familiar face in the crowd that I haven't seen before and he has his hand up. John L. Allen, publisher of *Crux Now*. What brought you out of the Vatican?"

"If your beat is to follow the pope, you have to go where he is. And I do have a question or two."

"You always do, John. What is it?"

"Since I know how many people attend Curia meetings, I am sure that it won't be held here. Where will it be?"

"You are correct, John. The Curia will meet at an off-site location."

"In the greater Washington, D.C. area."

"That would depend on how large one thinks the greater Washington, D.C. area is."

"Let's say thirty miles in all directions," said Allen.

"The Curia will meet at an off-site location. That is all I am permitted to say," said Parolin.

The next question came from David Corn of *Mother Jones*.

"Cardinal, thank you in advance for the press release regarding the Curia meeting. May we assume that there will be daily releases during the week and a summary news conference at its conclusion?"

"Does the president do that after cabinet meetings? Next question." Laughter.

"No … but I had to try." Laughter continues.

"We will be answering general questions about the meeting and its agenda following its completion. I will try to do a good job at that."

DeeDee rose, saying, "Thank you very much, Cardinal Parolin, and all of you for your questions. Please enjoy the hospitality tables near the building. We hope to see you next week."

The cardinal began some solo schmoozing and seemed to be enjoying it. Several of the press surrounded John Allen to get some inside information about what reactions in Vatican City have been. When he broke loose, he went looking for the cardinal. They greeted each other warmly.

"When did you arrive, John?"

"Late last night and then couldn't sleep, but I wanted to make your press conference. You did very well."

"Thank you. I have upped my game a bit since I have been here, I think. Better beware when we get back to Rome."

"Is there any chance that I could get a private interview with His Holiness?"

"I'll ask him, but he is pretty busy preparing for the Curia meeting."

"At an off-site location, I hear."

"Yes, an off-site location that I am unable to identify."

"Can I get a private interview with you?"

"Sure, as soon as you get some rest. When you have, call DeeDee. Her number is on the press releases. She'll set it up."

* * * * *

Parolin and Allen met on Friday, May 31at three in the afternoon.

"How long will you be in Washington, John?"

"That depends on how long the Holy Father will be. This is where the news is being made."

"Our initial plans were to stay until the new bishops were selected and consecrated, which will coincide with the new liturgical year."

"So around the first of December, then."

"Well, that was the plan. I personally think it will be sooner than that," said Parolin.

"What would cause that?"

"Well, several things. Although we have the best possible communications with our offices, it is becoming more and more difficult to manage day to day. Then there is the problem that we don't hear the undercurrents of the Vatican. We don't know what the people who are not involved are thinking. At some point these things will increase the motivation to return."

"Is security an issue?"

"Not really. At least not yet."

"What is the Curia meeting going to be about?"

"Again, several things. First is to deal with the issues the pope talked about in the Sunday interviews. Then, the next steps we are going to take and why. And an interesting concept: teaching them to 'play nicely' and get things done instead of just talking about them."

"Are you and the Holy Father satisfied with the progress thus far?"

"We are, but there is much more to be done and we must retain the momentum."

"One last question: Where will the Curia meeting be held?"

"At an off-site location," said Parolin smoothly.

They both laughed.

* * * * *

On Monday morning, June 3, Parolin and DeeDee were going over the topics for Wednesday's third press conference. "I really look forward to these planning meetings, Cardinal P, because you always have so many interesting topics."

"Well, you are going to like this week's list because there are some that might be rather controversial. I thought we would start with the results of the resignation request, a revision of the percentage requesting laicization, and what those numbers might be telling us. Then we will talk about the election rules we have sent to the chancellors in each diocese, and a slight wrinkle in that.

"Then there will be an announcement of a new letter being delivered to all of the current diocesan bishops warning of the consequences of their planned strike. Next an announcement reversing the position regarding the Tridentine Mass. We will end with an announcement of a letter circulated among the 3,000 archbishops and bishops of the world regarding their behavior during the period between now and the effective date of their resignations, and the pope's response.

"The press will love it," said DeeDee. "Lots of things to report. You'll have to tell me more about that last one. I'll develop some practice questions for tomorrow's meeting."

* * * * *

The press conference convened promptly at ten o'clock on June 5, with the usual large crowd; DeeDee introduced the dais, and

Cardinal Parolin went to the podium. "Good morning and thanks for your interest. As usual, I have some announcements and then we will get to the questions. First, the final signed resignation requests have been received and 100 percent took the deal. Several more people have sent their requests for laicization, separate from their resignation document. The new total for that is 42 percent.

"Second, the rules for the election of bishops have been sent to the chancellors in each diocese; a few have received requests from retired bishops for consideration. Some dioceses have received more than one such request. It has been decided that in the spirit of what we are trying to accomplish, only one former bishop will be allowed to run.

"Third, we will discuss some new developments in the former Archbishop Chaput matter.

"And last, the Holy Father has revoked Pope Benedict XVI's position on the Tridentine Mass.

"Now we will take some questions, starting with the numbers of bishops resigning."

DeeDee stood and announced, "Ann Compton from *ABC Radio.*"

"Cardinal, I know that last week you said that 37 percent requesting laicization was 'just that.' What do you say about it when 42 percent request it? That is around 1,200 people. Is this a rejection of the practice of celibacy?"

"Some of it may be. Some of the younger men, may want to take their lives in a different direction," he said.

"Do you think some of it may be to legitimatize existing relationships?"

There was some guarded laughter.

"Maybe, but I have no way to know and I will not judge. Let's move on to bishops running for bishop. DeeDee?"

"Sam Stein of *Huffington Post.*"

"Cardinal, in those dioceses where more than one bishop wants to run, how will that choice be made? And I have a follow-up question."

"We'd probably call a primary. I think you folks have some experience with them."

Laughter, including Stein.

"My second question is: will you be announcing a list of the bishops who are running for bishop?"

"As soon as all the nominations are made, we will announce the slates, by diocese."

"Now about the Chaput matter. He was disciplined for developing a plan that was circulated throughout the world, recommending that after signing the resignation to be effective in November, all the bishops would effectively go on strike to bring the church to a halt in some areas. Tomorrow, the Holy Father is sending a letter to the 2,851 archbishops and bishops of the world, warning them that if they participate in that practice, they will receive the same censure as Mr. Chaput."

There was silence and no hands were raised.

DeeDee asked, "Any questions about the Tridentine Mass? Major Garrett."

"What is it? And I do have a follow-up."

Parolin smiled and said, "The Tridentine Mass is the traditional Catholic Mass, said in Latin with the celebrant facing away from the congregation."

"My follow-up is: Where will the Curia meeting take place?"

"In an off-site location."

* * * * *

As DeeDee and the cardinal were finishing up, she said, "I have put together some thoughts about the Curia meeting, and some of the will require some lead time, so I need to get your approval on them."

"Let me see if the Holy Father can give us some time today, since he is the decision-maker."

About ten minutes later the cardinal called DeeDee and asked her to join them in the pope's office for about an hour.

Chapter Eight
A Curious Curia

The June 5 meeting with the Holy Father started at two in the afternoon. When DeeDee entered the room the pope stood and extended his hand, saying, "Good to see you, Ms. Myers. I understand you have some more interesting ideas for our meeting. Please tell us about them."

"Please, Your Holiness, call me DeeDee. Otherwise I don't know who you are talking to."

"Well, I will, and I suppose that maybe I ought to have you call me Frank or John, but people would talk. Tell me what you think about the Curia meeting."

"OK. Although I have never attended a meeting of the Curia, I have been to many the president's cabinet meetings and I have developed a sense of when to do things one way and when to do them another. My assumption is that Curia meetings are usually rather formal, almost ritualistic.

"I see them, for the most part, as status reports rather than opportunities to share ideas and make decisions. In this case you are trying, as you have said, to change roles and culture to bring the church into the twenty-first century. That means that the people involved in this change must first have changed themselves, and this meeting ought to result in your having more confidence that the changes can be made and the people involved will do it. In fact, that may be the most important thing on the agenda.

She continued, "To do that, you have to see if your people can adapt to that environment. To some extent, that is the reason that Camp David may be the perfect place for it to begin. It is not formal or ritualistic, but I would venture to say that in its seventy years it has been the venue and environment for more change truly affecting more people than the church has in seven centuries."

"Interesting thought, though I would like to think more about that," said the pontiff.

"More has to change than moving the venue for the meeting from a formal chamber in the Vatican to the rustic and casual environment of Camp David. That is why I said that you should require casual dress for the attendees. Some will welcome it; some will try it; some will give it lip service. Who does what will tell you volumes. But it can't stop at attire. It will extend to recreation. It will extend to mealtimes. And most importantly, it will extend to the way the meetings themselves are conducted."

"I'd like to hear more about that last one, please," said Parolin.

"Happy to do that. My guess is that your meetings consist at least in part in discussion of whether not you are going to do certain things. Everyone knows the subject before they arrive and has formed a position on it that they do not intend to ever change. Much study has been done on ways to make people take ownership of a problem and work with others to arrive at a conclusion. We need to force them into that modus."

"And how do you do that? Could you give us an example?"

"I think so, Your Holiness, if you give me a little latitude. Let's say that the subject before the Curia is whether to permit the ordination of women. Everyone comes prepared with reams of theology, the conversation is limited, nothing new is introduced, and the answer is no. Ironically, with most serious policy issues, the devil—and, incidentally, the angel—is in the details, when you begin the planning how to implement something you have decided to do. Sometimes you find problems that reinforce the position of *not* doing it. However, many more times you find benefits that wouldn't have been possible if you don't do it.

"After further thought I believe it's simpler to assign the members of the Ouellet or Stella teams by alphabetical order, rather than drawing lots, and to have them proceed directly to the conference rooms designated for their team.

"When they convene, they will be presented the following premise:

> It has been decided and made canon law that women are permitted ordination either as permanent deacons or as transitional deacons en route to the priesthood. This is no longer a subject for debate.

> Your task is to develop a detailed outline for an implementation plan, including but not limited to discernment, education, limitations, lodging, compensation and whatever else is considered essential.

> Your plan is to remain secret until tomorrow morning when you will meet with Cardinal Parolin.

"They will be thrown off-stride because that is not the way things usually happen. Their task is to develop an outline for its implementation; to identify issues and opportunities not considered before; and to propose resolutions for them. They are not used to thinking that way, and they don't want to make a mistake. You will have gotten their attention!

"They have all that day to complete the task, including, if necessary, after dinner or beyond. This gives them the chance to discover the real 'whys' and 'why nots' to make the initial decision to proceed.

"Cardinals Ouellet and Stella will coach their teams to be creative, not merely reflecting their personal experience. They should be vigilant in pointing out things that could go wrong, things that could be done better, and remembering there will be large numbers of candidates. I can teach them how to do that.

"On Friday, the two groups will merge, along with the cardinals, but this time under the guidance of Cardinal Parolin, to produce a final plan, perhaps with new ideas which have emerged. In addition, they must provide a policy on those women who have been illicitly ordained as deacons, priests or bishops.

"On Saturday, the Ouellet group will become the Stella group and vice versa. Their tasks will be the same for a different canon law: optional celibacy.

"Sunday will be a day off, but the teams will not share any of their work with one another.

"On Monday, the two groups will merge, along with the cardinals, again under the guidance of Cardinal Parolin, to produce a final plan, perhaps with new ideas which have emerged. On Tuesday, they will again come together with Cardinal Parolin to integrate and reconcile the two projects: ordination of women and optional celibacy. That should be an interesting day."

Her finish was greeted by ten or more seconds of silence, which seemed like several minutes.

"I like it," said the Pope. "It is certainly a different way of approaching a policy. Let's try it. Great job, DeeDee."

DeeDee and Parolin left and headed for the cardinal's office. He said, "That went very well, DeeDee."

"Yes. I decided not to bring up the rest of the stuff until another day."

"What other stuff?"

"Oh, the rugby jerseys, theme dinners, entertainment, the bocce tournament ... and a few more."

"We should talk first. And don't forget that we have to plan next week's press conference the day we leave for the off-site location."

* * * * *

About an hour later Cardinal Mamberti called Francis II.

"Good evening, Dominique. I am looking forward to seeing you next week and I suggest that you to stay with us for the following weekend."

"Well, I am pleased to accept the invitation, but I didn't call about that."

"Why then, do I have this pleasure?"

"I think Cardinal Law suspects that it was I who told you about Chaput. He asked us all at dinner last weekend and he has asked me for lunch at his place tomorrow. I expect that I will be tossed out of The Brethren. I may be wrong, but I don't think so."

"That would be better treatment than Parolin and Ouellet received," the pope replied. "We will talk more about it while you are here, if not before."

"One more thing. Law has instructed the cardinals attending the meeting to call as soon as they know where they are and to report daily on the proceedings by e-mail."

"Thanks for the information. I will have Col. Graf take care of that."

"Good night, Santità."

"Good night, Dominique."

* * * * *

Hans and Kate went to dinner at a small, intimate restaurant on Monday evening, June 10.

Over cocktails, Hans smiled and said, "It is really going to be really strange for us to see each other all day every day at a strange place for a week."

"But not all night?"

"Oh, God no!"

"When do you leave tomorrow?"

"We are taking two vans. One of them will pick me up tomorrow after dinner."

"Have you ever been to a Curia meeting?" Kate asked.

"A few, up at Castel Gandolfo. We stood guard."

"Did you wear your cute blue and yellow suit, funny hat, and carry your sword?" she giggled.

"Yes," he said smiling, "But since I am now a captain, my uniform is different."

"How so?"

"It is red with golden embroidery on the sleeves, and the breeches are a different style. Less baggy. I also have a longer sword."

Kate had just taken a large sip of wine, which ran up her nose in a burst of laughter.

"Oh, God, I wish I had a picture. Do you have that getup with you here in D.C.?"

"Of course," he said, "It's my uniform."

"Will you put it on some time and let me take a picture?"

"We'll see."

* * * * *

Following the plan, Capt. Fasel and eight guards left for Camp David after dinner on Tuesday, the next day.

It was still dark on Wednesday morning, June 12, when the van left for Camp David with guards Franz Buchs driving and Roland Pfyffer von Altishofen riding shotgun. In the back seats were the

204

Holy Father, his secretary Msgr. Menendez, Col. Graf and Lt. Keenan.

* * * * *

Cardinal Parolin's fourth press conference started promptly at ten. After DeeDee's usual preliminary remarks, Parolin went to the microphone. "Good morning and thank you for coming. As usual, I have some announcements to make, and then we will answer your questions.

"First, following up on developments in the Archdiocese of Philadelphia, the office of ordinary of the archdiocese will not be filled until the elections later this year. The chancellor will oversee day-to-day operations.

"Second, our own Cardinal Ouellet, whose day job is Prefect for Bishops, has been appointed to a temporary assignment so set up a placement office for the nearly 3,000 resigning bishops. Catholic and secular colleges and universities around the world will be asked to consider these resigning bishops and archbishops for faculty and administrative positions.

"Third, a meeting of most of the Curia convenes today and will run until next Tuesday at …?" He paused, cupping his ear with his hand.

"An off-site location," the press shouted in unison.

DeeDee stood up and laughing, said, "On the subject of Philadelphia, hands? Helene Cooper of the *New York Times*."

"Cardinal Parolin, is this the usual procedure when the office of archbishop or bishop is vacant?"

"That depends to some degree on what caused the vacancy. If a bishop—and this also applies to an archbishop—retires at the age of seventy-five as required, and a new bishop has been already designated or a coadjutor is in place, the new man just takes over.

"If no succeeding bishop has yet been selected, there are three alternatives: the retiring bishop may be asked to remain in office until his successor arrives. If the retiring bishop is ill and unable to continue, and his replacement will be available within a matter of months—which is the case in Philadelphia—that solution is chosen, usually with the chancellor presiding. If the period of not having a bishop is anticipated to be longer, a neighboring bishop may be asked to cover both for a time."

"May I have a follow-up?"

"Certainly."

"What is a coadjutor bishop?"

"Simply stated, coadjutor bishops are appointed because the bishop has health issues or something else limiting his competence. They rule jointly and when the bishop retires or dies, the coadjutor becomes the bishop.

"You may recall that a few years ago Bishop John Nienstedt was appointed coadjutor bishop to assist the ailing Archbishop of St. Paul and Minneapolis. When the ailing Archbishop died, Bishop Nienstedt took over. Ironically, a priest named Lee A. Piché was named *auxiliary* bishop to Nienstedt, not coadjutor bishop. As things later worked out, both men were forced to resign.

"Moving on to Cardinal Ouellet's added responsibilities," DeeDee said, "Any hands? Scott Horsely of *NPR*."

"Cardinal Parolin, will there be any prioritization of the retiring bishops and archbishops when it comes to placing them in new positions outside the hierarchy?"

"What a great question, Scott! I am going to call on Cardinal Ouellet to answer it. Actually, I want to find out if he knows what he is doing."

206

Laughter from the crowd, including Cardinal Ouellet, who stood and took the microphone.

"I think it is about time that I had this opportunity. Of the four of us temporary exiles here in your great country, only the Holy Father and I claim English as our primary language: he's from New Zealand and I'm Canadian. I agree that this is an excellent question, which has a very simple answer. The archbishops and bishops were not asked to resign because they specifically were doing a bad job; they were asked to resign because the culture in which they have had to work must change, and it would not be possible to do that one diocese at a time.

"The clear majority of bishops are very holy and good men. However, times have changed, and in far too many ways the church has *not* changed. When we were developing the plan we are now implementing, one of our greatest concerns was what is going to happen to these good men, especially the younger ones not ready to retire. I am very pleased that I have been given this assignment, especially since it is really a logical extension of my job as prefect for the Congregation for Bishops. I guarantee that I will make no moral judgments on anyone and will do my best to place all 3,000 in the best positions for them as people."

Strong applause.

"A follow-up, please?" asked Horsely.

"Go ahead," Parolin answered.

"Will *any* kind of prioritization be employed?"

"An interesting way to phase it, since the objective is to employ. We will try to start with the youngest and work up, simply because they are those who were not expecting to retire this early and the most likely to be hired. However, if Catholic University of America is looking for a seventy-year old chairman for their theology department, we would be happy to help them out."

DeeDee moved to the microphone and said, "Now to the topic you have all been waiting for, the Curia meeting at … ?" Mimicking Cardinal Parolin, she cupped her ear with her hand.

The press shouted again, "At an off-site location!"

"Since he has expressed so much interest in this subject, Major Garrett of *CBS News*."

"Cardinal, since the meeting convenes today and you have not exhibited any great urgency in this press conference, may we assume that the off-site location is quite nearby? And I would like a follow-up."

"Yes, Major, you may assume that, if you choose. What is your follow-up question?"

"Would we be correct?"

"No comment. Thank you all for coming. Please join us at the buffet and we hope to see you next week."

Cardinals Ouellet and Stella, DeeDee and Jackie stayed in the tent, working the crowd as it gradually moved toward the buffet. Then the four strolled slowly toward the rear driveway, then quickened their pace, trotted into the main parking lot and entered the van that was waiting for them, which then drove along the side of the embassy to a service entrance.

Parolin headed directly to the buffet, filling up a large plate. Major Garrett moved to his side and asked, "Could I have a few words with you, Cardinal?"

"Sure, if you would take my plate and find a table. I have to use the men's room and then I'll try to find you."

Garrett took the plate. Parolin went in the back entrance of the embassy, then downstairs and out the service entrance to the waiting van, which left immediately.

Major Garrett ate both platefuls from the buffet and chuckled that a cardinal had fooled him.

* * * * *

When the cardinals, DeeDee and Jackie arrived at Camp David, they learned that the pope was staying in the presidential cabin where they would all be joining him. Twenty-nine cardinals had arrived, all accompanied by their secretaries, and had been assigned to nearby cabins.

* * * * *

The charter plane from Rome arrived at BWI airport a little before 3:00 p.m., and the travelers were given special treatment through customs. They were surprised to be told that due to the nature of their meeting place, they needed to surrender all smartphones, computers and other electronic devices. They would be returned just before boarding their return flight.

Cardinal Law was going to have a quiet six days.

* * * * *

Sister Elizabeth Johnson and Brother Guy Consolmagno, SJ, arrived at Camp David around four in the afternoon. DeeDee and Jackie met them and gave each a folder with the schedule of all events, the lists of those assigned to the Ouellet and Stella conference teams, and other related information. They were also informed that the official greeting by the pope would be at six on the veranda outside the presidential cabin, followed by dinner at 6:30 and an opening talk at 7:30.

The vans from the airport arrived a little before five and their passengers received the same instructions.

* * * * *

When the twenty-six visiting cardinals and their secretaries—all in black cassocks, with the cardinals in their scarlet sashes and zucchettos—began to assemble on the veranda a little after five-thirty, they found the bar open, with DeeDee and Jackie inviting them to order before the program began.

Promptly at six, Cardinals Parolin, Ouellet and Stella came out of the cabin, followed by the Holy Father. They were greeted by enthusiastic applause. DeeDee looked at Jackie and held up two crossed fingers.

"I am pleased to see you all and that you have begun to share the hospitality of this beautiful and historic place. I will have more to say after we have eaten, so I will be brief with my greeting," began Parolin. "First, I would like to introduce two people whom you probably did not expect to see here. They are Sister Elizabeth Johnson and Brother Guy Consolmagno, SJ." Both raised their hands.

"Next week we will announce the addition of two new Curial congregations: science and other forms of revelation, with Brother Consolmagno as prefect; and equality of the baptized, with Sister Johnson as prefect. At the same time, we will announce a new group of cardinals, which will include both Brother Consolmagno and Sister Johnson."

Applause broke out among some of the Curia. Neither could hide the intelligence in their eyes: the nun with short graying hair and ready smile, and the bearded Jesuit brother with bushy eyebrows.

Parolin continued, "I welcome you all and hope you will enthusiastically join us in a new approach to collegiality. An essential part of that new collegiality is a sense of informality and relaxation. Some of you have already learned that I practice what I preach in that regard, especially my fellow exiles."

Parolin, Ouellet and Stella moved forward, removing their scarlet sashes and zucchettos, unbuttoning their cassocks to disclose their jeans and rugby jerseys— greeted first by laughter, then applause. They placed the cassocks and the other items on a nearby chair.

During the applause, the pope removed his white cassock, sash and zucchetto, disclosing his own jeans and rugby jersey. The laughter and applause continued until the pope raised his hand and spoke. Cardinal Stella added the pope's cassock and accoutrements to the pile on the chair.

"To make sure that the rest of you won't be embarrassed during your stay, while I have been speaking, three pairs of jeans and six jerseys have been delivered to each of your rooms. Now, let's enjoy our dinner. I'll have a little more to say after dessert."

Some cardinals were no longer smiling, but DeeDee and Jackie shared a fist bump.

* * * * *

Dinner was an American-style cookout with hot dogs, hamburgers, roasted corn, baked potatoes—the works. When dessert was served, the pontiff again went to the microphone to explain the way the program would proceed, and the alphabetical groupings. He did not, however, disclose the topics to be discussed. He urged them to enjoy their surroundings, especially on Sunday, which would be a free day.

By eight the travelers from Rome and most of the others were headed for their rooms in the various lodges.

* * * * *

The thirteen-cardinal teams, to be led alternatively by Cardinals Ouellet and Stella, had earlier been determined by alphabetical order, with Ouellet on Thursday having those from Braz de Aviz to Mamberti. Strictly by chance, that gave him six who had been appointed by Benedict XVI; two of those, Comastri of Italy and Koch of Switzerland, were considered very conservative. Five had been appointed by Francis I, and two, Sister Johnson and Brother Consolmagno, would soon be appointed by Francis II.

Cardinal Stella's first group was far more conservative, with four appointed by John Paul II and seven by Benedict XVI. The other two, Cardinal Ronald Peck from England and Cardinal Gerhardt Müller from Germany, were appointed by Francis I; Müller, probably the most conservative in the Curia, was a "Benedict XVI leftover," whose pleasant smile did not reach his eyes. The two groups would meet for the first time in separate conference rooms at 8:00 a.m. on Thursday, June 13.

* * * * *

The conference room was silent and the cardinals were already seated at the table when Cardinal Ouellet walked in. Behind each was his secretary in a chair against the wall. No one was smiling except Sister Johnson and Brother Consolmagno. Ouellet immediately noticed that cardinals Koch and Comastri were sitting side by side, dressed in their cassocks.

He smiled at them and said to Koch, "Were your casual clothes the wrong size, Kurt? I'm sure we can fix that."

"I didn't even try them on."

"Neither did I," said Comastri.

"Okay. The rest of you look quite comfortable." There was laughter.

He began to distribute a sheet of paper to the group, saying "These are the only ground rules for today's assignment. We have all day to complete it and if we don't, we will after dinner. Our main objective is to produce a more complete and prioritized outline for a plan than Cardinal Stella's group."

"I will read the assignment:

It has been decided and will be made canon law that women are permitted ordination either as permanent deacons or as transitional deacons en route to the priesthood. This is no longer a subject for debate.

Your task is to develop a detailed outline for an implementation plan, including but not limited to, discernment, education, limitations, lodging, compensation and whatever else is considered essential.

Your plan is to remain secret until tomorrow morning when you will meet with Cardinal Parolin.

"Any questions?"

"Are you saying that the decision to ordain is already made?" asked Koch. "That is a violation of canon law!"

"That is my assumption."

"Well it is not mine. This is ridiculous," Koch said, wadding up the paper and throwing it in the general direction of a wastebasket.

"I agree," said Comastri.

Ignoring them, Cardinal Ouellet said, "Let's take five minutes or so and each make a list of the issues you think need to be addressed."

* * * * *

In the Stella conference room, six cardinals and their secretaries were wearing cassocks. Three were on one side of the table at the end nearest the door and the other three were seated across from them. The seven others were in a similar formation, with the seventh seated at the other end of the table.

Thus, when Cardinal Stella walked in, he had to sit in the middle of the resistance. He smiled at the situation and walked around the table, handing out the assignment before sitting down. Then he read the assignment aloud. When he finished, as they had planned, he made the same suggestion as Cardinal Ouellet made to his group. The cassock crew just sat there. The others made their lists.

* * * * *

As the Ouellet group in turn read off their selected issues, he listed them on a whiteboard on the wall behind him. When there was a duplicate, he made a mark in front of the name of the issue.

Cardinal Mamberti was reading his list when the Holy Father walked in. In respect, everyone stood.

"Good morning. Please sit. I am just visiting." He sat in a chair off to the side, which had been placed there for him. "Please continue."

"My last suggestion," said Mamberti, "is that we should try to develop an estimate of how many new candidates we will have each year for the next ten years, and what the attrition rate we will have over that same period."

"Good question," Ouellet said. "That concludes this part of the process. Now we will begin to flesh out each suggestion."

"Excuse me, Marc," said the pope, "I would like to ask a question. Kurt, what do you think was your most important issue?"

Calmly, Cardinal Koch replied, "I didn't have any. I thought the list was quite complete."

"Why do you feel that way?"

"Well, frankly, I think this is a total waste of our time. This is never going to happen."

There was not a sound in the room for several seconds, until the pope said pleasantly. "Oh, it will happen."

More silence.

"Do you think the Curia will approve of this if it comes to that?" asked Koch.

The pope stood to leave, saying, "Perhaps not."

Everyone stood and he left.

Ouellet stood and said, "Let's talk more about Dominique's idea about estimating the ten-year flow of women candidates through the process to ordination."

* * * * *

Cardinal Stella followed the same agenda prepared by DeeDee, with little effort by the men in black. The others were trying hard to make things work. It was a struggle, but by lunchtime they had a pretty good list.

DeeDee's plan was to have each group eat box lunches together in the conference room while Parolin, Ouellet and Stella ate in another private room.

* * * * *

As soon as Ouellet had left his conference room for lunch, Cardinal Comastri excused himself; after nearly twenty minutes, he returned, wearing jeans and a rugby jersey. Cardinal Koch glared at him but said nothing.

When the Ouellet group reconvened, Ouellet casually remarked to Comastri that he looked much more comfortable but not fully relaxed.

Ouellet turned to Mamberti and said, "Dominique, why don't you lead us through your thinking about how and why what you call the flow of women through the preparation for ordination process is so important to all the other elements."

"Okay," said Mamberti, "everyone please write down the average number of women in the average diocese and archdiocese who would be interested is this program today." He paused. "How many wrote down ten or fewer?"

Two hands went up.

"How many think the number is at least twenty-five?"

Six hands were raised.

"How many think it is fifty or more?"

Five went up.

"If it is ten per diocese or archdiocese, the total is 28,510; if twenty-five, the total would be 71,275; and if fifty, that means 142,550. Now, if the usual duration of the education is eight years and the number is just twenty-five, by the end of three years, there could be 285,100 studying at the same time. Where are we going to find the resources to do that? And how long must it be sustained?"

"Let's say we could figure that all out. Do we have jobs for all those people? Can we afford to pay them all? That is one woman graduate for every 4,000 Catholics and climbing.

The cardinals struggled with that and the other elements all afternoon.

* * * * *

The Stella group also finished their task by the end of the day, but without the insights of their rivals. Reconciling the two plans would be Cardinal Parolin's task tomorrow.

At dinner Thursday, Cardinal Piacenza and Cardinal Sarah of the Stella group were in jeans and jerseys. Müller, Rodriguez, Sodano and Turkson from Stella's group and Koch from Ouellet's group were not.

A traditional American Thanksgiving dinner with all the trimmings was served and enjoyed by all. When it was over, Pope Francis II stood at the microphone.

"I'd like to take advantage of our having a traditional Thanksgiving dinner tonight, to express our thanks to this country and the way they have welcomed, kept us safe and guided us during our stay.

"First, of course is the president, who granted us political asylum within the embassy. Then there is Lt. Kate Keenan, sitting back there and her Navy Seals, whom we rarely see but we know they are always there keeping us safe.

"Next is David Andreatta, the assistant White House press secretary, who not only arranged for us to be here at historic Camp David, but who has guided us through the maze of the American press and introduced us to the mastermind of this event, DeeDee Myers.

"Finally, I thank the members of the Curia, who have made the long trip; adapted to a new way of working as a group on complex policy problems; and the many of you who have tried casual dress for comfort and creative thinking. I hope the rest will accept the advice of an American TV commercial: 'Try it ... you'll like it.'

"Now please, spend some time talking with each other, our staff and our hosts, to the music provided by the U.S. Marine Corps Jazz Band."

* * * * *

Friday morning, June 14, Cardinal Parolin greeted the Curia members and their secretaries at eight. in a large conference room. The first thing he noticed was that only Cardinals Koch and Müller and their secretaries were still wearing cassocks. He made no comment.

"The Holy Father is here to start the day and plans to stop in periodically to see how we are doing. Today we are supposed to reconcile the two plans that have been outlined. However, Cardinal Mamberti has presented us with a problem. He took our new problem-solving approach to another level and shown us a new problem. That problem is that we must first determine how many ordained women we need."

"Easy answer," shouted Müller, "NONE!"

There was no immediate response except some murmuring. Parolin, who had been facing in the other direction, turned slowly to face Müller. "Gerhard, I am going to take that as an extremely poor attempt at humor."

"It was not intended as that."

"Then I take it as an insult to all of us, and especially to the Holy Father and Sister Johnson. You owe an apology."

"I apologize for saying it aloud, but not for believing it. I will not continue to play this foolish game," said Müller, stalking out of the room.

There was more murmuring, and Cardinal Koch looked very uncomfortable.

Parolin said, "Let us get back to the reason we are all here. Cardinal Mamberti, what do you suggest to get us out of this dilemma?"

"Which one?" Mamberti asked, to relieved laughter.

"The ideal number of ordained women," responded a smiling Parolin.

"Actually, that may be the easier of the two. It requires determining the total number of ordained clergy we will need by say 2030; subtracting the number of current clergy we will lose by then; and projecting the number men and women we realistically can educate on a yearly basis to meet that 2030 goal."

"Excellent!" said Parolin, turning to the group. "It is now 8:45 a.m. You have until dinner to solve the issue. Cardinals Stella, Ouellet and I are here to help."

Standing, Francis II said, "I leave now, but you may be sure I will return. This is fascinating."

* * * * *

Cardinal Müller had gone immediately to the chapel, where he stayed for the rest of the morning. He then called and asked that lunch and dinner be delivered to his room. After lunch he visited the Camp David library and borrowed several books that had nothing to do with philosophy, theology, the Catholic church, or religion in general. He left with what he thought would be enough to last five more days.

* * * * *

The Curia organized itself, including the secretaries. Müller's secretary had not left and was pleased to be asked to join Mamberti and his secretary to do the people power projection that Dominique had made sound so easy.

The others organized by whatever topic interested them; this required some adjustments, but eventually ran smoothly.

Francis II dropped in a total of four times, to everyone's surprise.

At 5:30, Cardinal Parolin declared the project complete, to everyone's relief.

* * * * *

The Friday evening dinner was a Low Country Boil, a new experience for nearly all. They were fascinated that the shrimp, oysters, corn, lobsters, potatoes and who knows what else could all be all cooked together in those huge kettles on a charcoal fire. A strolling magician circulated through the tables doing tricks, but the cooking and eating process got more attention.

219

* * * * *

In Rome, on Saturday morning Cardinal Law was beside completely frustrated as he sat down for breakfast at a nearby restaurant with Cardinal Burke. He had called everyone he could think of who might know where the Curia members were and what they might be doing.

"It is if they had all ascended to heaven with the Holy Father!"

Burke scoffed, "Well, we both know that is unlikely."

"All we know is that they are in Washington."

"I guess it *is* too early to expect a card, but have you talked to Wuerl to see what he knows?"

"Of course."

"Are you really sure they are in Washington?"

"Well, the general Washington area."

"Are you sure?"

Law rasped, "What are you getting at, Ray?"

"What if they just changed planes in Washington?"

That ruined Law's entire weekend.

* * * * *

On Saturday, July 15 the Curia gathered in their assigned groups, in their assigned conference rooms at 8:00 a.m. This time, Ouellet had the Stella group, and vice versa.

Each read the new assignment to his group:

> "It has been decided and will be made canon law that beginning January 1, 2020, clerical celibacy will be optional except for religious orders. This is no longer a subject for debate. In addition, you are to assume that the

decisions made jointly with the other group in the previous assignment all apply.

Your task is to develop a detailed outline for an implementation plan, including but not limited to discernment, education, limitations, lodging, compensation and whatever else is considered essential.

Your plan is to remain secret until tomorrow morning when you will again meet with Cardinal Parolin."

The Ouellet group accepted the task as presented. But although it was a different group, Cardinal Stella was challenged again.

"Are we supposed to believe that this nonsense is ever going to happen?" asked Cardinal Koch, the only one in the room wearing a cassock.

"The assignment merely says that you are not to debate it. What you believe is up to you," Stella said calmly.

"It seems to me that this situation is essentially a matter of logistics, especially regarding lodging," said Cardinal Robert Fien.

"And equality," added Sister Johnson.

"Don't forget compensation!" said Cardinal John Considine.

"How so, John?" asked Brother Consolmagno.

"It is a matter of economics, Brother. A married priest has more expenses than a celibate one."

"I think you mean an unmarried priest."

"Not necessarily," replied Considine, to considerable laughter.

Stella said, "I think that this is a good time for us to begin the process we used on Thursday. For the next fifteen minutes, each of us will write down the issues we believe must be addressed.

* * * * *

In the more conservative conference room now monitored by Cardinal Ouellet, there was less initial humor. However, in the absence of Cardinal Müller, they seemed inclined to get to work and get it over with.

Cardinal O'Malley said, "It seems to me that unlike the previous assignment, every one of the mentioned sources of issues are in play and, in fact, often interact with each other. I suspect that while I agree it should done, the overring issue is whether the church can financially afford it."

"I totally agree. However, can we afford to not do it?" asked Cardinal Marx.

Ouellet replied, "I think it would be safe to say that the required funds will be found."

"Can we actually get away with four collections every week?" said Cardinal Sarah, to wry laughter.

"Let's each make our own list and get to work."

* * * * *

Pope Francis visited each group twice during the day, asking questions and offering a few suggestions. Both groups met the 5:30 p.m. completion deadline, agreeing that the major issue was funding. Since tomorrow would be Sunday, they'd have to wait until Monday to complete the final product. Some wonder what they will be doing on Tuesday.

* * * * *

Dinner was an authentic New Orleans dinner from the menu at Antoine's consisting of: *escargots á la Bourguignonne*; *bisque d'ecrevisses*; *salade de laitue au Roquefort*; *filet de boeuf en brochette marchand de vin*; and bread pudding *de Noix de Pecan*, with an appropriate selection of wines, and music by the Annapolis Midshipman Dixieland Band.

222

* * * * *

After the spectacular dinner, the pope had a few remarks.

"We have reached the halfway point in our conference and I must say that I am impressed with the progress thus far. At least part, if not most, of the credit for that goes to our new friend, DeeDee Myers. She convinced us to try a different approach to problem solving, which I believe is rather revealing; she was instrumental in procuring this very beautiful and historic venue; she has planned the meals, selected the meals and, I think, has even has controlled the weather. She figured out how to make the casual apparel work, at least for the most part, and has made Cardinal Parolin an excellent spokesman for our activities.

"As most of you know, at the end of this coming week, DeeDee will be leaving us to go back to her day job in California. While she is leaving us in the good hands of Jackie Ring, we owe her our sincere thanks. As a token of our appreciation DeeDee, please accept this simple signed picture for your office." He presented DeeDee with an autographed picture of Pope Francis I.

"Thank you, Your Holiness," said DeeDee, obviously moved. "You can be sure this will have a special place in my office. This has been the most incredible three months of my personal and professional life. I will miss you all greatly."

She started to sit down, but turned around, took the microphone and said, "I'm so happy, I am going to ask the Midshipmen Dixieland Band to stay another hour. Tomorrow is Sunday. What time is Mass, Your Holiness?"

"How about ten?"

"Great! Two hours, Middies!"

The Midshipmen exhausted their repertoire well before the additional two hours, but delighted the crowd by playing *When the Saints Come Marching In!* as they marched out.

* * * * *

Mass on Sunday, June 16 was on the veranda of the presidential cabin, followed by a breakfast buffet. The rest of the day was free and the attendees were enjoying the amenities of Camp David. Several played tennis; a few were riding horses on the trails through the woods. The pool was the most popular choice— but more for sitting than serious swimming.

German Cardinals Koch and Marx, with Guinean Cardinal Sarah, visited Cardinal Müller in his room.

"How are you doing, Gerhard?' asked Sarah.

"Pretty well. I have been doing quite a bit of non-clerical reading and spending time in the chapel when I know you are in *class,*" sneered Müller.

"You are a stubborn man," said Koch.

"But am I right?"

"That doesn't matter. You are only hurting yourself."

"Have you asked the Holy Father if you could see him?" asked Marx.

"No, but he hasn't invited me either."

"Did you expect him to?"

The conversation changed to what the cardinal had been reading and other less important matters. Then the visitors went for a long walk.

* * * * *

Sunday night dinner was a traditional Kansas City pork barbecue, with briskets, ribs, shoulders and assorted sauces, whose aromas had been tempting appetites since daylight. The music was a Kansas City jazz band. It was a relaxing end to a delightful day. When the pope spoke, he said he hoped they all had a pleasant afternoon. They had.

* * * * *

When the Curial conference came together with Cardinal Parolin on Monday, June 17, the mood was very positive. There were, of course, differences in their conclusions about costs, but they quickly reconciled them. By noon they had a final document.

As they were eating lunch, joined by Stella and Ouellet, Parolin said "I am pleased and grateful that you worked so quickly this morning. You have probably wondered what is on tomorrow's agenda. It is a subtly complex issue and, since we have some time constraints relative to your catching the plane back to Rome, I'd like to get started as soon as we finish lunch."

The suggestion was met with applause.

* * * * *

Earlier, Cardinal Law called his contact in the Vatican Travel Office.

"Good morning, Cardinal. What can I do for you?"

"I am curious as to whether the charter plane returning the Curia from Washington will be leaving on time tomorrow evening."

"As far as we know, that is correct and we anticipate that it will arrive in Rome early Wednesday morning."

"So the connecting flight to Washington is also expected to be on time?"

"There is no connecting flight, Your Eminence."

"I had heard that the meeting was at another location."

"Not that I know. I haven't heard that and I certainly would have."

"All right, thank you," said Law, hanging up. "DAMN!!"

* * * * *

After lunch Monday, Parolin laid out the agenda.

"This afternoon and tomorrow we will complete the overall task we have been assigned. On Thursday and Friday we dealt with the results of a decision to authorize the ordination of women. For Saturday and today, our attention has been on the decision to make celibacy optional. Now we will address what we must do if the two decisions are announced simultaneously."

There was a mixture of groans and laughter.

* * * * *

At one o'clock Cardinal Müller placed a call to Francis II's suite. Msgr. Menendez answered. "This is the office of His Holiness."

"Msgr. Menendez, this is Cardinal Müller. I would like to meet personally, briefly if necessary, with the Holy Father this afternoon."

"If I can put you on hold for a minute or so, I will ask if he is available."

"Certainly."

Moments later Msgr. Menendez returned and asked, "Could you come at one-thirty?"

"Yes, I will be there."

At the appointed time, Müller walked the short distance to the presidential cabin, wondering what he was going to say to the pope. The door to the Holy Father's private office was open; he was in the outside office waiting when Müller arrived. "Good afternoon, Gerhard. I am so pleased that you called. Come in and sit down."

"Thank you, Your Holiness. I am ashamed and embarrassed about my behavior last week."

"You are a passionate man."

"Yes, I am. Is that wrong?"

"No, but unwise sometimes. And you are also a stubborn man. Bad combination."

"I have been told that. Will you forgive me?"

"For what you did last week, of course. But you are not a team player, Gerhard, which was obvious when no one joined you. That must change."

"I will try."

The Holy Father extended his hand and said, "I hope so. Please join us for dinner tonight."

"I will."

* * * * *

The cardinals were in good spirits when the afternoon session began.

"Let's use the approach that has served us well so far," Parolin suggested. "Thirty minutes this time. Make your lists of topics."

They did more thinking than writing, but were ready to share after thirty minutes.

"Perhaps we should revisit contraception," said Cardinal O'Malley, which drew laughter.

"There is an additional financial component to this, for sure," added Cardinal Considine.

"How would we deal with, God forbid, if a priest—or a bishop for that matter—expressed his intent to marry and then disclosed that he had already married civilly and has three or four kids," asked Cardinal Peck.

"Ask him how he afforded it," suggested Cardinal Stella.

By three o'clock they had an impressive list of topics, and Francis II joined them.

The cardinals brought him up to speed with what they were doing; he was impressed and asked several questions. Then he asked if they had any for him.

Cardinal Robert Fien asked, "Your Holiness, should we be planning to write a code of conduct to accompany our plans?"

Francis laughed and said, "Is that a personal question or from the group?"

"I guess it is a professional question."

"I think you should probably discuss it and make a recommendation."

* * * * *

Dinner Monday evening was an authentic Texas steak and pot roast, with baked potatoes, corn, sauce and apple pie. The entertainment was country western couple Faith Hill and Tim McGraw.

Just before grace was to be said, Cardinal Müller walked in and approached the pope. He was wearing his cassock.

Francis II saw him and extended his hand.

"Good evening Your Holiness."

With a slightly forced smile, the pontiff took Müller's hand, saying, "Welcome back, Gerhard. Please join me at our table."

228

"Thank you, I'll be happy to join you."

In a quieter voice and the same smile, Francis murmured, "Gerhard, you are a stubborn man."

* * * * *

Cardinal Giuseppe Bertello said to his tablemates, "I feel like I have eaten myself halfway across the United States for the past six days. It has been wonderful, but I am really looking forward to a large plate of pasta—for breakfast."

"It has been an impressive display of the variety of our cuisine, although I have not had some of these things for decades, and I have sincerely enjoyed it," said Cardinal Considine.

"It has been a remarkable conference. Memorable, I'd say. What do you think of Gerhard showing up?" asked Bertello.

"Typical. Always willing to push the envelope until the postmaster says enough."

"Has he said enough?"

"Not here, but he will soon."

* * * * *

At a nearby table, Cardinal Peck asked, "What do you think led to Müller showing up?"

"He was probably wondering if he had a ride home," said Cardinal Farrell.

"He is a complex person, but so convinced of his positions that he cannot participate in any form of discussion," sighed Cardinal Comastri.

* * * * *

At still another table, Cardinal Fien asked, "Sister Johnson, what is your assessment of your first Curial conference?"

"I would say that it was more open and less dogmatic than I expected."

"Did you feel that you were listened to?"

"Yes, although I would anticipate that in future conferences I will have much more to say."

"I, for one, look forward to that."

Brother Consolmagno nodded cheerfully.

* * * * *

At a moment when their tablemates were engaged in conversation, Cardinal Müller leaned over to Francis II and asked, "Have you forgiven me, Santità?"

"Yes, but I have not yet decided on your penance."

"When will you decide?"

"Soon."

* * * * *

At the end of the dinner, the pope rose. "This is our last dinner together in this, which I consider an historic meeting of the Curia. Our discussions have been free, open and, most importantly, honest. We have made great progress. After tomorrow morning's session we will go back to work. Decisions will be made, plans will be put in action and undoubtedly modified, but we have moved forward. I thank you for your participation and diligence and hope that this indicates a welcome trend."

Many looked at Cardinal Müller, who showed no reaction.

"I will see you tomorrow before you leave, and look forward to working with you to save our church in the future."

* * * * *

The morning session on optional celibacy went smoothly, perhaps indicative of a desire to be done with it. In the end, they decided not to include a code of conduct.

* * * * *

During lunch on Tuesday, June 18, all the luggage was picked up from the rooms and delivered to three locations on the road near the presidential cabin: one for those leaving for Rome; one for those going back to the embassy, including Cardinal Mamberti; and one for those returning to the Swiss Guard quarters at Georgetown.

They departed in that order. The Curia council was over.

Chapter Nine

A Game Changer

After six days not following their routine, at 6:55 a.m. on Wednesday, July 19 the pope and Cardinal Parolin were getting ready for their morning walk. Swiss Guards Franz Buchs, their guide, and Roland Pfyffer von Altishofen, their driver, were waiting for them in the car; they had already established remote communications with the control center when their passengers came out.

"Good morning, Franz and Roland."

"Good morning, Your Holiness … Your Eminence."

The pope and the cardinal got into the back seat.

"Leaving the compound and turning right onto Thirty-fourth," Roland reported and the control center confirmed from the GPS.

"What a beautiful day," said the cardinal, "I am getting to appreciate these walks, especially on press conference days. They relax me."

"Turning right onto Fulton headed south."

"No traffic in sight."

"Stopping to disembark."

The pope and the cardinal got out of the car and began walking along the left side of the road facing traffic. Franz followed, walking on the right side, five paces behind.

"Proceeding east on Fulton to pick-up destination."

Two miles down the road, Roland made a U-turn and parked facing the walkers, who were not yet in sight.

"Parked at pick-up destination."

After about five minutes, a car with no license plate passed the embassy car and parked a quarter of a mile down the road.

"2014 Ford with no license plate passed and is parked a quarter mile ahead. Driver still in car."

After about five minutes, the driver of the other car had still neither left nor exited it. It was time to resolve the mystery.

"Leaving destination to investigate."

"Roger, Roland. D.C. police have been notified and are on the way. Seals will arrive first."

As Roland began to walk toward the parked car, the walkers came into view about half a mile away. Roland began to run. When he was about twenty yards away, the driver left the car and, without looking behind, ran toward the walkers.

"Driver out of car and headed for the walkers."

"Seals scrambled and headed for walkers."

Strangely, the suspect raised both arms and, extending his fingers, turned the open palms toward the walkers. He also began to shake his hands, seeming to indicate that he was unarmed.

"I see the suspect and Roland," Franz reported, and bellowed at the walkers, "TROUBLE AHEAD. STOP!" The pope and the cardinal stopped, looking at Franz, who had drawn his gun.

Roland was gaining on the runner, who didn't seem to notice. Suddenly, continuing to shake his left hand, he dropped his left arm to waist height. His right hand went to his waist. Franz saw something shiny in his right hand.

"GUN!!" Franz shouted. "GET DOWN!"

Parolin tripped as he moved to grab the pope and take him to the ground. Francis fell on his back as they had practiced but he trapped the cardinal's arm and prevented his effort to get on top of him as a human shield.

BA-BANGG! BANGBANG!

"Pietro!!"

"Shooter down. Two bullets to the head. One is mine," shouted Franz.

"The other is mine!"

Roland knelt over the shooter. Franz tended to the pope and the cardinal. Sirens were screaming.

"The shooter is dead."

The silence was broken only by wailing sirens.

"The cardinal was hit. Two bullets. One to the head, the other to the heart."

Two Seals were on the site. The shocked and grieving pope was helped into the first ambulance, and Franz climbed aboard.

"Pope in ambulance headed for Georgetown Hospital for examination. He was not wounded. I am aboard."

"Cardinal in second ambulance. Seriously wounded. I am with him," said Roland.

The third ambulance took the shooter to the morgue, accompanied by two Seals.

* * * * *

Word had spread quickly in the embassy, and people gathered in the large reception room at a little after eight.

Colonel Graf took charge.

"The pope was not hit, but suffered some bruises when Cardinal Parolin, following the training he was given, took him to the

235

ground to shield him from the attacker. Unfortunately, the cardinal was wounded severely. The assailant was killed. The pope and Cardinal Parolin have been taken to Georgetown Hospital for observation and examination. Guardsmen Franz Buchs and Roland Pfyffer von Altishofen accompanied them. The Holy Father is expected to be released this afternoon.

"There will be a meeting in the large conference room at ten o'clock for Capt. Fasel, Lt. Keenan and the control center shift leader at the time, who I understand was Navy Seal Chief Petty Officer Richard Tierney. I am told we will be joined by the commissioner of the D.C. Police Department, as well as agents from the CIA and the FBI," who are all on their way."

Lt. Keenan spoke up, "Colonel, my commanding officer, Lt. Cdr. James O'Reilly, is already here and would like to attend."

"Of course; he is welcome."

* * * * *

DeeDee Myers heard about the shooting from her car radio on her drive to the embassy around 8:30. Knowing the phones would be ringing off the wall, she decided to hold the press conference as planned.

She found Col. Graf and asked him to give her a quick briefing before his ten o'clock meeting; he did so, in more detail than he had shared with the people in the embassy.

The press tent was full and silent at ten when she stepped to the microphone.

Her voice shaking, she said, "Good morning. It is with a heavy heart that I speak with you this morning. As you have heard, an assassin attacked Pope Francis and Cardinal Parolin as they took their daily morning walk down Fulton Street, which runs in back of the trees behind me.

"Sadly, Cardinal Parolin was shot while trying to shield the Holy Father, and died instantly. The pope was shaken up and suffered some minor cuts and bruises from the cardinal's effort to protect him. He was taken to Georgetown Hospital for observation, but is expected to be released this afternoon.

"The assassin was shot and killed by the pope's two bodyguards, who accompanied the pope to the hospital.

"Since the pope is under political asylum in this country, the investigation is being conducted by the CIA. I know very little else, but I will take questions until they begin to repeat. Please remember that this is very difficult for me because I have become close to Cardinal Parolin and even the pope—and, of course, I am a Catholic. In the past several months, the cardinal has become a friend and mentor. I will miss him."

"But fire away … Oh, God, I can't believe I said that!" No one said a word. "Jonathan Karl, *ABC?*"

Karl asked, "Since they have been given political asylum by the president, why were the pope and the cardinal walking outside the compound, and what kind of security did they have?"

"The walk procedure was approved by the Navy Seals, and both the Holy Father and the cardinal were disguised. They were accompanied by two specially trained Swiss Guards and monitored by two Seals on motorbikes. I will be back when I know more." She left the podium and went back into the embassy.

* * * * *

Cardinal Law was watching the end of an afternoon TV movie when it was interrupted by breaking news about the shooting in Washington. He grabbed the phone and hit speed dial.

"Cardinal Burke speaking."

"Was this your misguided work, Raymond?"

"Of course not!"

"Ray, tell me the truth. Did you order a hit?"

"No, Bernie, I swear!"

"Then who did?"

"I have no idea."

Law slammed the phone down.

* * * * *

Col. Graf introduced everyone Wednesday and then said, "I am saddened to report that, unlike earlier reports, Cardinal Parolin died instantly.

"This will be a brief meeting because we have a hell of a lot of work to do in as short a period as we can. This horrendous event did not take place on embassy grounds, but Vatican City citizens under the protection of political asylum are involved, so it is an international event and the investigation will be led by CIA Special Agent John Ferris. Agent Ferris, the floor is yours."

"Thank you, Colonel," said Ferris. "I am hoping that this investigation will be finished very quickly. We have five on the scene witnesses: the Holy Father, the two Swiss Guards and two Seals. We also have an off-scene witness in the person of CPO Tierney, who was listening to everything in the control room. We will be taking their statements starting as soon as the pope, the two Guards and the Seals return. I will interview the pope privately. No one is to talk with the pope, the two Guards, the two Seals or CPO Tierney after their interviews until we all meet tomorrow morning.

"I understand that both Guards were wearing body cams that were turned on and their vehicle had a live dash cam. These videos should be available in an hour or so, to be reviewed by me and the Guards. They will be shown to the rest of you tomorrow morning.

"DNA samples and fingerprints of the shooter are already on their way to the FBI forensic lab here in D.C. And the shooter's clothing will also be sent to that lab to see if we can find out where it was purchased and, through that, where he may have come from. We hope to have preliminary information for tomorrow's meeting.

"The car will be turned over to the D.C. police department to identify the owner and where he lives. I understand that the car has already been towed to their holding area. We need that vehicle to be inspected to find anything. FBI Special Agent Cliff Donahower, to my left, is handling those details.

"If all goes well, we should have quite a comprehensive amount of information when we meet back here tomorrow at the same time. Any questions?"

There were none. Everyone left. It was only about ten-thirty.

* * * * *

Lt. Keenan walked Lt. Cdr. O'Reilly out to his car.

"That CIA guy was pretty impressive."

"Yeah, I have worked with him before. No-nonsense guy and smart as hell."

"I can't believe this happened. Did we screw up?"

"No, Kate, you didn't screw up. No one could have predicted this. A sniper, yes. Maybe even a mortar. But a guy trying that with two armed witnesses? Nobody could have anticipated that."

"I can't stop thinking that there must be something that we missed."

He got in the car and started it, saying "Take the rest of the day off, Kate. Go shopping or something. I'll see you in the morning." He drove off.

Kate shook her head as she fumed, "Why do men always suggest shopping? I'm going to the damned range and kill several paper silhouettes!"

* * * * *

Capt. Fasel walked around the embassy perimeter on Wednesday afternoon, speaking to the guards he met. Then he went to his room and shined his shoes. He turned on the TV and watched commentators pretending that they had the shooting all figured out.

He tried a movie and fell asleep. When he woke up it was around three. He took a shower and put on a pair of khakis and a golf shirt. Then he went downstairs and checked a car out of the motor pool and drove away.

* * * * *

Kate returned from the gun range about 2:30. She was still agitated and finally grabbed a swimsuit and headed out again, this time to the Y. She changed there and headed for the lap pool. After some stretches, she went to the edge of the pool, took a racing start stance, dove and swam a 400-meter medley as fast as she could.

She sat on the edge of the pool and rested. Then she did it again. And again. And one more time.

When she climbed out the last time, she felt like she had at practice when she was a midshipman at Annapolis in training for the Olympic trials. Finally, the events of the morning begin to fade a little.

She arrived home around five. Putting on a pair of gym shorts and a tee shirt, she looked in the cupboard for some comfort food. She decided that it was a pasta night and started some sauce.

As she was pouring a drink, the doorbell rang. When she opened it, it was Hans, just standing there.

He said, "I just had to get out of that place," He took her in his arms and held her very close. "I have been driving around for hours."

After a minute or so, Kate said, "I'm making pasta. Do you want a drink?"

The events of the morning began to recede as they sat and drank and talked. She served the dinner and poured some wine. He kidded her about her "American" pasta, and they laughed for the first time all day. He saw a guitar in the corner of the room, went over and started to play it softly as he sat back down.

He began to sing in Italian, then Swiss French, then English. They were folk songs, then ballads, then The Beatles. Kate joined in and soon they were trying a little "fake harmony," as she called it.

She was asleep when he got up and dressed. He kissed her lightly on the cheek and she smiled, but didn't wake up. He drove to the embassy without turning the radio on. The clock said ten to three. He slept well.

* * * * *

The meeting on the morning of Thursday, July 10, started on time with Agent Ferris again in charge.

"FBI Special Agent Donahower and I have interviewed Guards Buchs and Pfyffer von Altishofen at the hospital yesterday afternoon. I am satisfied that although Pfyffer von Altishofen violated protocol in leaving the vehicle to apprehend the alleged killer, considering the situation he acted appropriately and is to be commended on his judgment and his courage. These two men did everything possible to avoid the outcome; had they not, the outcome might have been even worse.

"We also spoke with the pope yesterday afternoon at the hospital. Obviously, he was very upset, but his memory was good. He verified the testimony of the bodyguards. He will, incidentally, be released today around noon.

"So far, after a search of the worldwide DNA databanks, no one has been found who had a match close enough to the suspect to be significant. No fingerprint match was found either. Because of the skilled shooting of the Guards to the suspect's head, no facial recognition is possible. We had the suspect's beard shaved and tried again with no success. However, we did discover a small tattoo of a strange design under the suspect's chin. It is being run through several databases searching a match.

"The suspect's pockets were empty and nothing was found either in the car or on his route from where it was parked. The car was stolen during the night before the incident from a used car lot in Silver Spring. Not even the clothes the suspect was wearing have given us a clue as to where he had been. It is like this person never existed before yesterday morning.

"Amidst all this lack of evidence, just one thing contradicts the assumption that this was an attempt of the pope's life and that is on the body cams of both Guards. Please look at the video as I explain. It will run in super slow motion.

"I just stopped where Guard Buchs shouted 'GUN!'

"Now watch Cardinal Parolin's foot slip as he starts to take down the pope. Now you see the cardinal landing on his back first with his left arm extended. Now the pope falls backward on the cardinal's left shoulder and chest, trapping the left arm, which makes it impossible for him to get on top of the pope. This is when the suspect fires. Comments?"

There were no substantive remarks and the facts were gone over a second time.

* * * * *

242

When the meeting was over, Lt. Cdr. O'Reilly said to Kate, "Lt. Keenan, could you wait a minute. I need to tell Col. Graf something and then I want to talk with you for a bit."

"Fine, sir. I'll stay right here."

O'Reilly returned quickly. "Did you go shopping as I suggested, Kate?"

"Uh ... something like that. I'm fine."

"You have been under a lot of stress. I know you knew Cardinal Parolin pretty well and I was pleased at the way you accepted responsibility, yet stood up for your men."

"It's my job, sir."

"Yes, it is, and you did and do it well. Look, tomorrow is Friday. I don't want to see you in here until Monday. Take a long weekend and come back recharged."

"I'm really okay."

"I'm sure you are, and you have done a great job throughout this project. Now get out of here. You deserve it. I will fill in, and I don't want to see you on site until Monday."

"It's only noon."

"I said get out!"

"All right, all right, I'll go! Thank you, sir."

On her way to her car, she looked for Hans, but didn't see him. When she arrived home, she called him. "Hi. Did Col. Graf by any chance give you the weekend off, starting immediately?"

"Yes, he did. In fact, I was going to call you."

"Let's get out of Washington for a couple of days."

"Where?"

"It's a secret. I know you are from Switzerland, but I want to show you that low mountains can be beautiful and teach you some American history at the same time. Throw whatever you think you might need for a couple of days in a bag and I'll pick you up tomorrow morning at nine on the corner of Massachusetts and 34th."

"Why on the corner?"

"My boss said I wasn't supposed to set foot on the property until Monday. See ya tomorrow."

* * * * *

The pope was released as planned around noon on Thursday, July 19, and arrived by van about half an hour later with Franz and Roland. He had a dressing on his left forearm. Franz helped him out of the car and it was clear that the pope's right leg was at least severely bruised. He was met by Cardinals Ouellet, Stella and Mamberti.

"Happy to see you, Papa Francesco," said Stella.

"Thank you. I would like to get to my room. Please join me there for a few minutes, Dominique."

On the way, the pope asked Cardinal Mamberti if arrangements had been made for Cardinal Parolin's body to be shipped to Rome. He was assured that Archbishop Pierre was already working on that.

When they reached the suite and Franz had left, the pope said his first words to anyone about the incident: "The killer looked me straight in the eye and then shot Pietro." He shook his head slowly and didn't speak for several seconds.

"I am pleased that you promised to stay a couple more days, but I am afraid it will be longer than that. I am immediately going to make you Secretary of State and Camerlengo."

"I understand," said Mamberti, "and I will do anything you want me to do."

"I had some time to think in the hospital while they were waiting for test and x-ray results. Tomorrow morning, we need to have a serious discussion about our next steps. I would like to begin with a detailed discussion of your thoughts about 'then what' now."

"I will be prepared."

"Good. Will you ask Cardinals Ouellet and Stella to come up for a few minutes so I can tell them your new role?"

"Certainly."

"Then good night, Dominique."

"Good night, John."

* * * * *

The Thursday noon news had reported that the pope suffered minor scrapes and bruises and was back at the embassy.

DeeDee Myers was waiting for Mamberti when he came downstairs.

"Cardinal, we haven't officially met. I am DeeDee Myers and have been working with Cardinal Parolin as press secretary for the Holy Father. I would like to discuss how you want to handle the press over the next few days and weeks. Could we talk a bit in my office?"

"Certainly."

They went to her office and she closed the door.

"I know that you are a friend of the Holy Father. Did he tell you who will be dealing with the press now?"

"I guess that would be me. I think he is telling Cardinal Ouellet and Cardinal Stella this now. He has appointed me to succeed Cardinal Parolin as Secretary of State and Camerlengo."

DeeDee nodded. "I think we should send out a press release assuring people that the pope is fine and that he has made these appointments."

"I will accept your judgment on that."

"Cardinal Parolin has been holding press conferences every Wednesday. Will you continue that practice?"

"Will you teach me how to do it?"

"I will."

"Then I will do it."

"Great, but we can't wait until next Wednesday. I have scheduled one for tomorrow at ten. We need to start right now."

* * * * *

Hans reached the designated corner about five minutes early and Kate was already there. For the first time, the top was down on her car. He tossed his bag in the back seat and noticed with a smile that her guitar was there along with her bag.

"Are we going to sing on the way?" he asked as he took his seat.

"No, wise guy, but we might get to that later. Or maybe not."

She was dressed in shorts and a tee shirt, with her hair pulled back and tied. She looked radiant.

"Where are we going?"

"Ultimately, Charlottesville, Virginia, and Thomas Jefferson's home, Monticello."

"Oh, I've heard of him. He was for a while your ambassador to France."

"Now I don't know whether you are still being a wise guy or not. He wrote the Declaration of Independence and was our third president. But we are taking the long way there. First we are going to Front Royal, where we will stop for lunch."

"Strange name. Is there a Back Royal?"

"Is this the way you are going to be all weekend? Front Royal was named '*le front royal*' by the French, meaning the western edge of the British colony of Virginia."

"I'll behave."

"Somehow, I doubt that," she laughed.

* * * * *

The press tent was nearly overflowing on Friday when DeeDee, Jackie and Cardinal Mamberti walked onto the podium at five minutes before ten. David Andreatta was in his usual spot in the front row between two empty chairs. Jackie sat in one and DeeDee walked to the microphone with assurance.

"Thank you all for being here on such short notice. This will be more of a briefing than a regular press conference because as you might imagine, there is a great deal more that we don't know than what we do.

"We have lost a holy and innocent man, a colleague, a mentor and a great friend. That may make sense to some, but I am not one of them.

"Today I introduce another man—not Cardinal Parolin's replacement, but his successor."

"His name is Cardinal Dominique Mamberti, prefect of the Apostolic Signatura, which is the Vatican equivalent of its Supreme Court. He happened to be with us at this tragic time simply because he is a close friend of the Holy Father, who invited

247

him to stay a few days with us after the recent meeting of the Roman Curia.

"Several things have happened to Cardinal Mamberti since then. He has been relieved of his duties at the Signatura; he has been named Vatican Secretary of State and Camerlengo, which we talked about several weeks ago, which seems like several months. He's my new boss."

There was tremendous applause from the calloused press, not for the cardinal who was an unknown quantity, but for DeeDee.

Cardinal Mamberti went to the microphone.

"Thank you very much, and thank you, DeeDee. By the way, DeeDee, I forgot to ask you this morning. Are you leaving for home tomorrow as you planned?"

"No Cardinal. I have postponed it again, for two weeks. Why do you ask?"

"I was just wondering. I passed the kitchen on my way out. That cake is going to be pretty stale."

Dave Andreatta leaned over to Jackie Ring and murmured, "A very classy first move."

Turning back to the crowd, the cardinal began. "I have a fairly large number of announcements to make, some of which I can comment upon, some I cannot. First, as DeeDee said, the Holy Father has seen fit to appoint me Vatican Secretary of State. Frankly, except for Archbishop Pierre, I have never met anyone on my staff, whatever their names are, and I am not sure where my Vatican office is. So, although there may be many questions to be asked, for which I may have no cogent answers.

"Second, the investigation of the tragic events of Wednesday morning is underway with great urgency, as you have probably assumed. I will try to answer about what I know.

"Third, I have a couple of Curia organization announcements to relay, which were made at the meeting.

"Finally, I have announcements of two policy decisions by the Holy Father suggested to him by committees at the Curia and now pending."

DeeDee stood again and said "Let's get started: how about the investigation of Wednesday's terrible events. Any hands?" A dozen shot up. "Bill Plante of *CBS News*."

"Cardinal, welcome to our weekly get-together."

"Thank you, Bill," said DeeDee, "which reminds me—this is actually Wednesday's press conference, being held on Friday. We will return to Wednesdays this coming week, hopefully with more information."

"That is good news indeed. My question is this: Since the administration felt the conditions surrounding the pope's visit warranted the decision to grant the pope's request for political asylum, why were the Holy Father and Cardinal Parolin allowed to just go for a walk?"

Mamberti replied gravely, "You are correct that we benefit from the protection of the highest qualified group in the world on such things, and the walks were approved by them after thorough study. Walking was not well known as an activity the Holy Father enjoys. Morning traffic at that hour on that two-mile stretch of road is very sparse.

"Neither the pope nor the cardinal was wearing clerical garb, and both were disguised.

"Two specially trained and well-armed members of the pope's Swiss Guards, also in clothing not identifiable, accompanied them and, in fact, killed the shooter. They were backed up by two Navy Seals on motorbikes. The whole operation was constantly monitored by radio in the embassy and body cams worn by the Guards at the site."

"And the cardinal died."

"Yes, the cardinal died. Next question, DeeDee."

"Home run," murmured Andreatta.

"On the same topic is the investigation … hands? … Helene Cooper, the *New York Times*."

"Cardinal Mamberti, it would seem that several jurisdictions are involved in this crime. Can you tell us which is in charge and what are they doing? And I have a follow-up question."

"You are correct that there are many jurisdictions involved. As I understand this, since the pope's party is under political asylum and the assailant is believed to be a foreign national, the CIA is heading the investigation. They are first trying to identify the assailant, so far without much success. However, that may be the tip of the iceberg."

"Was the pope the target?"

"That is the assumption."

"Were others involved?"

"That's not clear at this point."

DeeDee rose again and said, "Last question on this topic. It has been just over 48 hours since the attack. Hopefully we will have more information on Wednesday … Carol Lee, of the *Wall Street Journal*."

"Cardinal, who are some of the other agencies involved in the investigation?"

"Obviously, the FBI; since the overall protection of the embassy is by them, the Navy Seals, NCIS; Interpol; the Swiss Guard; and I may have missed some."

"Let's move on to the announcements from the Curia conference," said DeeDee.

Mamberti said, "There are four: two new Curia congregations and two new policies.

"The Holy Father has announced the establishment of two new congregations—you would call them cabinet departments. For example, Cardinal Ouellet is the prefect of the Congregation of Bishops and Cardinal Stella is the prefect of the Congregation of Priests.

"The first new congregation is for The Equality of All Baptized. Its prefect will be the internationally known American author and theologian Sister Elizabeth Johnson, currently a professor at Fordham University. Sister Johnson belongs to the Sisters of St. Joseph of Brentwood, and she will become the highest-ranking woman in the Roman Catholic Church.

"The other new congregation is for Science and Other Forms of Revelation. Its prefect will be Brother Guy Consolmagno, SJ. Brother Consolmagno is the current director of the Vatican Observatory at Castel Gandolfo and its subsidiary site outside Tucson, Arizona.

"Question, please!" shouted Kristen Welker from *NBC News*.

"Okay, Kirsten," said a smiling DeeDee, "You get the punchline."

"Cardinal, aren't the prefects of congregations always cardinals?"

"Yes, and so it will be. Sister Johnson and Brother Consolmagno will be on the list of new cardinals to be announced next month."

"Now I have an announcement of two significant policy changes recommended by Curia committees at the conference for the pope to consider. I will not take any questions because this is very much a work in progress. The two policies are: Ordination of Women and Optional Celibacy."

There was an immediate uproar, with Major Garrett of *CBS News* shouting "Last question, please! Last question, please!"

DeeDee warned, "Nothing about the policies!"

"I promise!"

"Okay."

"Cardinal, what was the name of the place where the Curia conference was held?"

"I think it was 'Off-site location,' but I'm not sure."

* * * * *

Kate and Hans made the 75-mile trip to Front Royal in about an hour and a half. They had lunch in a small restaurant Kate had found on the Internet.

"Well, that was okay, if not memorable," said Kate as they walked to the car. "But I hope that the place I found for us to stay in Charlottesville is significantly better."

"How far away is Charlottesville?"

"Only about a hundred and ten miles, but the speed limit is just thirty-five miles an hour."

"Why is that?"

"I promised you a drive through some beautiful low mountains. Skyline Drive runs the length of Shenandoah National Park, literarily from peak to peak of the Blue Ridge Mountains. Lots of ups and downs, twists and turns, and lots of places you are going to want to stop. But don't worry, we'll be there in time for dinner."

When they got on the road, Hans asked, "Can I ask you a question?"

"Sure."

"How did you end up as a Navy Seal?"

"Well, I hope I haven't ended up there, but the answer is, strictly by chance. In high school, I was on the swim team and did very well. A friend of my parents was our congressman and she asked if I would like to go to Annapolis—that is, the Naval Academy—and swim for them. I said sure. I made the swim team easily and was invited to try out for the 2012 Summer Olympics Team.

I made it and won a silver medal. When it came time to request assignments, two West Point women had made it through Ranger School, so I asked to go to Seal School. I made it through. Finished second in my class, actually, but since the Seals don't allow women in any combat billets, I have only had administrative assignments like this one."

"Does that annoy you?"

"You bet, but why do you ask?"

"Because sometimes, although I didn't know why, I can tell that it does."

"I'm glad my boss is not as perceptive as you are."

Kate was right; Hans did ask to stop several times. Once, as they were leaving a lookout, her phone rang.

"Look, at that and tell me who is calling, please."

"It is Kim McAuliff."

"Let it ring, and when she sends a text message, read it to me."

A couple of minutes later the text message arrived.

"She says: 'Heard all about the pope being attacked. Isn't that where you are? Please let me know you are okay.' Should I respond?"

"Yes. Tell her 'I am about as good as I can be. Talk to you soon,' and sign it Katie."

The trip took even longer than Kate said it would. The hotel was very nice and after a quick change of clothes, they lingered over dinner until the place closed. Back in their room, Kate said she was going to take a shower.

While she was doing that, Hans took a thick notebook out of his bag and began to write. It was a long shower and when she came out, ready for bed, he was just finishing.

"What are you doing?" she asked.

"Just writing in my journal."

"You keep a journal?"

"I have, since my first year of what you'd call high school. I really love to write"

"What do you do with what you write?"

"What do you mean?"

"Have you ever tried to publish anything?"

"No. Why do you ask?"

"I love to write, too. Not journals, but short stories, essays, I even tried a novel and I try to publish them. So far, no luck."

"How do you try to publish them?"

"Well, this is really pretty weird. Do you remember that call this afternoon?"

"Yes. It was from Kim something."

"McAuliff. She was a classmate, swim teammate and my best friend at Our Lady of Mercy High School. She went to Columbia School of Journalism and is now a literary agent. She has been trying to sell some of my stuff."

"That *is* kind of weird. My turn for a shower."

"Don't be too long. May I read your journal while you are in there?"

"Sure."

"In that case, take your time."

Later, as they were falling asleep, Kate said, "I liked what I read in your journal. Especially what you said about me. You write very well. Could I send some of your work to Kim?"

"I guess so," he said sleepily.

"Thanks for a very happy day and evening."

"Wait until you see tomorrow. We might get that guitar out."

* * * * *

They spent Saturday at Monticello, with Kate telling Hans more about Thomas Jefferson than he ever imagined there was to know. Around four they headed for the University of Virginia for more about Jefferson, but on the way, they saw people entering a Catholic church for the four-thirty vigil Mass. Kate pulled into the parking lot and they joined them.

During the liturgy, they held hands tightly and enjoyed the kiss of peace before receiving communion.

The University of Virginia could wait until tomorrow. They had a romantic dinner and a happy evening and sang a little to that guitar before falling asleep in each other's arms.

* * * * *

Cardinal Burke's cell phone rang in Rome. "Cardinal Burke speaking."

"The sample was free. The cost of the service is ten million euros. A cancellation fee would be one hundred million. A decision and payment are required by Sunday."

The phone went dead.

The cardinal threw up.

* * * * *

Cardinal Burke made an unannounced visit to Cardinal Law on Saturday afternoon. Law noticed Burke's anxiety immediately.

"Ray, you seem upset. Relax and tell me why you are here."

"You asked me on Wednesday whether I had anything to do with Pietro's murder and I told you the truth about it, that I did not. What I didn't tell you was that I had asked one of our friends in Sicily what the cost of doing such a thing might be so that we could have all options on the table. I had no reply.

"However, last evening I had a phone call from a voice I did not recognize; it said 'The sample was free. The cost of the service is ten million euros. A cancellation fee would be a hundred million. A decision is required by Sunday.' Then he hung up. Today is Saturday."

"Who did you ask for the quote?"

"I don't know."

"Then how do you know the call is legitimate?"

"I told you Salvatore Mastrangelo wanted to help. He came here last week. Stayed with me. They, and I don't know who, had given me a protocol to follow if I ever wanted a favor. I had Viganò ask Salvatore to follow it for me, so that it couldn't be traced. He followed the protocol without realizing it, and went back home. When I heard what happened in Washington I didn't know what to do. Now this. Can we get that much money to give them?"

"Probably, but I will not try and if you do, I will turn you in," warned Law.

"What should I do?"

256

"Tell them the truth. You can't get the money. Or take a chance and call their bluff. Do nothing."

When the terrified Burke arrived home, he followed the protocol for answering the demand, saying that he couldn't raise the money. The voice said, "You may regret that."

Burke had several drinks and went to bed.

* * * * *

After Sunday brunch at the hotel in Charlottesville, Kate and Hans spent a long afternoon at the University of Virginia and its serpentine brick wall before driving back to Washington. They arrived at the corner near the embassy about nine. As Hans kissed her goodnight, he whispered, "I love you, Lieutenant Katie."

She replied softly, "And I love you, Captain Hans."

It was nine-thirty when Hans entered the embassy; he went straight to bed.

Kate reached home about ten minutes later. She locked up and was heading for bed with a glass of milk and a couple of cookies when she decided to return Kim's cell phone message.

Kim answered with, "Three things: Are you okay? Where have you been for two days? And I am coming to visit you on Tuesday."

"I'm fine. Wednesday and Thursday were a nightmare, and my boss made me take a long weekend so Hans and I drove down to Monticello."

"Hans? Who the hell is Hans? And why Monticello, for God's sake!"

"Hans is the guy from the Swiss Guard I have been working with. I told you about him."

"Oh yeah. You said he was good-looking. After a weekend is he still good-looking?"

"Nope. He's wonderful."

"One question: Do you outrank him?"

"No, the Swiss Guard is like the U.S. Army."

"I'm sure they will be pleased to hear that."

"I mean ranks. Their captain is like a Navy lieutenant. And the subject has never come up."

"OK, enough about your boy toy. I have something important to talk with you about, and I'm coming to see you on Tuesday afternoon to tell you. I am in New York and should be back here on Friday morning. We may have time to talk about the Swiss guy."

"*Talk* about him!! You're going to *meet* him!"

"Oh God! This sounds serious. See you Tuesday afternoon when you get home. Will my key still work?"

* * * * *

The Sunday evening meeting of The Brethren was chaotic. Law told them he had cancelled Cardinal Mamberti's invitation to join. He demanded that they come up with at least twenty cardinals and archbishops to be considered as potential members.

They broke up early.

When Cardinal Burke arrived home, he noticed that there was a new doorman at his building. They spoke briefly. Friendly enough chap, he thought.

He unlocked the door to his apartment and switched on the foyer light as he closed the door. A man stepped out of the dark living room. There was the strange, muffled sound of two shots from a gun fitted with a silencer. Burke fell without saying a word.

Two shots. One to the head and one to the heart.

The gunman ran out the door to the waiting car with the 'new doorman' at the wheel. They drove to the driveway and turned right. The gunman hauled the bound-and-gagged regular doorman out of the back seat, tossed him onto the sidewalk and drove off.

Rosa discovered the cardinal's body in the morning when she came to work.

Chapter Ten

The Investigation

On Monday morning, June 24, Col. Graf called Hans, and Lt. Cdr. O'Reilly called Kate, to tell them that the investigation meeting was cancelled. Hans decided to spend the morning in the control center reviewing body cam footage of the cardinal's last minutes.

He had watched Roland's tape over and over at regular speed and as slow as he could. Finally, he called Kate.

"Hi, I don't know how to handle all this time off."

"Are you on-site?"

"Yeah."

"I'm in the command center watching tape from Wednesday. Can you come over? I want your opinion on something."

"Sure. I'll be right there."

She was true to her word.

"Something has been bothering me about this whole thing," said Hans. "There is no way that the shooter knew that we had trained the pope and the cardinal to do that takedown drill. Then the cardinal slips and screws it up anyway. Look at this film."

He ran it until just before the shots and stopped it. "I measured with a tape the diagonal across Parolin's chest where his heart was; it is less than half the size of the same area exposed on the pope. Now look at what the shooter is doing—shaking his hands to distract, making it impossible to hold his weapon with two hands. Could you make a shot like that?"

"Well, you got a dinner when I proved I probably couldn't."

"Yeah, but you were faking it. Let me run it again, very slowly. Isn't it more likely that he would hit the pope?"

They watched with complete attention as the pope and cardinal began to fall.

"Stop!!" Kate shouted.

"What?" Hans asked.

"Back it up as slowly as you can. Stop! Who is that man with the gun?"

"I don't know. Maybe one of your Seals?"

"Zoom in!" she said, *"That is not one of my Seals!* There was another shooter, probably to take out the first if he were captured!"

They sat dumbfounded. Hans said, "We have been watching the wrong body cams."

Within minutes they had the body cams of the two Seal backups on motorbikes. The first showed nothing unusual. The second was going up the left side of the road closer to where the man with the gun was standing. The Seal passed a yellow car.

"Wait a minute, how did that car get there?" Hans asked, backing up the video.

"What do you mean? The shooter parked it there?"

"It is heading in the wrong direction. It is a getaway car."

"Let's watch until the end. Maybe the Seal left it on coming back."

He had, and the car was gone.

Kate said, "We need to take our bosses to the movies."

* * * * *

Kate checked that Lt. Cdr. O'Reilly was at the embassy and very quickly arranged a meeting with O'Reilly, Col. Graf, Hans and herself.

"As you can see, Capt. Fasel has been able to clearly establish that Cardinal Parolin—and not the Holy Father—was the target of the shooter, who was highly skilled." explained Kate.

Hans said, "Lt. Keenan also discovered the presence of a not yet identified potential second shooter at the scene, and what may be a second car intended as a getaway vehicle."

"I have contacted the Metropolitan Police and they report that the shooter's car was stolen during the early morning hours on last Wednesday from a used car lot in Silver Spring, which has also reported the theft of a yellow car of the make and model of the possible getaway car in the video," Kate added.

With a half-smile, O'Reilly said, "I am willing to stipulate that you two are the greatest team of criminologists since Holmes and Watson, but what does all of this mean?"

"That the target of the shooting was *not* the Holy Father," said Hans.

O'Reilly replied, "Here are the e-mail addresses of CIA Special Agent John Ferris and FBI Special Agent Cliff Donahower. They are in Rome, looking for any connection between the fatal shootings of Cardinal Parolin on Wednesday and last night's similar attack on Cardinal Burke in Rome. Please see that they receive all this information reaches them as soon as possible."

Graf and O'Reilly left the room, and Kate and Hans began putting together the e-mail to Ferris and Donahower.

"I thought that went pretty well," said Hans.

"How did you like the remark about Holmes and Watson?"

263

"I thought it was funny. Who do you suppose he thinks is Holmes?"

"Well, since he is my boss and writes my fitness report, I hope he thinks it's me."

"I suppose."

"I talked to my friend Kim by phone last night after I got home. She is coming to town this afternoon and staying with me until Thursday."

"That's not good news."

"Well it may be. She didn't say why she is coming, but I think she may want to talk about an outline for a novel I sent her a couple of months ago. I hope that maybe has someone interested in it. She is going to tell me about it over dinner."

"I'm happy for you."

"Stop it. You are invited for dinner on tomorrow night to meet her. I have told her nice things about you."

"That's good."

"Hans, you are being a real pain. I also told her about your journals and how good I thought they were. Will you give me some for her to read while I am at work tomorrow?"

"Sure. I'll get them."

By the time Hans returned, Kate had sent the e-mails to Ferris and Donahower. He had three rather thick loose-leaf notebooks.

"Here are all of them, up to yesterday."

"Including the weekend?"

"Of course."

"That's kind of personal."

"No. I left the ten pages of the really personal stuff in my desk drawer."

"Ten pages!!!"

"Yeah. I got rather carried away."

"I'm sure what I have will be enough for Kim."

"I have to talk to Col. Graf."

"Sure. I need to get back to work, too. This was a very productive day," she grinned.

As Kate started out the door, she turned and said, "Umm, Hans, if I get some free time this afternoon, can I read those ten pages?"

"Sure ... give me a call."

She never got around to it.

* * * * *

CIA agent Ferris and FBI agent Donahower arrived in Rome Monday evening and went right to bed. The package from O'Reilly and Graf was there when they arrived, but they didn't read it until early Tuesday morning, June 25, before heading for Cardinal Burke's lavish condo.

On the way, Ferris asked, "What do you think about the new information?"

"A nice piece of police work and it certainly expands the investigation."

"It will be interesting to see if the cardinal's housekeeper and the doorman can shed more light on the whole thing."

They reached the condo at 8:25 a.m. and were greeted by the doorman.

"I am CIA Special Agent Ferris and this is FBI Special Agent Donahower, here to see the late Cardinal Burke's housekeeper."

"Oh yes, she told me she is expecting you."

"Are you by any chance the doorman who was on duty Sunday evening?"

"Yes, sir. My name is Mario DeSantis. I understand you want to talk with me. I will try to help, but most of the time I was tied up with a gag in my mouth."

"Is there a place we can talk privately?" Ferris asked.

"Yes, sir. There is a small office off the lobby. I will open it. When you are ready for me, just let me know." Mario announced Ferris and Donahower and opened the door. Rosa was standing at the top of the half flight of stairs leading to the condo. It was clear that she had been crying.

She pointed down the hall to the right, saying "The entrance and the living room are still considered a crime scene." They followed her in the back door and sat down at the kitchen table.

"Rosa, I am CIA Special Agent Ferris and this is FBI Special Agent Donahower, both from the United States. Let me express our sympathy for your loss."

"I have worked for the cardinal for twenty years. I don't know what to do."

"I'm sure that you will soon find a similar position and if we can help, please let us know."

"We will try to keep this as short as we can," said Donahower. "We have a report on what you told Rome police. Do you have anything you have remembered since then?"

"No."

"Tell us who are Cardinal Burke's friends in Rome."

"He has … had many friends, but most of them are … were members of The Brethren."

266

"Who are The Brethren?"

"Most of them are retired Curia cardinals. Cardinal Burke was one of the younger ones. They are very traditional Catholics. In fact, their real name is *Benedict's* Brethren. Cardinal Law is the leader. They meet at his condo for dinner at least once a month."

"Are they all cardinals?"

"Except for Archbishop Viganò."

"And who is he?"

"He was the apostolic nuncio to the United States. He embarrassed Pope Francis during his trip to Washington a few years ago, so although they allowed him to retire, he was essentially fired."

"Would you say that things around here have been pretty routine around here for the last month or so?"

Rosa paused and thought for a moment. "Last week I would have said yes, but since yesterday morning I have been over and over everything I could remember."

"And what have you remembered?"

"Cardinal Burke and Archbishop Viganò met much more often than usual and for longer times. From what little I heard, they seemed to be trying to convince Cardinal Law of something."

"Do you happen to have the archbishop's address?"

"Yes, I'll get it for you."

She returned quickly and handed Donahower a piece of paper with the address on it.

"Anything else?" he asked.

"There was a strange visit from Bishop Mastrangelo."

"Who is he?"

"He is the bishop of Winona."

"Winona, Minnesota, in the United States?"

"I guess so."

"How were they connected?"

"They were seminary classmates and lifelong friends. The cardinal was always his mentor. He was a success and Bishop Mastrangelo definitely was not."

"When and why did he visit Cardinal Burke?"

"It was a day or two after the pope fired all the bishops. He wanted counseling."

"Why do you refer to it as strange?"

"Because the bishop was left here for a day and a half by himself, while the cardinal and the archbishop met. Then the bishop took the train to Catania in regular clothes, which looked very strange on him. He came back very early in the very next morning before Cardinal Burke awoke, and Bishop Mastrangelo went home right away without even saying goodbye."

"How do you know that?"

"I had some cleaning to do, so I came to work early that morning, and the bishop was loading his luggage into a taxi."

"Thank you, Rosa. You have been very helpful. May we contact you again if we have more questions?"

"Certainly! I want to protect Cardinal Burke's reputation."

Ferris and Donahower left to look for DiSantis, the doorman. They found him in the lobby near the office he had mentioned.

"I called in a relief doorman so I can answer your questions without interruption."

"We will try to be brief, so you can get back to work."

"Don't worry. I went through a hell of an experience to get the information I have."

Ferris and Donahower laughed, and Ferris said, "I think we can probably get you to lunch. Then you are on your own. Tell us what happened."

"I came on duty at eight p.m. About an hour later a man came by and said that there were a couple of people down the driveway acting suspicious. His description made me think it might be a drug deal; we don't allow that stuff. He led me back around the corner and told the one guy we found to move on or I'd have to call the police."

"Then what happened?"

"One of them sucker-punched me. I went down and when I woke up, I was tied up, my keys were gone and I was gagged. They had loaded me into the back seat of a car. I thought I was going to die."

"Then what happened?"

"The guys left. I guess one of them took my position as doorman and the other shot the Cardinal."

"Do you know that for sure?"

"No."

"What happened next?"

"About eleven, the second man came back and got into the driver's seat. He drove to the front of the building and they dumped me onto the sidewalk."

"Was there anything unusual about the way either of the men looked?"

"Yes. The second man had a small, strange tattoo under his chin."

"Would you recognize it if you saw it again?"

"Wouldn't you?"

Ferris showed him a picture on his phone of the Parolin shooter's chin.

"Was it like this?"

"Exactly."

"Are you sure?"

"Positive!"

"We will be in touch."

* * * * *

When Kate arrived home around five, Kim was there and had already made herself comfortable. They shared a "best friend" hug, and Kim said, "I made a pitcher of Manhattans for us."

"I hope it's a big one."

"We can make more. There's plenty of bourbon."

"I know. I live here," was Kate's laughing reply. They spent some time catching up, and Kim wanted to hear all about Hans.

When Kate finished, she said, "I told you about his journals. He is a very good writer. At times, he is almost poetic."

"I'll bet," Kim replied, with a chuckle.

"You'll see. I asked him if I could show you some." She went to the table near the door, brought back the three journals and handed them to Kim.

"Oh, nice. I'll have something to read while you are at work tomorrow," said Kim halfheartedly.

"Dinner's ready."

"Great, I'm really hungry!"

After they sat down, Kate said, "So, what brings you to Washington? You are always so busy that you must have a purpose."

"Well I sort of do, but I suspect you would like to know about the outline for the novel that you sent me."

"Yes, tell me," she said with a trace of excitement.

"Sadly, I don't have any good news about that. I have been through my top list of prospects. They all thought it was an interesting concept and the sample was well written, but interesting concepts by unknown authors don't sell books, no matter how well-written they are. And if they do, they don't sell many. I'll keep trying, but I am not very optimistic."

"Don't worry. It's not my day job and I know you tried. In a way, I'm glad it is a social visit and that you are going to meet Hans."

They talked until very late.

* * * * *

Ferris and Donahower met for breakfast Wednesday morning, June 26. There was a breaking news bulletin on the coffee shop TV: "Archbishop Viganò has been found shot to death." The two men grabbed coffee and headed for the crime scene.

They found that the archbishop lived in a much less prosperous neighborhood than Burke's, in a small apartment in a fifth-floor walkup. They found the officer in charge and showed him their official IDs.

He wouldn't allow them to enter, but answered a few questions.

There was no doorman, and the officer told them that he had no housekeeper, but a cleaning woman who came every Wednesday had discovered the body. The officer said that the estimated time of death was late in the evening of last Sunday.

As they were walking back to their car, Ferris said, "I think it is time to pay Cardinal Law a visit."

* * * * *

Cardinal Law was waiting in his living room when Ferris and Donahower arrived. Maria showed them in.

"Good afternoon, gentlemen."

'Good afternoon, Your Eminence. I am CIA Special Agent Ferris and this is FBI Special Agent Donahower, both from the United States. We'd like to talk with you about Cardinals Parolin and Burke."

"Terrible tragedies, just terrible! And now Archbishop Vigano— terrible. I have already talked to our AISI and AISE authorities, your counterparts, about Pietro and Raymond. I assumed they are who you are here to talk about."

"Well, yes, and on our way here, we had a text message about Bishop Mastrangelo, whose body was also just discovered this morning. They believe he was also killed on last Sunday evening."

"I don't believe I knew Bishop Mastrangelo, but that is terrible, too."

"Really? Bishop Mastrangelo was a lifelong friend of Cardinal Burke, and we assumed that you knew him."

"No. I don't believe so."

"We are here to learn about your organization called The Benedict Brethren."

"It is just The Brethren, and I would hardly call it my organization. We do meet here, but that is just because I have enough room for all."

"What did you think about the pope's recent decision to fire all the world's bishops?"

"Well, of course, it didn't affect me, but I will be interested in how it all works out."

"You weren't upset about it?"

"At my age, one tries to not be upset about anything."

"There is word in the States that you recommended the worldwide adoption of a plan developed by Cardinal Chaput, who was subsequently fired by the Holy Father and laicized."

"I think this conversation is over, gentlemen. I don't have to answer these questions."

"All right, Cardinal. Let's change the subject a bit. We have heard from reliable sources that Cardinal Burke and Archbishop Viganò were trying very hard to get your support for a plan they developed to reverse the pope's decision regarding the bishops. And since they were part of the Benedict Brethren, others knew about that."

"It is The Brethren, not the Benedict Brethren," corrected Law. "And I don't know anything about what you are asking. I told you I will not answer any more questions and now I ask you to leave."

"Cardinal, Cardinal Parolin was murdered while in the United States while under political asylum by the order of our president. Cardinal Burke was an American citizen murdered, we believe, as a direct result of actions by his Brethren friends. Bishop Mastrangelo was also an American citizen who recently met with Cardinal Burke and was then sent by Burke to Catania.

"Agent Donahower and I have been charged with the responsibility to bring the murderers involved to justice and to depose anyone thought to have relevant information. You are going to answer our questions either here—and you can have your attorney present—or after extradition in the United States. I can think of a couple of hundred lawyers who would love to have your feet on U.S. soil again. Take it or leave it."

The cardinal sat there, his face ashen. After a minute or so, he said softly, "I will answer your questions."

"Thank you. It will take Agent Donahower just a few minutes to set up the recorder. In the meantime, I have some paperwork for you to sign."

* * * * *

Cardinal Mamberti, DeeDee and Jackie had worked very hard on Tuesday to put together the Wednesday press conference and were satisfied with the result. However, the news they received early Wednesday morning complicated things—the news about the murders of Archbishop Viganò and Bishop Mastrangelo, which was not yet known in the United States. They decided that the murders should be announced, and that questions should limited. The rest of the announcements should be limited or postponed.

DeeDee introduced the Cardinal Mamberti promptly at ten a.m.— four p.m. Rome time—where the latest fatalities had not yet been announced.

A somber-faced Mamberti walked to the microphone. "Good morning, my friends. This continues to be a very sad time for our church following the tragic murder last week of Cardinal Parolin and the similar fate of Cardinal Burke in Rome on Sunday night. This morning, we are again shocked, first by this morning's discovery of the murdered body of former apostolic nuncio to the United States, Archbishop Carlo Maria Viganò, in his Rome apartment."

There was a gasp throughout the tent.

"It is believed that he was killed on Sunday at approximately the time of Cardinal Burke's death. In addition, the body of Salvatore Mastrangelo, the American bishop of Winona, Minnesota, was found in his rectory last evening. Preliminary information indicates that he too was shot Sunday evening at about the same time as the others."

The murmuring grew louder.

Mamberti said, "I realize that this is shocking and a great deal to absorb. Although I have told you everything I know for sure, I will answer some questions."

Many hands went up. DeeDee said, "Major Garrett of *CBS News.*"

"Cardinal, you have my condolences and I'm sure those of everyone here. The obvious questions are: Given the similarities between the deaths of Cardinal Burke, the archbishop and the bishop of Winona, are they in fact connected otherwise? And are they related to the assassination of Cardinal Parolin?"

Mamberti responded "Certainly these are legitimate questions, but all I can say for sure is they are all being thoroughly investigated."

DeeDee said, "Jim Acosta of *CNN.*"

"Cardinal, I join with Major in expressing condolences. My question is, who is conducting the investigation?"

"Jim, that gets complicated. Cardinal Parolin was an Italian citizen; the crime was committed in the United States; and he was under political asylum here. The CIA and FBI are jointly leading that investigation with the support of their Italian counterparts AISE and AISI.

"Cardinal Burke, however, was an American citizen. The crime was committed in Italy, where the AISE and AISI are jointly leading the investigation with the support of the CIA and FBI.

"Archbishop Viganò and Bishop Mastrangelo are also opposites, but in a different way. The archbishop was an Italian citizen and the crime was committed there. The AISE and AISI are jointly leading the investigation and sharing information with the CIA and FBI. Bishop Mastrangelo was an American citizen, and the crime was committed here. The CIA and FBI are jointly leading the investigation and sharing information with the AISE and AISI.

"Finally, the Vatican City police are involved in the Burke and Viganò cases."

Acosta replied, "It sounds like we are in for a long investigation."

"Let's pray that you are wrong."

The press applauded and the press conference was over.

* * * * *

Col. Graf called Msgr. Menendez around noon on Wednesday asking for a private meeting that day with the Holy Father, lasting about half an hour.

"I can get you in at 4:30."

"That will be fine."

The pope welcomed the Colonel. "Christoph, please sit down. What can I do for you?"

"Your Holiness, ever since the death of Cardinal Parolin—and increasingly since the death of Cardinal Burke and now Archbishop Viganò—I have been doing a great deal of thinking about our overall situation."

"I suspect all of us have been doing the same thing. Please share your thoughts with me."

"As you know, I strongly supported the move here and the political asylum. I think the U.S. Navy has done a magnificent job assisting our security. However, we are now learning things that suggest that there could be a conspiracy to overthrow your papacy. For several reasons, one might conclude that Archbishop Viganò was a part of that conspiracy, and he knew more about the strengths and weaknesses of this building that anyone in this world.

"Lone gunmen we could probably handle, but a drone with a small bomb flown into your window we cannot. Nor could we handle a small mortar fired from across the street. It is unbelievably ironic, but the safest place for you—and by extension the rest of us—may be the city where those threatening you live."

"Very interesting. What is your plan?"

"I would like to immediately create a new position in the Swiss Guard of Vice Commander for Internal Security and promote Capt. Hans Fasel to that rank and position. After a few days of consultation with me, he will return to the Vatican to do a study to determine how to provide you and your associates, including the Curia, significantly more security and significantly more freedom than you have here. He will supervise all the work necessary to do that, and when he is finished, we will all move back to Vatican City."

"How long do you think that will take?"

"Vice Commander Fasel will have all the freedom and funding to do the job right. His target date for completion will be August 1, but it may take longer."

"Let's do it. I would like to personally congratulate the new Vice Commander tomorrow."

"I will arrange for that. Thank you, Your Holiness."

* * * * *

At Cardinal Law's condo, the papers had been signed and the recorder was turned on. Agents Donahower and Ferris began their questions.

"Cardinal Law, we have been told by a highly reliable witness that two of The Brethren, Cardinal Burke and Archbishop Viganò, had been trying to convince you to join them in something to do with the Holy Father. Is that correct?"

"They thought we ought to have more information about what the Holy Father was doing in the United States than he was providing."

"Do you mean surveillance?"

"Yes."

"Any discussion of violence or threats of violence?"

"I made it clear from the outset that there was to be nothing like that."

"Did they accept that?"

"I believe so."

"Did either of them ask you for money to fund that project?"

"Yes, and I refused."

That was not entirely true.

"Were you aware that Bishop Mastrangelo made a trip to Catania so brief that he came back on the return trip of the same train."

"As I said, I don't know anything about Bishop Mastrangelo."

"Do you think that Cardinal Burke had anything to do with the death of Cardinal Parolin?"

"I did wonder and confronted him with that."

"What did he say?"

"That he did not. He said he had only asked for a quote for surveillance of the people who were in Washington."

"Was that the last conversation you had with Cardinal Burke?"

"I talked with him again the next day."

"About what?"

"He told me he had a threat from the people he had talked to."

"What did they say?"

"I think the exact words were: 'The sample was free. The cost of the service is ten million euros. A cancellation fee would be one hundred million. A decision and payment are required by before Sunday.'"

"What did you tell him to do?"

"I couldn't believe they would do that, so I told him to call their bluff and ignore them."

"Was that the last time you saw Cardinal Burke? And if so, how did he seem?"

"He was at meeting of The Brethren on the Sunday he was murdered. He seemed fine."

"That will be all for today, Cardinal. We will be in touch as soon as we have any other questions. Thank you for cooperating."

Donahower had received a text message during the questioning, and signaled Ferris to wrap up the conversation. When they got to their car, he said, "I had a text from a guy named Alberto Manenti, who is the director of AISE, the Italian equivalent of CIA. He wants us to meet as soon as possible with him and General Mario Parente, who runs their version of the FBI. I texted back that we were on the way."

"I hope that either your boss or mine told him we were here."

"How else would he know?"

"I suppose. If the situation were reversed, you and I would know."

"I hope so."

* * * * *

Kim began to read Hans' journals after breakfast on Wednesday morning. At first, she just read, but was soon writing notes and the process slowed. She was impressed by his attention to detail and his comfortable writing style.

She had expected to be finished by noon but was just starting the second volume after lunch. She was still reading and writing when Kate arrived.

"Oh, I see you have been reading Hans's journals. Weren't they good?"

"I thought they were great, and I see what you mean about sometimes poetic. Especially in the last few pages of volume three about Charlottesville."

"What!! he told me he removed them! I haven't even read them!! I can't believe he would do this to me!!!"

"Calm down. I have already talked with him about it."

"You talked to him about it!! You're supposed to be my friend!! *You talked to him about it?"*

"Yes, he called just before you got here to say he would be on time. I love his accent."

"Will you please give us a few minutes alone when he arrives?"

"Wait. Here they are. Read them."

Kate read the three pages concerned and said, "That is what you meant?"

"Of course. What did you think I meant?"

"Oh my God, he just drove in the driveway. Please don't tell him I lost my mind."

"OK."

Hans rang the doorbell.

Kim looked quickly at Kate and said, "He rings the doorbell? Don't tell me he doesn't have a key."

"Yes, he has a key, but he is being very proper. Isn't that sweet?"

"I guess."

Kate greeted Hans with a quick kiss and said, "Hans, this is my absolutely best friend, Kim McAuliff."

"A pleasure to meet you, Kim. I have heard a lot about you."

"And it is a pleasure to meet you, Hans. Kate has talked about you, and I read your recent journals today and feel like I know you. You write very well."

They continued to get to know one another through cocktails and dinner. When Kate served dessert, Kim said, "Sit down Kate. I want to tell you both why you have the pleasure of my company this evening. Ironically, what I am going to tell you is not what I had planned, but it is even better."

"As I told Kate last evening, I have not been able to find a publisher for her novel. However, we talked for so long last evening, some of it about you I might add, that we never got to some good news. However, since then, I have changed my mind.

"Publishers sometimes are looking for books about very current events, especially when they are not expected. They want them quickly and they pay very well for them. Periodically, I stop by and check out what they are looking for, hoping I might have a match with one of my clients.

"I made the rounds last Friday in New York and four of the top houses: Harcourt, Harper Collins, Random House and Simon & Schuster are looking for books about the pope's self-imposed exile in the United States, although they were not yet very interested prior to Cardinal Parolin's murder. Now with the shooting of Cardinal Burke, this is *hot*.

"That's why I called Kate the other day. I wanted to see if she was interested in trying to make a proposal. However, as I said before, I have changed my mind. Now, I want you both to co-write it, and with Hans's journals you already have a great start. What do you think?"

"Oh my God, that is wonderful!" exclaimed Kate.

Hans said, "I'm not sure I heard what I think I did. How long would we have?"

"An outline about a week after we get a contract signed. I'm going to pitch all four houses on Friday. I'll call you that evening and let you know what it looks like it. In these cases, they either love it or don't, and they are very competitive. The best part is that I can almost guarantee that they will love it. I'll call you here on Friday evening to report what happens."

"I can't believe this," said Kate "It is what I have wanted for so long!"

"I think I have a title," Hans offered. "How about *It Happened on Our Watch?*"

"Perfect!"

Kate stood and said, "We need some more dessert—and champagne!!

* * * * *

AISE (Agency for External Intelligence and Security), a somewhat less sophisticated Italian version of the American CIA led by Albert Manenti, collected relevant *external* intelligence, performed counterespionage work in other countries, and monitored proliferation of weapons for mass destruction. AISI (Agency for Internal Intelligence and Security), a counterpart of the American FBI led by Gen. Mario Parente, collected relevant *internal* intelligence; conducted counterespionage activities within Italy; and sought out subversion, criminal and terrorist activities within the country. Both agencies regularly interacted with their American counterparts.

When agents Ferris and Donahower arrived at AISE headquarters, they were ushered into Mr. Manenti's office where he and the AISI director, Gen. Parente, were seated.

"Welcome, gentlemen," said Manenti, extending his hand. "It is a pleasure to have you here."

"Welcome indeed," said the general, "We are pleased to have your help and the renowned expertise and capability of your organization to help us solve this strange case, which we just learned has another victim."

Manenti said, "Every aspect of our investigation is available to you and we hope you will return that favor. Sadly, we have nothing but a series of coincidences."

Ferris glanced quickly at Donahower and said, "So far, we have only one fact that may not be coincidental. The shooters of Cardinal Parolin and Cardinal Burke each had a small tattoo under their chins."

"What was it like?"

Ferris showed them the picture.

"The Gordian Gang!" the general nearly shouted.

"What is that?" Donahower asked.

"I'm sure you have heard of the mythical Gordian knot. Of course, there was never any such thing, but for literally centuries, artists have drawn pictures of what they think it looked like. Several years ago we arrested a man with a fairly simple tattoo. We thought it might be a gang symbol we hadn't seen before and it looked like a knot. We assigned an agent to research it. He worked several weeks and he found it in a collection of artists' renderings of the Gordian knot."

"What happened to the suspect?"

"He turned out to be innocent; he was just a Gordian knot buff. We have never seen another tattoo like that."

"So it was nothing. But now we have two in a week—and maybe four."

Ferris and Donahower then told the others the information from the interviews today and promised to provide updates.

* * * * *

Col. Graf called Hans to the pope's office first thing on Thursday morning. The Holy Father had a broad smile on his face, which was reassuring.

"Captain Hans Fasel," Graf began formally, "it is my great privilege, with the blessing of His Holiness, Pope Francis II, to inform you that you have been promoted to Vice Commander for Internal Security of the Pontifical Swiss Guard. As you well know, this is a new rank and position for us, which you and I will be discussing for the rest of the day and perhaps into the evening. Congratulations."

"Thank you, Colonel. I am privileged to serve and, frankly, astounded,"

"Congratulations, Vice Commander," said the pope. "Your promotion is greatly deserved and you have a very bright future ahead. I have especially appreciated your previous work and, in particular your service during this current period in Washington."

Hans and Graf adjourned to the Colonel's office. Hans's head was spinning.

"I can't believe what has just happened."

"You will when we're finished today. As soon as I have briefed you and you are ready, you will return to Vatican City. You will design and build a completely safe and comfortable environment for the Holy Father, within the Vatican palace and its grounds, without destroying any of their elements. You will have complete access to all the Vatican architects and the money to consult with others. In fact, you will have access to all the resources it takes."

"I am overwhelmed. Are you sure I can do this?"

"If I don't think so by tonight, you will be the first to know."

The two men worked until ten that night, with meals brought in. When they finished, Graf said, "This is a very good start. I think you will be ready to leave for Rome next week."

Hans went to his room and fell on his bed, thoughts stampeding through his head. "What am I going to tell Kate? What about the book opportunity? Do I want to stay in the Swiss Guard all my life? Do I know any other life? Can I live without Kate? Do I want to? How the hell can the Holy Father walk for two miles inside the palace wearing jeans and a rugby jersey, even with a beard? Do I give a damn?"

He awoke with no answers.

* * * * *

Hans and Graf spent most of the day together.

About four, Hans told him that he needed to leave for a while to take care of a personal matter.

Graf said with a smile, "It wouldn't have anything to do with Lt. Keenan, would it?"

"Yes, sir, we are going out to dinner together."

"Have you told her about your promotion and new assignment?"

"No, sir."

"How do you think she will respond?"

"I think she will be proud of me and pleased for my promotion."

"And the new assignment?"

"I don't know, but I am very afraid she might have problems with that."

"When I was about your age, I had a very similar situation, although she was the one with the new assignment."

"But you were able to work it out?"

"No. She was a wonderful woman but I lost her. She followed her heart."

"You are happily married now."

"Yes, but it will never be the same. Follow your heart, Hans. I will understand."

* * * * *

Hans arrived at Kate's house at five.

"I'm so happy you got here a little early. I am so excited and I didn't want to be alone when Kim called. Aren't you excited?"

"Who could not be?"

"Stay right here. I'll fix us a drink."

"I can do that."

"No it will keep me busy. Besides you were locked up all day with Col. Graf."

"How did you know that?"

"I stopped by to say hello, and his secretary told me. It must have been important. She said you were on whatever it was for two days."

"Yes—kind of."

When she came back with the drinks, he kissed her and the phone rang.

"Hi, Kim!" Kate said, "Hans is here and I have you on speaker."

"Hi to both of you, I do have news! Are you sitting down?"

"Yes!"

"On the couch?"

"Yes!"

"OK! Here is the story: I set my opening bid at a hundred thousand dollars in advance and a million guaranteed. Delivery of manuscript September 15."

Hans frowned slightly at the timing, but Kate didn't notice.

"Oh my God!" said Kate. "I can't believe it!"

"Stay with me now. This is without any book-signing tour. I went to all four of the houses I mentioned. Honestly, I thought I could see the last over lunch. Instead, I didn't get back to my room until twenty minutes ago.

"They all loved that there are two of you; that you are 'insiders'; that you are both military (I didn't mention your uniform, Hans); that you are from different countries; and you are good-looking (I added that). In other words, you had a leg up, right out of the box, to grossly mix a metaphor. They even loved your *It Happened on Our Watch* title idea, Hans, and most publishers want to choose their own titles.

"When we got to the book, they were excited that you didn't just have access to information about the political asylum stuff, which could be done with research, you have been involved in the tragic aftermath stuff of Cardinals Parolin and Burke's assassination and now these other two that I don't even know about. Do I sound excited?"

"Yes!" they both shouted.

"Good, that was what I was going for. My first stop was Random House. I never got to my opening bid. They offered twice what I had in mind on the spot. I tried to look disappointed and said I would talk with you about it."

"Are we going to take it?" Hans asked.

"Hell, no! My second stop was Harcourt. I told her that I already had a bid and she never blinked. I went through the same pitch and she listened with no expression. When I finished, she said, 'I'll give you twice the offer you have if you sign right now.' I asked, 'Sight unseen?' and she said yes."

"So it's Harcourt?" Kate asked.

"If it were, I would have called you at 10:30 this morning. I still had two more fish to fry."

"You are killing us, Kim!" Hans laughed.

"Next stop, Simon & Schuster for lunch and I stuck them with the hefty bill to show where I was coming from."

"And?" said Kate.

"Same reaction, different approach. This smart lady didn't want to know about other offers and gave me a substantially higher one. I told her I had one more stop and she was fine with that. The final stop was Harper Collins. The guy must have seen that I was flying high and offered a new option. He wants an open auction among the four. This is the deal: The previous bids are now fixed as the opening bids in an auction I will run. He gets the first bid. The others can counter, if they choose, and all can offer things other than cash. The rest, who had nothing to lose, agreed to participate. It will take place Monday at ten. I will call you as soon as I have the results.

* * * * *

When they hung up, Kate said, "I just don't feel like going out to dinner to celebrate as we planned. What would you think about ordering a pizza to go with our champagne?"

"Do you have enough champagne?"

"Three bottles."

"That should be enough."

When the pizza was finished, Kate went to the kitchen for a second bottle of champagne. When she returned, Hans was sitting as if deep in thought, with no telltale expression on his face.

She filled their glasses and sat down next to him.

"Thinking about our book?" she asked.

After a couple of seconds, Hans said, "Not really … well, maybe a little."

"What then?"

"Well, I too had some news today."

"I'm sorry, I should have asked."

"No, that's all right. We were both excited. And there is no way you could have known."

"What is it?"

"This morning the pope and Col. Graf promoted me to Vice Commander of the Swiss Guard."

"That is fantastic! Aren't you excited? What is that, a two-rank jump? Why didn't you call me?"

"I was in meetings all day and all evening with Graf yesterday and until just before I came here. About my new assignment."

"Can you tell me about it?"

"Yes, but first I'd like to ask you a question."

She could see he was serious, perhaps a bit sad.

"Sure. Go ahead,"

There was the trace of a tear in her eye.

"Kate Keenan, will you marry me?"

She was stunned.

"You haven't answered. Do I have to get down on my knees? I can't really do that because I don't have a ring yet."

She threw her arms around his neck. "Of course, it is yes! I will, and now you can afford to buy a *huge* one!"

When he left, he still hadn't told her about his new assignment.

Chapter Eleven

Time to Go Home

On Monday, July 1 Kate and Hans were eating lunch at the embassy when both of their phones rang. It was Kim.

"We have a winner!" she shouted. "If you have something to write on, you may want to take some notes. There are a lot of elements to the deal."

"We're ready."

"As you might have guessed, it quickly came down to two, Random House and Harper Collins. Random House won, which pleased me greatly. They are great people to work with.

"Here is the deal: $500,000 advance and $3 million guaranteed; between eight and twelve major TV interviews; thirty-day national book-signing tour with first class air reservations, at topnotch hotels, and essentially with unlimited expenses paid; two-week stay at a resort of your choice anywhere in the world after the book tour. I call it my Honeymoon Special."

"How did you know?" Kate asked.

"How did I know what?"

"Hans asked me to marry him."

"Damn! If I had known that, I could have gotten another fifty grand! Are you ready for the terms?"

"Sure."

"A twenty-page synopsis by a week from today; a hundred pages of a first draft by July 29; rewrites and the rest of first draft by the end of August."

"Wow!" said Hans.

"I've sent the contract for you to sign by FedEx. As soon as I give them the signed copy, they will cut the two advance checks. Now, I must go and find another client to make happy. I'll call in another couple of days. Get to work!"

They all hung up.

"Do you know what I am going to buy first with my advance check?" Kate asked.

"What?"

"My wedding dress. How about you?"

"My own guitar."

They both laughed.

* * * * *

As soon as Hans left Kate, he went to Col. Graf's office.

"Are you ready for another briefing session?"

"No, sir. But there is something I very much need to talk to you about."

"Come in and sit down."

Hans described the book deal in detail, including the terms and schedule. He also told Graf that he and Kate were going to be married. Graf listened intently, making neat notes on a sheet of paper.

"I have decided that in everyone's best interest, I should resign immediately from the Guard."

There was a pause before Graf responded. "Well, you are certainly following your heart in many ways. I both envy and deeply respect that. Congratulations, Vice Commander. I will inform the pope of your intentions immediately."

* * * * *

Col. Graf met with the Holy Father that afternoon.

"Well, Colonel, how are the briefings going?"

"They have been going quite well, but we have some adjustments to make."

"Tell me about them."

Only occasionally looking at his notes, Graf recounted his meeting with Hans almost word for word, including the terms of the book contract. The Holy Father listened closely, and when Graf finished, he thought for a moment before responding.

"This is certainly an opportunity of a lifetime for this young couple. Even if the book is not successful—and I can't imagine it won't be—they will have many options and little pressure to make quick decisions. I am very happy for them. What adjustments do you have in mind?"

"Before we get into the adjustments, Your Holiness, I believe that if this book is successful, it *could* be immeasurably helpful to what you are trying to accomplish; in a way, it could be another voice for you. I think we should give them all the assistance they need to tell the story truthfully and clearly."

"You may be correct. How do we do that and still come close to moving back to Rome on the schedule you proposed?"

"I think I have a plan that will work," said Graf. "First, I asked to promote Hans in order to provide him with what Americans call the 'clout' to deal effectively with the Vatican architects and others needed to do the project. But his greater value is his experience and ability to analyze and critique the planning. I can obviously provide the clout, and we can put an architect in a leadership place. We can ask Hans to review. He can do that on his schedule. I am certain that he would do the best he can.

"Finally, Hans has been with us for over ten years and I don't recall his ever taking any annual leave. I haven't checked yet, but I think he probably has at least four or five months of unused leave. I suggest that we allow him to go on leave immediately with the understanding that we will ask his advice and counsel occasionally. Each day he spends with us will be subtracted from his unused leave.

"He will maintain his Vice Commander rank of Lieutenant Colonel until the unused leave or the book tasks are completed. If he then still wants to leave, we allow him to retire at that rank with full benefits. I suspect that rank will enhance his credibility and sell a few more books."

Francis agreed. "I think we have a workable and attractive counterproposal for the Vice Commander. Please set up a meeting with him tomorrow at ten."

"I will."

"And invite Lt. Keenan also."

* * * * *

At eight a.m. Washington time on Tuesday, July 2, Pope Francis II had Msgr. Menendez place a call to Cardinal Müller.

"Cardinal Müller."

"Good morning, Gerhart."

"Your Holiness, what can I do for you today?"

"It is what I can do for you. As I am sure you remember, I owe you a penance for your behavior at the Curia conference. I have thought carefully about this. I have always felt that the best penance is more corrective than punitive."

"I would agree."

The pope continued, "The problem here is that what we were trying to demonstrate at the conference was a new way of working as a team and thinking creatively, rather than reactively. I believe that is critical to the success of the things I want to accomplish during my papacy. We are going to learn and practice teamwork. By your own admission, you are not a team player, even in something as harmless as what we were all asked to wear. You wouldn't do that. Even on that day when you asked for forgiveness, you were still wearing a cassock.

"You don't *get* it, or if you do, you don't accept it and never will. I have thought long and hard for an appropriate penance. Now sadly, quite by chance, I have a position to fill that meets that criterion. Effectively immediately, you are relieved of your duties as prefect of the Congregation for the Doctrine of the Faith and appointed as patron of the Sovereign Military Order of Malta, an office formerly held by the late Cardinal Burke.

"Cardinal Blase Cupich, formerly Archbishop of Chicago, has been appointed as your successor as prefect of the Congregation for the Doctrine of the Faith. He will arrive in the Vatican this Friday afternoon. Please relocate your office prior to his arrival."

"But Your Holiness!"

"Go and sin no more, Gerhard. You are forgiven and have my blessing. Goodbye."

"Goodbye, Your Holiness."

* * * * *

Kate stopped at FedEx on the way to work Tuesday morning to send the contract she and Hans had signed last evening. Arriving at her office she learned about the ten o'clock meeting in the pope's office. She immediately called Hans.

"Good morning."

"Good morning to you. Did you sleep well?"

"No. Trying to decide what to do first. I wish we had talked more last night. I have scheduled a meeting with Lt. Cdr. O'Reilly at one. I wanted to do it earlier, but I have been called to a meeting with the pope at ten. Are you going to that?"

"Yes, Graf told me about it."

"Any idea what it is about?"

"I thought I did, but if you are going, I don't know."

"OK. I should go. See you there. I sent the contract. Love you."

"I love you, too."

* * * * *

Col. Graf was already in the pope's office when Kate and Hans arrived. When they walked in, the pope rose and extended his hand to Kate.

"Lt. Keenan, I understand that best wishes are in order, for you. You have chosen a remarkable man."

"Your Holiness, I prefer to think that the remarkable man chose me," Kate responded, smiling.

"I will accept that construction. And Vice Commander, my congratulations to you. I wish you both, a long and happy life together. I am also pleased at the news that you people have been asked to write a book about our exile in Washington. You have certainly been an essential part of it. I want you to know that if you need clarification, or anything else with which I can help, my door is open."

"Thank you, Your Holiness. We want it to describe the reasons and the plan behind your efforts."

"Now, Vice Commander, Col. Graf has told me of your generous offer to resign from the Swiss Guard. We have talked about it in significant detail and would like your thoughts on an alternative approach, which he will now explain to you both. Let's all sit down."

Graf began, "Hans and Kate, the Holy Father asked that you both be here because we believe that this should be your joint decision." He went through the whole proposal, answering questions as he went along. Hans and Kate looked at each other and smiled several times.

When Graf was finished, he said, "Well, what do you folks think?"

"I think it is wonderful. I know that being a Swiss Guard is very important to Hans and I respect that."

"Hans?"

"This is very generous, and I would be foolish to turn it down. I thank you both. I accept."

Both the pope and the colonel clapped. Hans took Kate's hand. The pope smiled and said, "Vice Commander, you have my permission to kiss the Lieutenant."

He did.

"Now, there is one more thing," said the Holy Father. "If it can be worked out that your wedding takes place before we return to the Vatican, you are welcome to hold the wedding and reception here at the embassy and I would be honored to witness the nuptials."

Kate said, "Your Holiness, I would very much like to kiss you!"

He laughed and, with arms outstretched, said happily, "You may!"

Graf said, "Kate, if I may ask, how are you going to handle *your* situation?"

"I have been so busy, and so has Lt. Cdr. O'Reilly, with the investigation that I haven't even had a chance to tell him we are getting married. I have an appointment with him at one."

The happy couple left.

"I'm surprised that she hasn't even been able to tell her boss anything," said the Holy Father.

"She is right. He has been difficult to find these days. I called him this morning and told him what we were going to offer Hans. He's going to give her the same deal."

Both men laughed.

* * * * *

As soon as Kate's meeting with Lt. Cdr. O'Reilly was over, she called Hans.

"Hi, how did your meeting go?"

"Hi, guess what!"

"OK, what?"

"He gave me exactly the same offer you have."

"That's great! Aren't you pleased?"

"I guess—maybe a little disappointed."

"Disappointed? Why?"

"I was kind of hoping it would include a promotion to admiral."

"You *are* funny."

"Would you like to come over for dinner tonight?"

"Why don't we go to La Chaumière in Georgetown to celebrate? We can afford it."

"But it's Tuesday."

"Aren't they open on Tuesdays?"

"Celebrations should be on weekends!"

"We might not be this happy by the weekend."

"Are you kidding?"

"I'll pick you up at seven-thirty."

"What if we *are* happier this weekend?"

"Then I'll find another place."

"Why don't you come over at seven? Kim said she would call around then."

"I'll be there at 6:45."

* * * * *

Graf had a briefing meeting with Ferris and Donahower at two.

"Colonel, we just arrived from Italy last night and wanted to bring you up to date with the now four investigations. Strangely, this is moving must faster than we expected.

"The murder of Cardinal Parolin is now considered closed by the AISE and AISI, except for the identity of the assailant, who is deceased. There are no clues other than his Gordian knot tattoo. The CIA and FBI are classifying the case as unsolved and it will be periodically reviewed.

"Investigation of the murders of Cardinal Burke and Archbishop Viganò has also been closed by the AISE and AISI for the same reason. However, there is some evidence—from Cardinal Law, of all people—that Burke and Viganò may have been in touch with some secret and essentially unknown group to obtain information about the Holy Father in the United States, and that they sent Bishop Mastrangelo to Catania, Sicily, as a messenger.

"In other words, the AISE and AISI investigating is now focused on finding the organization using a very specific Gordian knot image—of which there are thousands—as a trademark. Of course, if that organization just changes to a different Gordian knot image, we are back to ground zero. Finally, the Mastrangelo murder, which is ours alone, will proceed for a while although we have practically nothing to work on."

"Pretty discouraging. May I inform the pope and ask Cardinal Mamberti to announce this in tomorrow's press conference?" asked the colonel.

"Sure. Maybe someone will come forward."

When the investigators left, Graf told the pope and asked if he wanted to release it. He said yes, and Graf gave it to Cardinal Mamberti, who, with DeeDee and Jackie, was preparing for the press conference at the time.

* * * * *

After Col. Graf left the pope's office, the Holy Father had Msgr. Menendez place a call to Cardinal Law in Rome.

When he reached him, the pope picked up the phone.

"Good evening Bernard."

"Good afternoon to you, Your Holiness. How can I help you?"

"Bernard, I am going to tell you several things and I want you to listen carefully."

"Of course," said Law.

"I have learned these things and consider them accurate. They are not debatable."

"All right."

"You are to do exactly as I say. If you do not, there will be consequences."

"I will."

"Tomorrow morning you are to call General Mario Parente of the AISI and make an appointment. You are to tell him everything you know and what you suspect about the activities of Cardinal Burke and Archbishop Viganò to enlist the assistance of an organization to provide services for surveillance of our activities here in the United States. You are to tell him of any money requested for those services.

"You are to tell him everything you know or have heard about the trip made by Bishop Mastrangelo to Catania on behalf of the cardinals. You are to tell him everything you know about any organization that uses a Gordian knot image as a symbol. You are to answer truthfully any, and all other questions you may be asked. When you are finished with the interview, I will ask General Parente if he feels that you withheld any information. If he says yes, there will be consequences.

"Now on another matter. By this time tomorrow, you will have ceased all external activities of the Benedict Brethren, such as the Chaput fiasco, wherever they may be located. You may continue to meet socially in Rome, but not engage in activities counterproductive to my papacy.

"Now for the consequences. I know that CIA Agent Ferris discussed this with you. If you fail to do any of the things I have mentioned in the time allotted, I will personally inform Agent Ferris what I believe to be true about two of your deceased members and suggest that he start extradition proceedings for you, which I, as head of the Vatican City State, will personally endorse."

There was a pause then Francis asked, "Have I made myself clear, Bernard?"

"Yes, Your Holiness."

"Good night, Bernard. Sleep well."

Law hung up.

* * * * *

As promised, Hans arrived at Kate's house at 6:45. She was ready to leave as soon as they talked to Kim.

"You look great."

"Thank you. As my father used to say, 'You clean up pretty well yourself,' Vice Commander."

"Thank you, Honorary Admiral."

She threw a sofa pillow at him.

"You know what?"

"What?"

"Kim doesn't know about your promotion."

"That's right. How much do you think she will say she could have gotten for that?"

The phone rang.

"Hi, Kim. Hans is here and you're on speaker."

"Thanks for the warning. I'll watch my language."

"Guess what Hans told me after we hung up last evening."

"Will I be embarrassed if you tell me?"

"He has been promoted, I think two ranks, to Vice Commander of the Vatican Swiss Guard!"

"Vice as in number two guy?"

"Yep. How much do you think you could have gotten if you had known that?"

"Don't ask! So now he *does* outrank you. Not a good omen. Congratulations, Hans."

"Thank you, Kim."

"And you know what else?"

"Is this *Twenty Questions*? I don't want to play anymore."

"The pope has offered to marry us!"

"Are you kidding?"

"He told us today."

"Pictures. Pictures! The book *must* have lots of pictures. Don't worry about that. I'll get Random House to hire the best damn photographer in the country. This is even better than Hans's promotion."

"I sent the signed contracts this morning."

"Excellent. I'll wire the checks tomorrow if I can. Any other news?"

"Yes. As of today, Hans and I are both on leave until the book is finished."

"Wonderful! I had wondered about that."

"OK. One more thing and then we must hang up, because we have an eight o'clock dinner reservation. I would like you to be my maid of honor."

"Well, I should think so! Where are you folks going for dinner?"

"La Chaumière"

"Ni-i-i-i-ice!!! Have fun. Call me when the checks arrive. Goodbye."

"Thank you. We will. Bye."

* * * * *

They ordered and toasted one another with their cocktails.

Hans said, "I hadn't realized until I was on my way to your house tonight that we have a very complicated schedule to construct, if we are going to pull this thing off."

303

"Well, it certainly became a lot easier today. We're free as birds."

"True, but the problem, which also happened today, has nothing to do with the book."

"Get to the point."

"We have a deadline for a twenty-page synopsis a week from today and a hundred-page first draft due on the twenty-ninth."

"Oh, I already have a solution for that."

"How so?"

"I have written several synopses and I don't think you have written any, so that should be my first assignment. I plan to start tomorrow, working at home. The core of that book is going to be based on your journals. That should be your assignment, but as soon as the synopsis is delivered, I can help full time. What is the problem?"

"You don't know this, but the project I was assigned calls for the pope and his entourage to be back in the Vatican on or about August 1. When do we get married? Or where?"

"Oh, my God!" Kate gasped.

"OK. We can work this out, but I obviously have your attention. I assume that you want to be married by the Holy Father—and *I* certainly do."

"Absolutely."

"From my assessment of the task, I think that an August 1 move is impossible. Now that the head architect is going to be in charge, I know that he will have the task determine the date, rather than the date determining the task. That said, I still think August 15 is more realistic and it might even be a little later. I wonder how long the edit of the first hundred-page draft will take. My guess is the better part of a week."

"We need some input from Kim. We could call her tomorrow."

"Shouldn't we have a plan in mind?"

"Well, it would seem to me that if your estimate is correct, the safest date for us is August 3. Random House will have what we have promised and we just have to manage our time to meet the schedule for the rest of the first draft."

"What if we concentrated on working as fast as we can and could finish the draft two or three days earlier? Then the wedding could be July 27. Remember, the reception is already taken care of. Could you be ready by then?"

"We need a wedding planner!"

"We can afford one," said Hans calmly.

"Yes. I can be ready by then. And that would give us time for a short, two or three-day honeymoon."

"Where?"

"How about back to Monticello? The real honeymoon will be after the book tour and on Random House. I'm thinking about Switzerland."

* * * * *

On Wednesday morning, July 3, Cardinal Mamberti felt well prepared for the press conference, and the attendance was much larger than the past few weeks. Promptly at ten he stepped to the microphone. "Good morning. We have several things to talk about today. A couple of them are things we weren't at liberty to talk about before and some of them are brand new. We will begin with an update on the investigation into the deaths of Cardinals Parolin and Burke. Then we will talk about an interesting connection between the investigation and Cardinal Law, whose name is familiar to some of you. We will follow that with a couple of personnel changes in the Curia stemming from the recent conference at that famous 'off-site location.' The last subject will be a surprise for all of you. Let's get started.

"As you know, the FBI and CIA have been working very closely with their counterparts in Italy, the AISE and the AISI. The results regarding Cardinal Parolin have been frustratingly simple. He was shot and killed by a man about whom nothing is known, who is also dead; his fingerprints and DNA had no matches in any country.

"Careful analysis of body cams worn by the Swiss Guards and those worn by the Navy Seals, have led to the conclusion that the target was Cardinal Parolin—not the Holy Father, as initially thought.

"The only evidence that exists is a tattoo of a Gordian knot, found under the chin of the shooter. Now as you know, the Gordian knot is a myth, but that has not bothered hundreds of artists who have produced their concept of what it looked like. Several years ago AISI arrested a man who had a tattoo on his arm, which they thought might be some kind of a gang symbol; they searched and found it to be one of those artist's impressions of the Gordian knot. The man was found to not be involved in any wrongdoing and was released. AISI had not seen the image again until this week. Your press packages contain a picture of the symbol and we urge you to publish it in the hope that someone will come forward with some valuable information.

"Regarding the murders of Archbishop Viganò and Bishop Mastrangelo, there were no witnesses; the crime scenes were clean of any evidence of the presence of any person; and suicide has been ruled out because no weapons were found. AISI and AISE have closed the investigation of the Viganò case. The FBI and CIA have suspended the investigation of the Mastrangelo case but have not closed it.

"There are also some new assignments to announce because of the Curia conference, so let's get started."

DeeDee stood and said, "Regarding the investigation—hands?" Several were raised. "Andrea Mitchell of *NBC News*."

"Cardinal, is there any connection between these four murders within such a short time? And I would like a follow-up."

"Well, there certainly seems to have been a connection between the shootings of the two cardinals because of the tattoos, but we don't have any witnesses of that in the other two. However, all four were shot in the same way: one shot to the heart and one to the head."

"Did the four victims all know each other well?"

"We believe so. Obviously, the cardinals did. Cardinal Parolin was the archbishop's superior and Mastrangelo knew Viganò as apostolic nuncio to the United States."

DeeDee said, "John Allen of *Crux Now*."

"Cardinal, a couple of questions. Since Archbishop Viganò and Cardinal Burke were both members of The Brethren and, until recently, Cardinal Parolin also was, is there any thought that The Brethren as a group were involved in some way? My second question is: Are you and Cardinal Ouellet still members of The Brethren? My third question is: Are The Brethren currently under investigation and by whom?"

"Spoken like a true Vatican insider, John," said Mamberti. "I will tell you what I know. There have been conversations with at least one of The Brethren. Cardinal Ouellet left The Brethren when he came to Washington with the Holy Father. I was invited to join, but then the offer was cancelled."

DeeDee said "Anyone else? ... Katy Tur of *NBC News*."

"Cardinal, who are The Brethren? And I'm sure I will want a follow-up."

"The Benedict Brethren are a group of generally conservative, mostly Rome-based cardinals. As the name suggests, they were strong supporters of Pope Benedict XVI. Many of them are retired; they meet frequently for dinner and discussion. Former Archbishop Chaput used them to distribute his plan for sabotaging the pope's plan to replace the bishops."

"My first follow-up is, who is the head of The Benedict Brethren?"

"The founder and leader is the American cardinal, Bernard Law."

There was a reaction from the press.

Tur continued, "Is Cardinal Law being investigated?"

"He has been interviewed and, at the urging of the Holy Father, is cooperating. That is all I can tell you at this point."

"Let's move along to the personnel changes in the Curia," DeeDee suggested.

Mamberti said, "Cardinal Müller, prefect of the Congregation for the Doctrine of the Faith, has become the successor to the late Cardinal Burke as patron of the Sovereign Military Order of Malta. Cardinal Müller's successor as prefect of the Congregation for the Doctrine of the Faith will be Cardinal Blase Cupich, the former Archbishop of Chicago.

"Questions?" asked DeeDee … Peter Baker of the *New York Times.*"

"Cardinal, isn't this a significant demotion for Cardinal Müller?"

"Yes. Next question?"

"Will you tell us the reason?"

"That is between the pope and the cardinal."

Dee stepped in. "David Boyer of the *Washington Times*."

"Will the Holy Father be releasing an announcement about this?"

"I don't believe so, but I do have another announcement. Although I haven't known her very long, I am sorry to say that today is DeeDee's last Vatican-in-exile press conference. We have kept her here much longer than she expected, and she has found us a very capable replacement in Jackie Ring, but DeeDee Myers is going back to her day job. DeeDee, would you like to say something?"

"Yes, Cardinal, I would. This has been one of the most interesting experiences of my life and one of the main reason for this is the people in this tent. Another was my friend, mentor and partner Cardinal Parolin, and my supporters, Cardinals Ouellet and Stella, and, if you can believe it … I hardly can … the Holy Father. Now, I am going finally home to my family and, as the cardinal said, my wonderful day job. Thank you all."

They gave her a standing ovation.

*　*　*　*　*

Cardinal Mamberti planned a farewell dinner for DeeDee on Friday, July 5. All the Vatican contingent, including the pope, the Guards and the Seals attended. Several people spoke, as did DeeDee. Toward the end of the evening, Mamberti talked to Jackie and assured her that he had great confidence in her as DeeDee's successor.

"Jackie, I'm sure that you are aware that we are considering a return to Rome earlier than we had thought. I'd like you to consider coming with us and heading up a new organization, the Pope's personal press office. You don't need to commit now. Think it over and let me know."

"Thank you very much for considering me," said Jackie. "This would be a great opportunity and I don't need to think it over. I'm all in—and thank you, 2020 Vision."

Chapter Twelve
<u>Now What</u>

As planned, Kate had been writing the synopsis at home for nearly a week. Hans had been working on the draft of the first hundred pages in his office at the embassy. They talked by phone often but hadn't seen each other since their dinner at the restaurant.

Around three in the afternoon on Sunday, July 7, Kate made a phone call.

"This is Captain Fasel."

"What, I let you out of my sight for a few days and you get demoted?"

"Sorry, I'm still not used to it. How are you doing?"

"The synopsis is finished and is due tomorrow. How would you like to come over now to read and critique it before I send it? Bring what you have done and your journals and we'll decide how to divide up the rest of the work. I'll fix dinner for us. I'm tired of soup and sandwiches."

"Sounds good to me. I'll be there in about half an hour."

* * * * *

The Brethren met at Cardinal Law's apartment for dinner on Sunday, July 7. The tone was noticeably somber, and at times conversation was awkward because no one was sure what anyone else knew or didn't know. After just one cocktail they had their usual excellent dinner before settling back in the living room for after-dinner drinks. They were clearly waiting for Law to say something.

"As I understand our colleague Cardinal Müller did this week, I too received a call on Friday from the Holy Father," he began.

Müller mumbled, "I hope yours brought better news than mine did."

"It did not. It appears that His Holiness knows a great deal more about our little group than we thought he did, and he also knows about the connections among the four murders."

"Tell us about the connections with the murders," said Cardinal Levada. "More in particular, tell us what *you* knew about this tragedy."

"You know what my position was throughout, Bill. I don't appreciate your comment."

"Just start at the beginning, Bernard. There may be two fewer listeners than when we last met, but we are interested and deserve to know."

"All right. You know that I tried to shut down Burke's talk of a 'solution' every time he brought it up. I think you also know that Cardinal Burke and Archbishop Viganò had been privately trying to repair relations with 'our friends down south' ever since Francis I excommunicated some of them at the beginning of his papacy. They apparently contacted someone in Catania recently—I don't know who—and they asked how much it would cost to put the pope under surveillance in Washington. I don't know that they asked, but the quote included an option to go further than just surveillance."

"When did you learn this?" Levada asked.

"A few weeks ago. Burke heard from his contact that Pietro's shooting was a 'free sample of their work' and they wanted $100 million for 'us' to get out of 'the deal.' I told Ray to call their bluff—and the next day he and Viganò were dead."

"What about this Mastrangelo guy, the bishop from the U.S.?" Cardinal Bertone asked.

"Collateral damage. He was a longtime friend and protégé of Burke's who happened to be visiting Ray while he and Vigano were talking to their friends. They sent Mastrangelo as their courier to Catania, and that trip connected Burke and Vigano to the murderers."

"What did the pope say to you?" asked Cardinal Stafford.

"He said he knew that I had been questioned by the CIA, FBI, AISI and AISE and had not told them everything. I felt comfortable with that, but he ordered me to contact AISI and tell them the whole story, including things that I believe but cannot confirm."

"Are you going to do it?" Stafford asked.

"I already have. Since Burke and Mastrangelo were both Americans, the FBI threatened me with extradition. You know I can't do that."

"What else did the pope tell you?" asked Bertone.

"The Brethren must become a strictly social group. No campaigns. No strategy development. No snooping!"

"Did he really say snooping?"

"I think so, yes."

"What do you think about that?"

"I have considered and, yes, prayed seriously about that, and now I think that is the right thing for us to do. Our church has changed because of the Holy Father's strategy. Instead of endlessly arguing against traditional theology with the Curia, he is engaging the laity in revolutionary ways. His firing all the world's bishops in the way he did was pure genius. Who can argue that the people of a diocese should not be led by one of their own and of their own choice?

"His quick reaction to Chaput's plan has clearly demonstrated that he is in charge. Is that not a good thing?

"His treatment of Gerhard has sent an explicit message to the entire Curia that he will not tolerate defiance. Why should he? Are they not supposed to assist and faithfully advise him? At this point, our opposition is defenseless.

"I expect that we have not seen the last of the changes increasing the laity's influence and reducing the Curia's. That has strong support. The church of John Paul and Benedict is over. We may not like that, but it is a new church, with an excellent chance to survive."

"Does this mean the end of The Brethren?" asked Levada.

"That is up to all of you. I would like to continue it in the way the Holy Father has stated, and in fact I would like to expand it, here in Rome. It is good to share ideas—and who knows, perhaps Francis II will convince us that his is the right way to go, or vice versa."

* * * * *

Hans arrived with a bottle of wine and was greeted appropriately.

"OK, I'll show you mine if you'll show me yours," Kate said playfully, handing him the synopsis.

"Here are thirty-five pages of the first draft and the supporting journals, and there are many ways to fill that out to perhaps fifty. I think I can meet our schedule." he replied.

Each proceeded to read the other's work, making a few notations in the manuscripts. Hans finished first, saying, "I think you did a great job on this. You set the bar high and it is very complete."

"Thank you. I think the journal really does operate as a detailed outline for the book."

"On Wednesday after the cardinal's press conference, I went down to Jackie's office to see what she had in the way of records. It turns out that there is a complete transcript of every one of the press conferences. She asked Mamberti if she could give us copies, and he said sure.

"I also talked to my boss and he is going to give us copies of the investigation, except for some details on the Gordian knot tattoos, which is still an open issue."

"This book is getting fatter every day. I just hope *I* don't, with all the soup and sandwiches."

"Don't worry. I'll still love you."

"Ah, how sweet! Speaking of eating, dinner is ready. No book stuff while we're eating."

When they were seated, Kate said, "I have some non-book things to announce. Yesterday, I found a wedding planner. She was very highly recommended and will do almost everything but marry you. That's my job. She said that the first thing she needs is a list of the wedding party and the invitees. She nearly had a stroke when I told her the pope is going to marry us, with three cardinals and an archbishop concelebrating the Mass. Kim is set as maid of honor. Have you decided on a best man?"

"My younger brother."

"Please don't tell me his name is Fritz" she laughed.

"No, his name is Gunnar."

"How old is he?"

"Twenty-eight."

"Oh nice! So is Kim. I assume that your parents are coming. Who else?"

"Yes they are. I'll get a list. It won't be long. Switzerland is a long way away."

"Mine may be long. I'm from Canandaigua, New York, which is near Rochester. That isn't very far. Beware of great scrutiny. Is your brother good-looking?"

"Not as handsome as I am," he grinned.

"Excellent!"

* * * * *

On Monday, July 8, old friends Cardinal Müller and Cardinal Koch had lunch together at a favorite restaurant. Müller told him about the conversation at the meeting yesterday evening.

"What do you think about this turn of events, Gerhard?"

"I'm not satisfied that resistance is not still warranted."

"Ineffective resistance can be deeply frustrating."

"Law wants to expand the group. Are you interested?"

"Yes, and I know some others who would be."

"I will talk to Law about that."

* * * * *

On Tuesday, the 9th, Jackie and Cardinal Mamberti were planning the press conference. There would be just be two topics: a change the pope was making in how future popes would be chosen; and the announcement of the move back to Rome. It didn't take them very long to develop the list of probable questions and find answers for them.

As the meeting was ending, the cardinal asked, "Are you having any second thoughts about moving to Rome, Jackie?"

"Not about moving there, but wondering what to do when I get there. Ordinary stuff like finding a place to live; finding a grocery store and a place to get my hair done; selling my car here and buying one over there. And then there are the job-related things: what will be different from what I am doing now? To whom will I report? Where will my office be? Will I have a staff? Will I be travelling? Will I be able to develop friends at work? Then there are the after-work things: will I find a social life? What are the local customs? Will I be able to find my way around? Does everybody always eat pasta?"

"That sounds like many second thoughts. Adequately answering the job-related questions is my responsibility, and we will begin doing that immediately. Regarding the other things, I will have one of my secretaries in Rome start doing some research on the rest. Then, perhaps as soon as the afternoon of next week's press conference, we will send you to Rome to look around for a long weekend and provide you a guide."

"That sounds wonderful. Do you have a handsome male guide, about my age, who isn't a priest?"

"I'll see if that can be arranged." The cardinal laughed, but made a mental note.

* * * * *

The press conference on Wednesday, July 10, again drew a large crowd. Jackie stepped to the microphone promptly at ten and introduced Cardinal Mamberti.

"Good morning, everyone. We have only two announcements today, but I suspect they will produce a significant number of questions each. The first is that Pope Francis II has issued an Apostolic Letter *in motu proprio* regarding the election of future popes. Those of you who are Latin scholars will know that '*in motu proprio*' literally translates as 'on his own impulse.' A more appropriate translation would be 'on his own initiative and personally signed by him.' It carries the full force of canon law.

317

The second is an announcement about the duration of the Holy Father's stay in your country.

"I will first provide you with some more information regarding the Apostolic Letter and then take your questions. Such a letter is not unusual, nor is its subject. Pope John Paul II and Pope Benedict XVI also issued *in motu proprio* letters on the same subject. This letter is issued to further implement the policy of the election of bishops from the priests of the diocesan priests by the people of the diocese.

"This may be a little difficult to understand, but it is laid out very clearly in the press release. I suggest that you listen to my explanation and then ask questions. I will not go over the similar letters of Popes John Paul and Benedict, since they will also be summarized in the press release.

"The pope will still be elected by cardinals, with two limitations: only cardinals who are the ordinaries of an active diocese may vote; and the maximum number of electors will be raised to 200, determined by seniority in office. Prior to the promulgation of this letter, the maximum of cardinals was 120, and all who had not yet reached the age of eighty could vote.

"Another benefit of this change is that more Catholics will be represented in the voting for the next pope.

"Ninety-nine countries have large enough Catholic populations to warrant diplomatic relationships with the Vatican. There is no current correlation between the number of Catholics in any country and the number of cardinals representing them. We have ranked the ninety-nine countries by Catholic population; each will have one cardinal elector. The seventy-six countries with the largest Catholic populations will have a second elector. The top twenty-five most populous will have a third. Any questions?"

Several hands went up Jackie called "Peter Alexander of *NBC News.*"

"Cardinal, since there are 1.2 billion Catholics in the world, what was the logic of 120 cardinal electors currently?"

"To tell you the truth, Peter, I have no idea. In fact, in the current system there are several things that are biased against the representation of large numbers of Catholics in the voting. However, I do think there is an improvement in the new system. The next pope will be elected by bishops who were all elected by the laity of their dioceses."

Jackie called, "John Allen of *Crux Now.*"

"Cardinal, you didn't specifically mention it, for some reason, but this change obviously excludes cardinals of the Curia from the election of the pope. Could you explain that?"

Mamberti replied, "I was just trying to see if you were paying attention, John. You are correct. The principle involved here is that the baptized need to be more involved in the church. Currently more than thirty cardinals in the Curia are eligible to vote for the next pope, but none are representative of the laity in general. That is more than 25 percent of the total number eligible to vote, and they represent no active dioceses."

"I'd like a follow-up question," Allen said.

"Go ahead."

"Isn't this discrimination against Curia cardinals?"

"Good question. It depends on what you see as the role of the Curia. They are roughly analogous to the cabinet of your president, rather than governors of states. They represent no constituency, yet they currently have an inordinate influence on who becomes the pope. This change remedies that situation."

Jackie called "Cheryl Bolen of *Bloomberg BNA.*"

"Cardinal, since ordinaries of active dioceses are required to retire at seventy-five, is this not a de facto reduction of the maximum age for voting cardinals?"

"Jackie, these people are really paying attention today!" smiled Mamberti. "Cheryl, you are correct. It is an effort for consistency and more equal representation of the laity.

"Let's move on to our other topic. As you may recall, we originally planned to stay here in the United States until around November. This has not been a hardship. The welcome we have had has been remarkable and very enjoyable. Our purpose was the safety of the Holy Father and the combination of the Navy Seals and our Swiss Guards has been so successful that their two leaders are actually going to get married.

"However, recent tragic events have made us question whether *anyone* can provide full protection to a building not usually needing it, in an urban neighborhood. Ironically, the Vatican Palace is a better place to do that, although some additional safeguards must first be put in place. These changes will take some time, so this is what Americans call a 'heads up' that we will be returning to Vatican City sometime in August.

"Questions?"

Jackie called "Hallie Jackson of *NBC News*."

"Cardinal, you and your predecessor have been outstanding in your innate candor and for the most part in answering our questions. Will that continue when you get back to Rome, and how will we get that information?"

"Thank you, Hallie. The American press has taught us the value of a balanced respect for each other, and I think that will continue. I do have another announcement. I have offered our Jackie Ring a position in the Vatican and she has accepted. She will reorganize and then manage a new Papal Press and Public Relations Office, which will be much more open, informative and cooperative. I'm sure she will be open to suggestions."

* * * * *

Pope Francis II, the three cardinals and the archbishop were enjoying an after-dinner drink on Wednesday evening in the pope's conference room. Cardinal Mamberti reviewed the press conference. The conversation shifted to the investigation and the Gordian Knot tattoo.

Francis said, "I find the Gordian knot to be a fascinating and appropriate metaphor for the entire hierarchy of the church, especially for the Curia. My predecessor had tried mightily to untie it, but it seemed to be getting tighter. I believe that we are making progress, but there is a long way to go. There is no chance for a reformed hierarchy and a surviving church until someone pulls out a sword and chops that metaphoric knot in half. Perhaps I should have chosen Alexander as my name."

"I think you are doing just fine, Santità," said Mamberti. The others agreed.

"I appreciate that. Now I have a question. It would be relatively easy to produce a church that would please either those who want to remain the same *or* those who want to create a church for the ages. How do we do both? Do we not need measured and reasonable input from both points of view?

"How are we going to do that? On the one hand, we have the Benedict Brethren, with newly limited constraints on their activity. Cardinal Mamberti has done significant work on developing the Francis Fellows, albeit with an absence of representation in Rome. Should we not try to bring these two entities into parity, with the same constraints, at least in Rome?

"I would look forward to meeting for dinner on Sunday night with the Rome representatives of the Benedict Brethren on week one;

the Rome representatives of the Francis Fellows on week two; and Rome representatives of both on week three, ad infinitum."

* * * * *

On Thursday morning, Col. Graf had a call from the Vatican's chief architect, Antonio Jannotta. "Good morning Commander. I have some news for you."

"Good morning, Antonio. I hope it is good news."

"It is, indeed. I needed to check on a few things before responding to your request on the security project. Now I can tell you. As soon as I heard that the pope had sought political asylum in the United States, I knew that there would have to be a limit on that, and that we would have to be prepared for his return. I immediately launched a project with the utmost priority to make needed changes in the Vatican palace and its grounds to provide the highest level of security possible.

"The recent tragic events have made us redouble our efforts and add even more elements. We discovered many ways to do it and have made most of them reality. I am certain that we can be ready for your return on Monday, August 5."

"That is good news, Antonio. I will inform His Holiness that we can return that week and call you with the details."

Before calling the pope, Graf told Hans that the wedding could be on Saturday, August 3.

It was difficult to tell whether Kate or the wedding planner were happier.

* * * * *

The next morning Msgr. Menendez made a call. "Good afternoon, Cardinal Law."

"Good morning, Monsignor. What can I do for you?"

322

"We have just learned that we will be returning to Rome on the morning of August 6. The Holy Father would like for you and the Benedict Brethren to join him for dinner at seven on Sunday August 11 at the Vatican Palace."

"We would be pleased to do so. I will notify the others. Thank you."

When he hung up, the cardinal murmured, "Well, I'll be damned," and began to call his colleagues.

* * * * *

The wedding, on Saturday, August 3, was proper, unusual, colorful, unconventional and perfect.

The ceremony was conducted in the largest room used for receptions and other events in the nunciature. The altar from the chapel was moved to the area furthest from the rear door opening onto to the yard where the press tent was located.

As the ceremony began, one of the Swiss Guards began to play the chapel piano. The Holy Father entered from the left to join Hans, in his red uniform, and his brother Gunnar at the end of the center aisle.

From the back entrance, Col. Graf on the right and Lt. Cdr. O'Reilly on the left started up the aisle. Graf was followed by newly-promoted Captain Franz Buchs and Lt. Cdr. Kay Naumann.

Then came newly promoted Captain Roland Pfyffer von Altishofen and Lt. Cdr. Trish Gerace.

All the Swiss Guard officers wore dress red uniforms. The U.S. Navy officers were in dinner dress whites, including swords.

Trish and Kay had been juniors at the Naval Academy and co-captains of the swimming team when Kate arrived; they had been her mentors as she progressed to the 2008 Olympic team.

Then came the maid of honor Kim McAuliff, and the bride, escorted by her father, retired Rear Admiral James J. Keenan, USN. Kate was wearing a simple, elegant white gown, with flowers in her hair.

The Holy Father welcomed the attendees. He was the celebrant for the Mass, with Cardinals Mamberti, Ouellet, Sella and Archbishop Pierre as concelebrants. After the readings from scripture, the pope gave a brief homily, then witnessed the joyful exchange of vows between Kate and Hans. The Mass continued with a special Eucharistic prayer.

At the end, Col. Graf and Lt. Cdr. O'Reilly led the other officers down the aisle to the door to the garden, followed by the radiant bride and groom and the wedding party, who proceeded to the tent.

The lavish reception by Chef Bourg was underway.

* * * * *

Kate and Hans pulled out of the nunciature parking lot around two-thirty, headed for the Boar's Head Resort in Charlottesville. It was a beautiful day and the top of Kate's convertible was down. Hans was driving.

"Whew! I feel like I am just getting out of a wind tunnel," she said. "Isn't it great to know all the rushing is over and we don't have any pressure on us for four whole days?"

"Yes, but don't you feel like we have forgotten something?"

"Like what?"

"I don't know. Maybe like where are we going to live,"

"Now that's silly; we're going to live in my house. It is okay for us to do that now. I already have converted the third bedroom into work space for our writing. Besides, I think my lease isn't up until January."

"I didn't mean while we write the book. I mean, then where? Do you want to stay in Washington? And what are we going to do for the rest of our lives?"

"Well, assuming the book is a success, I'd like to continue writing. Wouldn't you?"

"I guess so, but I'm not sure what I would write about. I'm just writing more detailed journals. What is the likelihood of getting away with that again? I'm going to need a job. I think we ought to decide where we want to live."

"Today? That's boring. Don't you any more interesting things in mind to do today?"

"While I'm driving?"

* * * * *

They arrived in Charlottesville about five and checked into the Boar's Head. Their suite had a porch that ran the width of the large bedroom and the comfortable living room, giving a view of the golf course. Sliding glass doors opened onto the porch from each room. A complementary bottle of champagne chilling was on the table. Saving the champagne for later, they freshened up and headed for the Old Mill Room for dinner.

* * * * *

Kate and Hans slept late Sunday morning, barely making eleven o'clock Mass. After a leisurely breakfast, they revisited Monticello and were astounded at what they had missed on their first trip.

Monday morning, Kate decided that she was going to go swimming. She asked Hans if he would like to join her; he readily agreed.

When they reached the lap pool they learned that it was smaller than Olympic size; Kate was clearly disappointed. They jumped in and swam a little to warm up. Kate was a little surprised at the form Hans displayed.

"Are you up for a little workout?" Kate asked.

"Sure. What do you have in mind?"

"How about a hundred-meter freestyle for lunch?"

"Fine with me.'"

They lined up at the end of the pool.

Hans said "Your call."

"Really?" asked Kate, followed by "On your mark. Ready. *Go!*"

They both dove into the water, and Kate came up about a half-length ahead. At the turn, she was two-lengths ahead; coming out of the turn, she led by three lengths. Hans held position on the second turn and Kate turned it on. When Hans made the third turn, he looked up and saw Kate sitting on the edge of the end of the pool.

"Have you ever played bocce?" he asked.

* * * * *

Hans was up early on Tuesday morning, August sixth. He knew that the pope's return to Rome was being televised and went into the small living room of their suite to watch. The crowds were enormous and the pope's motorcade was just arriving.

The announcer said that the pope would be making a short address from the balcony of the papal apartment. Within ten minutes the Holy Father appeared.

Kate came out of the bedroom in her robe and sat down on the couch next to Hans.

"Good afternoon, my friends, and thank you for this wonderful greeting. I am pleased to be back among you. I think you realize that my absence was the most efficient way to accomplish the early things we had to accomplish. We are now ready to move forward without losing the momentum we have attained. We have a long way to go.

"To assure that happens, I am pleased to announce that the Third Vatican Council will convene on October 1, 2020. This session will conclude on November 28. It is anticipated that the entire council will conclude just before Advent in 2023, with two sessions of two months each, in the spring and fall of 2021and 2022.

"Vatican III will address and resolve a great many fundamental organizational issues including, but not limited to: The adoption of a worldwide Roman Catholic Constitution clearly stating the equal rights, privileges, duties and responsibilities of the baptized and confirmed men and women; a new Code of Canon Law consistent with the Constitution; and an official and scientifically accurate *History of the Catholic Church.*

"Other issues of great interest to the laity will be addressed and resolved, not merely theologically but practically. There is no reason for our church to die from the impracticality of its theology.

"Among these issues are the ordination of women; optional celibacy; divorce and re-marriage; contraception; even same-gender marriage. After all, where is it written that there can be only seven sacraments?

"We must rid our charge of the stain of clerical sexual abuse while not tarnishing the reputations of the innocent, quickly and clearly admitting our mistakes in judgment.

"There is a policy in place that prosecution of a known abuser continues to a conclusion even if he or she dies before the laicization is completed. However, if the case is believed to be leading to an exoneration, it is ended when the subject dies. This practice cannot continue. We are dedicated to unquestioned equality for all the baptized.

"There is a great deal of work to be done and it must begin today. We need your prayers and understanding.

"Thank you very much for your welcome. May God bless our church!"

The ovation was overwhelming.

Hans reached for Kate's hand and asked, "How about living in Rome for a few years?"

2020 Vision

Francis I

When at the age of 75 Jorge Mario Bergoglio from Argentina, succeeded the resigned Pope Benedict XVI on March 13, 2013 he immediately became the most popular pontiff since St. John XXIII. His humor, energy, humility, confidence and optimism were infectious.

He had inherited a church that was clearly on a downward spiral. He seemed to instinctively know that the root cause of the problem was not so much a matter of faith and morals, but a failure of the governance and management by the institutional Catholic church from top to bottom to identify with a rapidly changing world and adapt to it. He also knew that the structure of the top tier of the institutional church, the Roman Curia, was such that it could *only* be reformed by the pope personally and that must be addressed first. If the system doesn't work well the individuals don't have a chance.

The premise that the doctrines of the church can remain immutable is no longer operable.

Complicating that task, but at the same time supporting its need to be done was that every single person in that institutional church structure, from cardinal to carpet sweeper owed his or her career to either John Paul II or Benedict XVI, with their determination to take the church back to pre-Vatican II and further if possible.

Despite all this, Francis almost immediately and bravely embarked on a task, which just eight years earlier his predecessor had declared impossible. He was going to reform the Curia, which had been rocked with charges of corruption several years earlier and had been exposed by the alleged leaking of the findings of

Archbishop Carlo Maria Viganò, who had been given that task of investigating.

Viganò had been sent packing to the United States as apostolic nuncio. The corruption charges were essentially dismissed. The fallout, in the form of the so-called Vatileaks, put terrible pressure on Pope Benedict XVI, and may have led to his decision to resign.

Clearly, this situation deserved high priority, although Francis obviously realized that another, related problem was the major contributor to the disaffection of the laity and the primary reason for so many to leave the church either physically or intellectually.

Most Catholics are not directly affected by the machinations of the Curia and don't know what the Curia is or does. They are concerned by their perceived need for a voice in the decision making of the institutional church. They are frustrated by the lack of interest on the part of most of their bishops in their needs, opinions and wishes.

We know from the Acts of the Apostles that in the early church, the faithful chose their own bishops based on their perception of the leadership capabilities of those chosen. We also know that Peter and Paul occasionally had to step in and advise those bishops. But not even the often-blustery Paul attempted to rule the faithful with edicts sent to their bishops. Discussion was his mode and for the most part that prevailed.

Two things indicated that Francis completely understood this problem. The first was that since then he has been somewhat of a "sound bite" pope, in a good way. This became apparent very early and the press was always ready to cooperate.

When asked about homosexuality, he responded with "Who am I to judge?" When asked about optional celibacy for priests, his answer was to the effect that if the bishops thought that was a good idea, they should take a position and initiate a dialogue with each other and him on it.

He has indicated that he believes evolution and the "big bang" theory are not inconsistent with the belief that God created everything. He has issued an encyclical supporting the reality of the human role in climate change.

It has been interesting that almost immediately after he has said such things one or another traditionalist Vatican official or bishop or archbishop will release a statement saying that we have all mistaken what the Pope "really meant." Francis has just smiled and ignored the disclaimers.

The other indication of Francis' understanding of the unease on the part of the faithful with their bishops was his early appointment of a council of nine cardinals to advise him. They were a rather interesting and diverse group:

- Óscar Andrés Rodríguez Maradiaga SDB, Cardinal, Archbishop of Tegucigalpa (coordinator)
- Marcello Semeraro, Cardinal, Bishop of Albano (secretary)
- Giuseppe Bertello, Cardinal, President of the Pontifical Commission for the Vatican City State
- Francisco Javier Errázuriz Ossa, Cardinal, Archbishop-Emeritus of Santigo de Chile
- Oswald Gracias, Cardinal, Archbishop of Bombay, India
- Reinhard Marx, Cardinal, Archbishop of Munich
- Laurent Monsengwo Pasinya, Cardinal, Archbishop of Kinshasa
- Seán Patrick O'Malley, Cardinal, Archbishop of Boston
- George Pell, Cardinal Prefect of the Secretariat for the Economy
- Pietro Parolin, Cardinal, Secretary of State

However, to any observer, this group did not seem to be people who could help very much with Curia reform. In addition, only the last two were part of the curia and Cardinal Pell was appointed to a new post, created by Francis.

Although that has been a minor part of their work, it seems more likely that the rest of them were chosen to be the Pope's eyes and ears on the other major segment of the institutional church, the mistrust of the faithful in the bishops who are supposed to be shepherding them.

The cardinals' council has been studying this phenomenon through many synods, questionnaires and such. However, they have not done anything that would significantly improve the status of the faithful or their ability to communicate upward except for those questionnaires.

2020 Vision

Afterword

2020 Vision: The Plot to Change the Catholic Church is a relatively new kind of fiction. Some people have called it "reality fiction". It is a mixture of fact and fiction that uses the names of real persons, living and dead to tell an interesting story and make a point.

I first encountered this genre in my friend Robert Blair Kaiser's 2007 novel *Cardinal Mahony*. Yes, *that* Cardinal Mahony and I found the concept very intriguing.

There is a challenge to finding a proper way to do it, which is fair to the real persons in the story beyond getting their names, descriptions and views correct. As the author, I must respect their offices, their reputations and their probable choices, while at the same time retaining my own right to exercise my imagination.

First, the story must occur in the future. You cannot attribute anything to a character in the past unless they have done it.

In this story, Pope Francis II is obviously fictional. However, the cardinal who is selected to become Francis II is real. He is a New Zealander named John Atcherley Dew who in real-life publicly described himself as "a fairly ordinary Kiwi kind of a bloke." I have tried to keep him that way, although without the accent.

Another rule for "reality fiction" is that one must keep all the characters borrowed from real-life "in character." Cardinal Law must think like Cardinal Law and Cardinal Burke like Cardinal Burke – not only in the way they speak, but, as the plot unfolds, in the substance of what they do.

And if Francis II seems to act out of character, I try to create a scenario that makes the real/fictional pope's actions reasonable.

The fourth caveat for "reality fiction" is that one cannot give the real character special talents, which they don't possess. Cardinal Parolin cannot run a four-minute mile, although on one occasion that might have come in handy. They also can't do things that they personally wouldn't, like Cardinal Müller having a mistress.

There are also many fictional characters and some have real names although you won't realize it. I tried making up names as I went along, but I kept forgetting who was who. So, I got rid of all those made-up names and substituted names of friends just because there was some vague reminder in the character, without any necessary connection to appearance or age. It worked.

So, if you and I are mutual friends of a person in the story with the same name, smile and the next time you see them, congratulate them on their few minutes of fame.

I wrote this story to try to convince those billions of Catholics like me who want to believe that our church can be saved if it just stops being so traditional and becomes more practical.

I hope you enjoyed it.

Acknowledgements

To Father Tom Doyle: A major part of the story takes place in Washington, D.C. at the Apostolic Nunciature, a place I have never been. I had never met Father Doyle, but I learned from a mutual friend that he had worked there for eight years, from the late seventies to the early eighties.

I am a visualizer. I always try to picture the place I am writing about. I don't always describe it, but I am more comfortable writing about it if I can see it in my mind. If I am describing a conversation I want to see what each participant sees, when someone else is speaking.

I sent Father Tom an e-mail asking if he could give me a "feeling" of the inside of the Embassy. He sent me almost forty pictures he had personally taken. Perfect.

To my friend, the late Robert Blair Kaiser: I had never heard of "reality fiction" until I read Bob's 2007 novel *Cardinal Mahony*. When I began to think about writing this book, I knew that was the only way to tell this story. I think the result was the most fun I have ever had writing anything.

To my friends and family: They have put up with my endless chatter for a year and a half about writing this book, without really knowing what its story was. What they don't know is that about nine months ago, I scrapped the whole thing and started over, so it hasn't taken as much time as they may think.

To my good friend, Barbara Reynolds: We met about eleven years ago, when she called me about the illness of our mutual friend Father Bill O'Malley SJ. She was Bill's colleague on the faculty of Fordham Prep. About ten minutes after we hung up, she called back to ask if I was from Syracuse, N.Y. When I said yes, she said her parents had friends in Syracuse named Betterton, whom they visited from time to time.

It turned out that when she was five and I was twelve, she lived in the upstairs flat of a two-family house in the Eastwood section and I lived downstairs. Since then we have become great friends with frequent phone calls and e-mails and discovered that our thoughts about the Catholic church are virtually identical. I should add that we have only seen each in person twice.

She has become my critic and my cheerleader, reading each chapter as I finished it and critiquing it. (I never told her what they were about before she read them).

To my Editor, M.D. Ridge: She uses "txtmaven" in her e-mail address and it could just as accurately be "TextNazi. She won't let me get away with anything. She is an author and composer of liturgical music. M.D. also edits my monthly *Saving the Catholic Church Newsletter* and our on-line quarterly *OMG! A Journal of Religion and Culture*.